SHEILA ROBERTS

The Tea Shop on
Lavender Lane

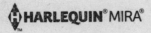

Recycling programs
for this product may
not exist in your area.

ISBN-13: 978-0-7783-1618-3

THE TEA SHOP ON LAVENDER LANE

Printed in U.S.A.

For Jill, the next best thing to a sister

Dear Reader,

Thanks so much for joining me again in Icicle Falls. You're just in time for summer fun with Bailey Sterling, who's returning home to pick up the pieces of her life. Sadly, Bailey discovered that being a caterer to the stars in L.A. wasn't all it was cracked up to be. So when the going gets tough the tough get going...back home to family and friends and new beginnings.

And speaking of new beginnings, Bailey's sister Cecily is working on some herself—with Todd Black, the sexy owner of The Man Cave. Everything is going smoothly, or so it seems, until her baby sister hits town and decides to open a tea shop on Lavender Lane. Suddenly, Bailey's new business takes an interesting turn, while Cecily's well-planned life takes a nosedive, thanks to small-town complications and unexpected sibling rivalry.

But I have a feeling everything will work out here in Icicle Falls. Meanwhile, I hope you'll brew yourself a cup of tea, enjoy a scone and join my friends on their newest adventure here in my favorite mountain town.

Please check out my website, www.sheilasplace.com, for information on upcoming books, contests, recipes and more. And I'd be delighted if you followed me on Twitter and Facebook (look for Sheila Roberts, author).

Sheila

The Tea Shop on
Lavender Lane

Chapter One

The party was going perfectly until the hostess clutched her stomach with an agonized cry and crumpled to the floor.

Rory Rourke, her boyfriend and star of the new TV series *Man Handled,* knelt by the woman's side and barked, "Someone, call 911."

"Call her doctor," said someone else.

"Call the *Star Reporter,*" the victim said faintly.

And that was when Bailey Sterling knew she was in trouble.

She'd been so excited to land this gig catering Samba Barrett's party. Samba wasn't an Emma Stone or Kristen Stewart, but she was...someone. Sort of. And with her catlike green eyes and red hair, she was on her way up, like the rest of her party guests. It was what everyone said. And surely that had meant Bailey was on her way up, too. The West Hollywood apartment had been packed with hot young actors and actresses. As she'd slipped among them bearing trays of goodies, she'd heard more than one person rave about the food and had envisioned a whole string of catering gigs after this one.

The shrimp salsa in phyllo cups had been an especially big hit. "Oh, my God, this is to die for," Angelica Winston (from the new reality show *Hard Ass*) had raved. Bailey had smiled modestly and kept circulating, while her assistant Giorgio served up stuffed mushrooms. She'd been working for the past three years to earn a reputation as caterer to the stars, and things were finally starting to happen.

Except here was Samba Barrett, writhing on her living room floor, groaning in agony. Twenty minutes ago she'd been eating those shrimp cups and laughing. Did she have food allergies she hadn't told Bailey about? Samba had gone over the menu with her, approved everything. How could this have *happened*? Was Bailey going to be known as killer of the stars?

Thirty people gathered around the actress, some offering advice, some taking pictures with their cell phones, others texting wildly. Bailey stood on the fringe and nervously downed one of her own appetizers.

"You'll be okay, baby," Rory Rourke assured Samba.

"I think I ate something bad," she whimpered.

"Oh, no, that's not possible," Bailey protested, and everyone turned to look at her. One woman aimed her cell phone at Bailey, capturing her miserable expression. This *couldn't* be happening.

But it could. And it was. Now Bailey felt sick. She lost her grip on the tray of canapés she was carrying and down they went, the tray landing on the Jimmy Choos of one of the party guests busily recording her hostess's misery on her cell phone.

The woman next to her let out a yelp and jumped back, then glared at Bailey.

"Sorry," Bailey muttered and bent to scoop the

mess onto the tray. In the process she managed to get in the way of another guest, nearly tripping him.

He didn't settle for glaring. He swore at her.

Catering hell—that was what this was. Bailey made a dash for the kitchen and hid out, watching the drama unfold from behind the counter.

The ambulance arrived, and the EMTs showed up to take Samba's vitals and load her onto a stretcher. Then away she went, a pitiful—but gorgeous—victim of Sterling Catering.

The guests switched from eating to drinking. Rory told Bailey she could clean up and leave, and not in the kindest tone of voice. He didn't offer to pay her, and she didn't ask. All she wanted to do was get out of that cramped apartment full of the young and the beautiful.

By the time she left, the media was waiting. Photographers snapped her picture, and reporters stuck microphones in her face. "Have you catered for Samba before?"… "Has Samba threatened to sue?"… "What's your relationship with Rory Rourke?"

Bailey stood there like Bambi staring at the headlights of a Mack truck, her toque askew, offering quotable quotes such as, "What?"

She quickly realized that it was time to scram and bolted for the van where Giorgio was loading up boxes of supplies…and telling a reporter that he wasn't involved with any of the food prep. "I'm only doing this while I wait to hear from my agent. We've got something big in the works. Giorgio Romano. R-o-m…"

Bailey tossed in the last of her serving equipment, then tugged on his double-breasted white jacket and growled, "Get in the van," even as the vultures who'd been talking to him now turned their attention to her.

He scowled at her but got moving.

They drove away with photographers pointing their cameras and shooting. "What were you thinking?" she demanded, swerving to avoid one.

"I wasn't thinking anything. I was just answering questions."

"Well, thanks a lot," she snapped.

He held out both hands. "What did you want me to do?"

"How about saying that Sterling Catering was not responsible for Samba Barrett's illness?" she suggested, her voice rising.

"I can't be sure of that," Giorgio said sullenly.

"You've been working for me for six months now, Giorgio. You know how good I am. You could have said something." Was there no loyalty in the world? She brushed away a tear.

"I told you, I'm only here until I get my break."

"And I suppose that was it," she said in disgust. "Getting your name in the paper as a caterer?"

"Every little bit helps," he retorted. "Publicity is great, even if it's bad."

Not for a caterer. She had a small liability policy, but it didn't cover bad press. Overwhelmed with misery, Bailey pulled off the road and began to cry in earnest.

Giorgio sat there in what she thought was silent sympathy. Until he said, "Here, let me drive. I've got a date."

She raised her tearstained face from the steering wheel. "A date? You were working the party."

"Yeah. But when it ended early..." He shrugged. "Sorry."

Sorry about summed it up.

After a long day of work punctuated hourly by texts from her miserable little sister, Cecily Sterling was standing in line at the Icicle Falls Safeway with her recharge essentials—a pint of mint chocolate chip ice cream and a bag of Cheetos. It seemed everyone else in Icicle Falls had had a long day at work, too, and the store was packed.

She'd already run into Dot Morrison, who'd eyed her purchases and said, "Now, that's my kind of dinner."

She'd planned on adding more to her "dinner," but she'd spotted Luke Goodman, the production manager at her family's chocolate company, in the cookie department with his daughter, Serena, and had decided to skip the cookies.

Not that she didn't want to see little Serena or, as Serena would insist, Big Serena now that she'd "graduated" from kindergarten. Serena's visits to the Sweet Dreams Chocolates office with her grandma gave Cecily her kid fix on a regular basis.

But Serena's daddy was another matter.

Luke Goodman was a nice guy. He had the husky build of a wrestler (which he'd been in high school), kind blue eyes and a great smile. He was a widower, and he'd been interested in Cecily ever since she'd moved back home to Icicle Falls. The only problem was that she wasn't interested in him as anything more than a friend.

She should have been. What was wrong with her,

anyway? She had such a gift for matching up other people. She'd brought together friends in high school and in college; thanks to her, a lot of weddings had taken place. She'd even been in the matchmaking business, for crying out loud. She could size people up and instinctively know who should be with whom. But when it came to herself she knew nothing. She'd been engaged twice, and each man had turned out to be a loser and a user. Pathetic.

Luke was neither of those, and he wanted her. So why did her stupid hormones do the happy dance every time she got anywhere near Todd Black?

Todd had also been after her ever since she'd moved home. He owned The Man Cave, a seedy tavern at the edge of town, and he was no Luke Goodman. He looked like Johnny Depp's kid brother, and he was a heartbreak waiting to happen. He had bad boy written all over him, from the double entendres he was so good at throwing Cecily's way to how he looked at her, as if she were a chocolate bar he'd like to unwrap. Slowly. Luke Goodman was the kind of man who married a girl, but Todd Black was the kind who slept with her and then conveniently forgot to call the next day.

She should have no interest whatsoever in Todd Black. And she certainly should never have agreed to stop by his tavern on Friday night to play pinball when she'd run into him earlier that day at Bavarian Brews.

But he'd caught her in a weak moment. She'd been worried about her younger sister, Bailey, and she'd said yes without thinking. At least that was her excuse. She really couldn't blame her moment of weakness on preoccupation, though. Insanity was the true culprit. Anytime she was around that man he heated up her hormones and fried her brain. Now she was going to go home and rewire the synapses with junk food and a long bubble bath. She enjoyed making bath salts and bubble bath and could hardly wait to indulge in her latest creation—lavender-vanilla.

She'd barely gotten in line when Cass Wilkes walked up behind her and said hi. "Ice cream—food of the gods."

Cass was Cecily's sister Samantha's BFF, but she'd opened the door of friendship to Cecily, too, and they saw each other every Sunday at Cass's chick-flick nights and during their monthly book-club meetings.

Cecily smiled, feeling slightly embarrassed. That was both the beauty and the curse of living in a small town. Everyone knew your business. "Not exactly the diet special, is it?"

"No, but I can't exactly say anything." Cass held up her shopping basket, which contained a pizza and a two-liter bottle of root beer. "You can see we're eating well tonight."

The basket also held a bag of ready-made salad. "It's not all bad," Cecily said, pointing to the salad. "And pizza has good things on it."

"That's what I keep telling myself. I also keep telling myself that I'm only going to eat the salad and leave the pizza for the kids. But I'm lying."

"Life's too short not to eat pizza," Cecily said with a smile. The smile fell away when her cell phone started singing Bailey's ringtone, "Girls Just Want to Have Fun."

Bailey's life had been anything but fun the past couple of days. She had called Cecily the evening of the disastrous party, practically hysterical. They'd pulled in Samantha, who had found Bailey a tough L.A. lawyer, but no legal shark could save her from bad publicity. Of course, the story had made the papers, and all the TV stations had repeatedly run the footage of her van driving away, leaving the scene of the "crime." Naturally, they'd zoomed in on Sterling Catering painted on the side of the van. Word of mouth had added to the avalanche of bad press. People who'd booked her for their events had been calling right and left and canceling.

Cecily answered, bracing herself for more bad news.

Sure enough. "Have you seen the *Star Reporter?*"

Oh, no. What now? Cecily turned to the magazine rack near the cash register. There, on the front of the latest popular celebrity news rag, was a picture of Bailey in her white caterer's coat, standing outside Samba Barrett's apartment building. She was wearing an expression of shock, along with her chef's toque, her big hazel eyes wide and her mouth dangling open. She looked more confused than crazy. In fact, she looked like the village idiot. The bold print above the picture proclaimed, Samba Barrett Poisoned? Crazy Caterer Tries to Take Out the Competition.

"Oh, no." Cecily dropped her junk food on the checkout conveyor belt and grabbed the magazine.

Cass, standing right next to her, took one, too, muttering, "Those creeps."

"This is the worst yet. I'm ruined!" Bailey wailed.

"That headline doesn't make sense. What competition are they talking about?" Cecily asked, trying to balance her cell phone, calm her sister and turn to the article all at the same time.

"They're saying I had a thing for Rory Rourke, which is ridiculous. I don't even know Rory Rourke. I didn't know any of those people!"

During the past forty-eight hours, Bailey's moods had swung between grim resignation and wild hysteria. It wasn't hard to tell what mode she was in now. "This is a gossip rag," Cecily reminded her. "You can't believe what you read in papers like this. Nobody takes this stuff seriously."

"My business is trashed. My life is trashed. I don't even have money to pay for the lawyer."

"Samantha and I told you not to worry about that," Cecily told her. "It's being taken care of." News had traveled as fast around Icicle Falls as it had in L.A., and Dot Morrison and Pat Wilder, two of the town's older businesswomen, had already set up a special bank account for Bailey's defense fund.

Not that she was going to need it. Anyone with eyes could see the actress had pulled a cheap publicity stunt. The lawyer was on top of things, and Cecily was sure that before the month was over, Bailey would be out from under this. She said as much, hoping to calm her sister.

"It's just...this article," Bailey said between sobs. "I'm nothing like that. And I worked so hard to build my business. Now it's...gone."

Cecily wished she could reassure her, but in Hollywood, where making an impression was everything, well, it didn't look good for Sterling Catering. "Come home," she said.

"I can't."

Cecily knew how hard it was to give up a dream. She also knew how hard it was to come full circle, right back to where you started. She'd done it herself. It had turned out to be exactly what she needed, and she was much happier working in the family business than she'd been trying to match up gold diggers with shallow men who wanted Playboy bunnies.

"Think about it," she urged. "Everyone here loves you."

"That's for sure," Cass said over her shoulder.

"I can't even leave my apartment. There are reporters hiding in the bushes."

"They won't hide there forever. And I can guarantee they won't follow you here," Cecily said. At least she hoped they wouldn't. "The story will die down as soon as the next manufactured scandal hits. Which, I predict, will be sometime within the next seventy-two hours."

"I asked her if she had any allergies," Bailey said. "I have all kinds of menus to choose from, and she chose that one."

"Don't worry. This will all work out," Cecily promised.

It was as if Bailey hadn't heard. "I'm ruined," she said again.

"Only temporarily."

"Well, how long is temporary?" Bailey cried.

That was something for which Cecily had no answer.

Ruined, Bailey thought miserably as she ended the call with her sister. She'd gone to the hospital to see Samba, thinking maybe they could talk, that she could explain why her food couldn't possibly have made the actress sick. She'd even brought flowers. She'd encountered a hired guard at the door of Samba's private room, and all he'd allowed in had been the flowers, along with the get-well card on which Bailey had written, *I hope you feel better soon.* But now she hoped Samba contracted terminal acne.

Well, okay, not really. She liked to think she was better than that.

Samba was out of the hospital the next day, shopping on Rodeo Drive, pretending to look annoyed when photographers took her picture. Of course, she'd given a quote to any paper that was interested. "I really don't know what happened."

Bailey knew what had happened. She'd been duped.

"All I want is to put this behind me," Samba said, posing like a tragic heroine.

Sure, now that she'd milked all the free publicity she could out of ruining Bailey. Rumor had it that Samba had been offered a part in a pilot for a new TV series, some sort of female detective show. (That was rich. Samba Barrett, who had just faked her own food poisoning, solving crimes.)

Meanwhile, Bailey couldn't even get a job catering to street people. She'd been dubbed "the party poisoner," and not only had she lost business, but she was also the butt of everyone's jokes. One late-night TV host had cracked that he'd planned to hire a caterer for his birthday party but changed his mind since he wanted to live to see his next birthday. Ha-ha.

She'd finally given a quote to the *Star Reporter,* a diplomatic but strongly worded quote, insisting, "I don't know what happened to Samba, but I know it wasn't my food that made her sick. No one else at that party got ill."

The paper had run with it, and the next headline proclaimed, Caterer Claims Samba Barrett Faked Food Poisoning. Great. That was almost as good for business as the original incident.

This will all work out, she told herself. Just like Cecily had said. *When life gives you lemons make lemonade. Or eat chocolate.* Except her chocolate stash was gone. Okay, she needed a drink.

She went to her fridge to pull out a Coke. None left. The refrigerator was a giant, near-empty cave, containing a bag with a few spinach leaves, half a tomato, some canned olives and pickles and a dab of Gruyère. At some point she was going to have to go out and get groceries.

Not today, though—at least, not in broad daylight. She'd have to wait until nightfall.

Around ten-thirty, she deemed it safe to leave her apartment. No one jumped up out of the bushes as she dashed to her car, and she convinced herself that she was being paranoid.

She drove to the supermarket; once inside, she hurried through the store, picking up produce, milk and juice. No photographer dogged her, and she let out her breath.

But when Bailey went to pay, the checker kept studying her, all the while trying to appear as if she wasn't. She could almost hear the checker thinking, *Why does this woman look so familiar?*

The customer behind her had a copy of the *Star Reporter* and was eyeballing her, too.

Now another shopper joined them, and he, also, began staring inquisitively.

It was all Bailey could do not to pull out her hair

and shriek. Instead, she paid for her groceries and said, "I didn't poison Samba Barrett. She just got sick. Okay?" She didn't stick around to find out whether it was okay or not. She grabbed her bag and left.

As the doors swooshed open, she heard one of the gawkers say, "Do you think she did?"

She rushed to her car, tripped in the process and dropped her grocery bag. A head of cabbage went rolling, and she dived to rescue it. As she plopped it back in the bag, she looked over her shoulder to check whether anyone had seen her clumsy moment.

That was when she spotted the man with the camera lurking on the other side of the parking lot. Great. She could see the headlines now. Crazy Caterer Cracks Up at Supermarket.

It wasn't right. It wasn't fair. She hadn't done anything to anybody. And these buzzards knew it. Frustration and anger finally took over, and she did something she'd never done in her life. She lifted her hand and saluted the rat across the lot with one finger, and it wasn't her index finger. There. That said it all.

That would probably say it all in the next issue of the *Star Reporter,* too.

But it didn't make her feel any better. With a sob, she put her groceries in the car and drove away. How long was this going to go on? How long were people going to look at her as if she were some kind of sicko?

How long was her money going to last?

Chapter Two

Not for the first time, Cecily asked herself what she was doing as she walked into the murky interior of The Man Cave on a lovely spring Friday evening. It was, of course, a rhetorical question. She knew what she was doing here. She'd been moving in this direction ever since she'd hit town and encountered Todd Black. It had been only a matter of time until she gave in and agreed to do more than trade insults with him.

It was eight o'clock, and the place was full, mostly with men. The mechanic from Swede's gas station was playing pool with Billy Williams and one of Billy's cowboy pals, Jinx Woeburn, as well as a skinny woman with long, stringy hair wearing Daisy Duke shorts, cowgirl boots and a tight tank top. A couple of bikers and their babes stood in a corner, playing darts and drinking beer. The rest of The Man Cave's patrons were lined up along the bar, draped over drinks, watching a baseball game on the TV that hung over the array of booze bottles. They ranged in age from men in their twenties to grizzled old guys looking to get out of the house for a while. The vibe here sure was different from the bar at Zelda's. That place buzzed with success and hospitality. The Man Cave was more of an "Aw, what the hell" kind of retreat.

The clack of pool balls acted as a rhythm section for Trace Adkins's "Honky Tonk Badonkadonk," which was blasting from speakers in all four corners of the tavern, and that competed with the noise of the baseball game playing on the TV. The place smelled musty, as if no one had thrown open a door or a window in months. The pinball machine, Todd's excuse for luring her over, sat in the far corner with an out-of-order sign on it. So much for his invitation to come in and show him what sort of pinball wizard she was.

She felt several pairs of male eyes on her as she walked in. This was nothing new. She'd always attracted male attention. But here, in this tavern, she felt as if she were the one in the tight tank top instead of a conservative pink sweater and loose-fitting jeans. This place, it was just so...ugh.

Todd had been behind the bar helping his bartender, Pete, but at the sight of her he came around and started moving toward her. He was dressed casually in jeans, loafers and a black T-shirt. It wasn't so tight it looked spray-painted on like the one Bill Will was wearing, but it clung enough to let a girl know he was sporting some splendid pecs beneath it.

He smiled at her, sending a jolt through her that ran all the way from her bra to her panties. What was it about this man? Did he have pheromone overload?

She shouldn't have come. If he kissed her, that would be it; she was bound to do something stupid and get her heart broken for the third time.

Well, she had a great excuse to leave. There was no sense staying if the pinball machine was out of order.

"You're looking especially pretty tonight," he greeted her, taking in her pink sweater. "Why do I look at you and think cupcakes?"

She motioned to his black T-shirt. "And why do I look at you and think devil's food?"

Of course, he wasn't insulted. Her comment served only to produce a grin on that handsome face of his.

She didn't give him a chance to say any more. "I might as well go. Your pinball machine is broken."

"No, it's not. I just put the sign up there to keep everybody else off it."

She shook her head. "You could've put up a sign that said Reserved."

One dark eyebrow shot up. "What does this look like, Schwangau?"

Good point. The Man Cave was hardly an upscale restaurant.

He nodded toward the bar. "What would you like to drink?"

"Coke." If she were at Zelda's she'd have indulged in some girlie drink like a Chocolate Kiss or a huckleberry martini, but his place was no Zelda's. Anyway, it was a given that an evening of verbal sparring with Todd Black would require her brain to be in top working order. She wasn't about to cloud it with alcohol.

"Rum and Coke?"

"Just Coke."

"You live dangerously, Cecily Sterling." He held out some coins and said, "Go on over and warm up. I'll get the Cokes."

"Thanks. Don't mind if I do." She took the coins and walked over to the corner. It was a vintage model from the seventies called Pin Up—a sexy name for a game with a bowling theme. This was going to be fun. By the time Todd joined her she'd studied the landscape of the machine and was ready to rock and roll.

He set their drinks on a nearby empty table and said, "Okay, let's see how long you can go."

"Are you sure you don't want to go first? I'll last a lot longer than you," she taunted him.

He leaned in close, his breath tickling her ear. "You have no idea how long I can last."

That hit her zing-o-meter. She made a determined effort to ignore it and turned her back on him. "Okay, you had your chance."

She positioned herself in front of the machine, standing straight. Then she put the ball in play, waiting patiently, not overworking the flippers, nudging the machine enough to get it to work with her but not to the point where it would tilt and end her game. The play went on. And on. Oh, this *was* fun!

At some point she became aware of the fact that she'd gathered a crowd. And soon the crowd began whooping and clapping. It finally messed up her concentration. Her game ended, and she stepped back from the machine with a frown.

"That was something else, Cec," Bill Will said reverently.

"Impressive," Todd admitted.

"I thought this was broken," one of the bikers said, glaring at Todd.

The man wasn't much taller than Todd, but he was twice as big and he looked like a block of cement with legs. And attitude. Weren't most bikers these days supposed to be nice, middle-aged men? Dentists who'd always wanted to own a Harley? Maybe this particular specimen hadn't gotten the memo.

Todd wasn't fazed by the customer's ire. He merely shrugged and said, "I guess she fixed it." He motioned to the game with his hand, and the big guy pushed his way up to it.

"That was convenient," Cecily teased. "Now you don't have to compete with me."

He grinned. "I can think of other things I'd rather do than compete."

Zing! So could she. Meanwhile, Jake O'Brien's new hit song, "Hot and Bothered," boomed from the speaker.

Todd picked up her glass from the table and handed it to her. "The darts corner is empty. Wanna give it a try?"

"Try is about all I can do," she said.

She proved it right away. She could barely hit the dartboard, let alone the bull's-eye, and he beat her soundly.

He was about to give her some pointers when things got noisy over at the pinball machine. The big biker was not happy, and the whole room (with the exception of the TV and the music coming through the speakers) got quiet. Cecily watched as Bill Will, his buddy and the tank top chick casually moved away to the relative safety of the bar. The men on the barstools hunched even lower over their drinks. Meanwhile the biker animal was swearing and pounding on the machine. Bad pinball etiquette.

"He's going to break that," Cecily predicted. If her big sister, Samantha, had been here she would've fearlessly strode over to the creep and let him have it. Cecily was not her sister.

Todd didn't have a problem, though. He went to the bar and had a quiet word with his bartender, Pete, then strolled across the tavern to where the gorilla's friends stood nonchalantly watching as he tried to beat up the pinball machine. Trying to get in touch with her inner Samantha, Cecily followed, not sure what she'd be able to do if things got ugly.

"Sorry, pal, but I'm gonna have to ask you to stop beating on that," Todd told the man. "It can't take that kind of abuse."

The biker stopped, and the way he scowled was clearly a challenge. "The machine's rigged."

"What, to favor women?"

Now the biker gorilla loomed over Todd. "Are you trying to make me look like a dick?"

"Not at all," Todd said easily. "It looks like you don't need any help with that."

A couple of the older patrons at the bar snickered. Everyone else in the room braced for the fight that was about to begin.

The biker poked Todd in the chest. "I don't like smart-asses."

"And I don't like jerks. I guess we're not gonna be friends, so you may as well leave."

Todd's antagonist puffed out his mammoth chest. "Yeah? Who's gonna make me?"

"The cops. We already called them."

"We haven't done anything," protested one of the biker chicks.

Todd nodded. "So far, you're good to go. I suggest you do that."

The big man stood for a moment, obviously torn between his desire to pummel Todd and the wiser choice, which was to leave. Finally with a snort of disgust, he smashed his beer bottle on the floor, turned around and marched out of the tavern. His companions followed him out.

Todd shook his head and went to his back room. A few minutes later he returned with a broom and dustpan and a garbage pail.

That was when Tilda Morrison and Jamal Lincoln, two of Icicle Falls's finest, made their entrance. Cecily watched as he stood talking with them, still unfazed by his close encounter with Godzilla. The man had nerves of steel. He also wasn't above doing his own menial labor. There was more to Todd Black than a gift for flirting.

"That little confrontation was either very brave or very dumb," Cecily said after Tilda and Jamal had left. She took the dustpan to hold it for him.

"You can't wimp out with guys like that. Otherwise they eat you for lunch." He smiled. "Anyway, it's easy to be brave when you know the cops are on the way."

"I suppose," she said dubiously. "Although he could have done some damage to you before they got here."

"Could have but didn't." He cleaned up the last of the mess and took back the dustpan. "Let's get out of here."

"Where?" she asked.

"Someplace where I don't have to stop what we're doing to mop up beer. Let me get my stuff out of the office."

Talk about assuming that she was up for whatever

he suggested! Well, maybe she was, since she hadn't protested.

He disappeared into the nether regions to stow away the broom and garbage, then reappeared wearing a black leather jacket and carrying two motorcycle helmets. After talking briefly with Pete, he walked over to Cecily and handed her one. "Want to take a ride?"

She'd run into Todd around town more times than she cared to count, but she'd usually seen him in a truck. Why was she not surprised to learn that he rode a motorcycle?

"So that's why you weren't afraid of that guy. You're one of them," she teased.

"Right," he said.

Next thing she knew she was seated behind him on the bike, holding on for dear life as they rumbled off down the road. No wonder men loved motorcycles. Feeling that power under you as you sped down the highway—it was like an aphrodisiac.

Just what she didn't need. He hadn't told her where he wanted to take her, but she had her suspicions.

Sure enough, partway down River Street he stopped the bike in front of a two-story house with a neglected patch of lawn. The porch light was on, spotlighting the fact that the place was obviously in bad shape. Thirsty for paint, it was an eyesore in a popular old neighborhood of Victorian and Craftsman-style homes, some of which had been around since the thirties, most of them restored. Fixed up, it could be really cute, Cecily thought. A fresh coat of white paint, some green trim, a rocker on that front porch...

To her surprise, the inside of the house looked good,

with photographs of mountain scenery on cream-colored walls, area rugs scattered over hardwood floors and expensive leather furniture. Funky ceramic art topped the mantelpiece—a raccoon holding a beer bottle and a biker elephant and his lady wearing Harley jackets, sitting astride a motorcycle with two flat tires.

"This is nice," she said, taking it all in.

"I can guess what you were expecting," he said. "I'll get to the outside of the place this summer. How about another Coke?"

"Sure."

He walked around the corner into the kitchen, then reappeared carrying a couple of glasses and a can of pop. "The big-girl version this time?" He went to a liquor cabinet in the small dining area and pulled out a bottle of rum and held it up, the expression on his face a dare.

"Okay," she agreed. "But if you're thinking it'll help you seduce me, you're wrong."

He poured their drinks and returned to where she stood checking out one of the photographs. "You really think I need help?" he asked, his voice a purr as he handed her a glass.

He was standing so close she could smell his aftershave, feel the heat coming off his body. Her heart rate picked up.

Part of her wanted to grab him and wrap her legs around him, but caution made her step away and position herself in front of another picture. Like the one she'd just been studying, it was a masterpiece of camera special effects, this one showing a mountain flower in sharp full bloom with Sleeping Lady

Mountain a soft blur in the background. "Did you take all these?"

Now there he was, right next to her again. "Yeah."

"They're really good."

"Don't sound so shocked. I have other interests besides my business."

She cocked her head. "Yeah?"

He went to the couch, sat down and patted the cushion beside his. "Yeah."

She joined him—at the other end, simply to prove she wasn't going to be some easy lay. "You have quite an eye."

He shrugged. "I was an art major in college."

"How could an art major..." She stopped midsentence, realizing it would be insulting to ask how someone with real talent could end up owning a seedy tavern.

He'd seen where she was going, though, and finished the sentence for her. "...wind up owning a tavern? It's a sound business investment. Anyway, I get a kick out of the place. And I still dabble in photography and painting."

"The Neanderthal in lederhosen on the side of the building," she said.

"Self-portrait," he joked.

"An art major," she mused. "I never would have guessed."

"You probably never would have guessed a lot of things about me. But then, that's because you've been too busy running away from me."

"So, if a woman doesn't fall all over you, she's running away from you?"

"We're not talking about *a* woman. We're talking

about *one* woman. You." He set his drink on the coffee table and scooted over, closing the distance between them.

She cast her gaze around the room, looking for something else to comment on. Of course, that would only postpone the inevitable. What was she doing here?

He rested an arm on the back of the couch and began playing with her hair, stirring up her nerve endings.

She took a long drink of her rum and Coke to settle them down. It didn't work.

He removed the glass from her hand and gently nudged her chin in his direction. "I've wanted to kiss you ever since I first saw you. Are you gonna let me?"

And then, assuming the answer would be yes, he did just that, and her nerve endings went from stirred to shaken. Oh, she was in trouble. Against her better judgment, she was falling hard for this man. She felt his hand drifting along her midriff, moving upward, and her nerve endings went into delirium. If she didn't stop this right now, she never would. And she wasn't ready to make that leap yet. She had to be sure.

She pulled away. "That was quite a kiss."

"You're quite a woman," he said and started to move in for more.

She placed a hand on his chest. "I think I've had enough fun for one night."

"Don't like to kiss on the first date?" he teased.

"I'm not sure playing pinball at your tavern and then coming over here for a grope fest counts as a date."

"Who groped? You never let me get that far."

"It's time for me to go home," she said and stood.

He stood, too. Now they were just a breath away from each other. He reached up and began playing with her hair again. "Have I mentioned that I'm a sucker for blondes?"

And she was a sucker for having someone play with her hair. But she wasn't about to be suckered by Todd Black—at least not tonight. "Thanks for sharing," she said and removed his fingers from her hair.

"And you are truly the most beautiful blonde I've ever seen."

Men had been telling her she was beautiful since puberty, and she wanted more than someone who was turned on by her appearance. She wasn't interested in a relationship where sex was the driving force. Although, if that kiss was any indication, sex with Todd Black would be amazing.

Stop it! she scolded herself. To him she said, "I've heard that before." And it didn't move her. She needed to be with a man who wanted more.

"I bet you have. I bet men have been telling you you're beautiful since the day you got your first training bra."

She frowned at him. "That was poetic."

"I try."

"Try harder. I'm not looking for someone to sleep with."

"Aw, and I put clean sheets on the bed and everything."

Cecily frowned at him again. "Can't you ever be serious?"

"Yeah, actually, I can. You'll have to go out with me, so I can show you my serious side."

"It's a little hard to date when I work days and you work nights, doncha think?"

"I own the place. I can take a night off. I can take tomorrow night off. Let's go out to dinner. Zelda's, and a movie after."

She should derail this train before it went any farther down the track. Instead, she said, "All right. Zelda's, and a movie after. With popcorn. Don't cheap out on me."

"I wouldn't dream of it." He put his hand to the small of her back and gently steered her toward the front door. "Come on, Beauty. Let's get you out of here before the beast ravishes you."

And before her nerve endings betrayed her.

Who was she kidding? They already had.

The ride back to The Man Cave on his Harley didn't calm them down any. Todd Black in leather, seated astride a big rumbling machine, was like a romance-novel cover come to life, and the minute she climbed on behind him, her zing-o-meter took another hit. What was she doing? Who was in charge here, anyway, her brains or her hormones?

As if she needed to ask that question? Oh, boy.

Bailey's bank account was dwindling, and she was down to her last catering job.

The detective hired by her L.A. lawyer had learned that the doctors found no evidence of food poisoning when Samba Barrett came in and played her *General Hospital* scene. Big surprise. Bailey's lawyer had sent Samba a letter threatening to sue her for slander and that had been enough to shut up her collagen-plumped mouth as she made the late-night talk TV circuit. It was one thing to be a tragic victim. Quite another to get taken to court for being a fake.

Sadly, it was all too late to bring back Bailey's customers.

You still have the Amora Bliss baby shower, she reminded herself. That would have several Hollywood people at it, and if all went well, maybe she could rebuild her reputation.

Or not. Saturday morning, the day before the shower, Melinda Spooner, the hostess, called her. "It turns out we're not going to need you," she said.

Seriously? She was canceling the day before the event? After Bailey had purchased the food, begun making preparations? "But I've already started on the baby bootee cakes," Bailey protested. "And they're adorable."

"I'm sure they are, but we won't be needing you."

This woman was an actress friend of Bailey's high school pal Bitsy (also an aspiring actress—in Los Angeles, who wasn't?). It was enough of a connection that Bailey felt she could fight to keep this gig. "Melinda, does this have anything to do with what happened at Samba Barrett's party?"

There was a betraying moment of silence before Melinda spoke. "No, of course not."

"You know Bitsy wouldn't have referred you to someone incompetent," Bailey pushed. "And you know you can't believe everything you read in the *Star Reporter.*"

"I know. It's just that, well, uh, Amora's having labor pains, and we're not sure if she'll even be around for the party tomorrow."

"I thought she wasn't due for another two months."

"They're premature."

Right.

"I'd better go," Melinda said. She ended the call before Bailey could say anything more.

Bailey looked around her rented commercial kitchen at the piles of fruit, waiting to get made into salad, the fresh herbs, the half-decorated little cakes, and burst into tears. And then she called her big sister.

Samantha answered on the first ring. "How are you doing?"

"Horrible," Bailey sobbed. "I lost my last client."

"Okay, that's it, end of story. You're coming home."

"I can't afford to come home." She also couldn't afford rent. Or food. Heck, she couldn't afford to breathe.

"Oh, yes, you can," Samantha said briskly. "I'm going online and buying you a ticket. You can stay with Cec."

That was her big sister, making decisions for everyone. It was in Samantha's nature to take charge.

But that was exactly what Bailey needed right now. It seemed she was no longer able to run her own life.

"I'll call Cec. You start packing. Okay?"

Bailey had so wanted to make a success of her catering business. She'd had everything all planned. She'd begin as a caterer to the stars and move from there into having her own restaurant and becoming a star herself, a celebrity chef with restaurants in L.A. and Vegas. That dream was dead.

"We've all missed you," Samantha said. "You belong in Icicle Falls. Come home."

Home. Suddenly, that was the sweetest word in the English language. Her family would dress her emotional wounds with encouragement and wrap her in love, and she desperately needed a dose of love.

She sure wasn't feeling it in L.A. "Get me out of here as soon as you can," she said. Dorothy was right. There was no place like home, and the sooner Bailey got there, the happier she'd be.

"Todd, I don't know what we'd do without you," Millie Halverson said, handing Todd a glass of iced tea.

He took it and wiped his sweaty brow. "Aw, Mrs. H., there you go, swelling my head again."

"I don't think that's possible," the old woman said with a smile. "I really do appreciate you coming over to help me. That lawn is too much for me with my darned hip."

Not just the lawn—the whole house, he thought, but he didn't say anything. Sadly, the time would come soon enough when the Halversons would have to admit defeat and give up the place. And now that her husband had had a stroke, Todd expected it was imminent. So far, the Halversons had been holding on with all their might.

He didn't blame them. It was a great old place. And talk about a perfect location. The house was on a street that was now zoned commercial, and it sat right around the corner from the block the locals called Foodie Paradise, which housed everything from Sweet Dreams Chocolates and a spice shop to Bavarian Brews, the town's favorite coffee shop.

Once upon a time this had been a neighborhood filled with families raising their children, but the families had moved on. Some had left during the years the town was struggling economically; others had relocated farther out when Icicle Falls began to prosper, building bigger houses in other parts of town, selling their places to businesspeople anxious to open shops and take advantage of the tourist boom.

Like his house, this one had been around for at least a century and was showing its age. Over the past couple of years, since he'd gotten to know the couple, he'd done some minor repairs, but the kitchen needed updating and the whole place needed painting. Although Todd had offered to do that, Millie and Mike had declined. He suspected it was because of money and had wanted to pay for the paint, but they'd still said no. Hard to accept help, even from someone who'd become a friend.

"If we'd had a son, I'd have wanted him to be just like you," Millie said.

Too bad his old man wasn't around to hear that. He looked at her in mock surprise. "I'm not?"

She smiled at him, shaking her head. "You're such a cutup. But I do want to talk to you seriously when you're done. If you've got a minute."

"For you? Of course." She nodded briskly and hobbled into the house, while he went back to mowing her lawn, wondering what she wanted to talk about.

He found out half an hour later when he'd finished, and she invited him inside to sit on her worn, blue velvet sofa.

"Mike and I have been talking. We think it's time for assisted living, for both of us."

"Aw, crap." They'd wanted to stay in this place until they died. Not practical, of course, but Todd still felt bad for them.

He remembered how his grandpa had fought the whole business of aging, tootling around in his Caddy, trying to take out half the population in his small town. After Gramps had run a stop sign and T-boned a truck, Mom had finally convinced him to turn over his car keys, but it had sent him into a depression that lasted for three months. The only thing that pulled him out was getting rides to the senior center from the widow down the road who drove a 1950 MG. Cruising around in a sports car with a sexy seventy-year-old had eased the pain.

What was going to ease the pain for the Halversons? They didn't have any kids. All they had was each other, and with Mike barely recovering in the nursing home, Todd wasn't sure how long that would last.

"We were hoping you might like to buy the house." Millie said timidly.

Just what he needed—another old Victorian to fix up.

She must have seen his hesitation. "We'll give you a good deal."

"Millie, I don't want to screw you guys over. But, well, I've got a place."

"I know," she said. "But only last fall you were talking with Mike about finding some more business investments. And this is commercially zoned."

Except that he couldn't see himself setting up some fussy little shop. "Aw, Millie, I appreciate the offer but…"

"Prime location. You could rent it out to someone wanting to have a shop."

Of course, she was right. He'd be a fool not to scoop this place up. "What do you want for it?"

The number she gave him was pathetically low. Good Lord, did the woman have no idea what property values were in Icicle Falls these days? "Uh-uh. I'm not out to steal from you."

"Well, then, make *me* an offer."

He did.

She shook her head. "Too high."

He had to laugh. "Mrs. H., you do know that this isn't how you do a real-estate deal? The idea is to get the most money you can."

"You've been awfully good to us since Mike had his stroke—even before. We've talked it over and we'd like to help you a little."

"You'll need that money," he said. "Assisted living isn't cheap."

"We have money, dear," she told him. "We just need to unload this house."

Yeah, right. Who did she think she was kidding? He named another figure, and she countered. At last he threw out a final number he thought he could live with. It was still a bargain, but at least not so much of a steal that he'd feel like a robber. "And that's my final offer."

She nodded. "Done."

"Do you want to talk to your husband about my offer?" Not that Mike could talk so well these days.

"No, I have power of attorney. Anyway, we've already discussed this. He'll be relieved. I'll have our lawyer draw up the papers. If you can arrange financing, we can get this settled pretty quickly."

"There's no rush," he assured her.

She smiled sadly. "Oh, yes, there is. My sister and

her husband are coming here next week to help us move. We found a lovely place in Bremerton."

"Oh." He sat back, shocked.

She smiled sadly at him. "Mike's not getting any better. There was no point letting grass grow under our feet."

"I'd have kept mowing it," he said, trying to lighten the moment.

She patted his arm. "I know. You've been a good friend to us. Mike sure loved going over to The Man Cave on Thursday nights and playing pool with you. It was something to look forward to."

"Same here," Todd said. Mike had reminded him a lot of his grandpa, and he'd enjoyed the old guy. "I'm gonna miss you two."

"Life moves on, dear," she said. She gave him another pat. "Do something wonderful with this place and make us proud."

He nodded, fighting the urge to go all wimpy and cry. "I will."

"I know you will. You're a smart young man."

"That's what my mama always says," he cracked. Too bad he'd never heard those words from his dad.

He and Millie shook hands, and then he left, mentally adding a visit to the bank to the day's to-do list. As he walked to his Harley, he glanced around the street, looking at the various shops. Yep, this was a sweet location. What could he put in that house? Something food-related? He didn't yet know what the old Victorian would become, what should be done with it, but he'd know when he saw it. Oh, yeah, the Halversons had given him an incredible deal.

He smiled. A new business acquisition this morning and a date with the delicious Cecily Sterling tonight. Life was good.

Chapter Three

Cecily was poking around in her closet, trying to decide what to wear on her date with Todd, when Samantha called to tell her their little sister was coming home.

"Thank God," Cecily said. "She needs to be here with people who care about her."

"She also needs a place to stay. Mom's is too small."

"She can stay with me." Cecily had bought Samantha's condo when Samantha married Blake Preston. The condo had two bedrooms, and she wasn't really using the spare one other than as a catchall for her extra clothes and some of her craft supplies.

"That's what I told her."

"You did?" Their big sister would have made an excellent dictator.

"I knew you'd offer," Samantha said in her own defense.

"Oh, so you're psychic. For a minute there, I thought you were just being bossy."

"That, too," Samantha admitted. "Really, I knew you'd offer to take her in. But she can also stay with Blake and me for a while."

They did have three bedrooms. One was an office, but the other they used as a guest room. Now that she thought about it, Cecily was surprised her sister hadn't insisted Bailey stay with them. What was up with that?

"No, it's okay," Cecily said. "I'm fine with having her."

She and Bailey had hung out often when they were both in L.A. Bailey had even catered some mixers for Cecily's matchmaking company. Their relationship, Cecily supposed, had the same ebb and flow as that of most sisters. As kids they'd had their squabbles, but just as often they'd banded together against a common enemy—their older sister. As they moved toward puberty they'd fought more, and sharing a room hadn't helped. But as they'd settled into adulthood and set aside teenage pettiness, they'd come full circle to the camaraderie they'd enjoyed as little girls. It would be fun having her sister stay with her now that they didn't have to share a room, Cecily decided.

"I booked her flight home," Samantha said. "She'll come in on Friday. Want to go to the airport with me to pick her up?"

"You're leaving the office?" Cecily teased.

"Her flight doesn't arrive until 4:30. I'll still get some work in. Anyway, want to ride shotgun?"

"Of course. You knew I would."

She could hear the smile in her sister's voice when she said, "Yes, I did. I'm glad she's coming back." Samantha added, "She belongs here."

As far as Samantha was concerned, Icicle Falls was the center of the universe. She wasn't a big-city kind of girl, and she'd never understood when Cecily moved away to start her business.

But she'd had to get out from under the shadow of Samantha Sterling, Super Achiever, and establish her own identity. Maybe it had been the same for Bailey.

Or it could have had something to do with Bailey's best friends, the twins Mitsy and Bitsy, moving down there. They'd filled her head with dreams of riches and success and her eyes full of stars. Literally.

Cecily felt bad for her little sister. Bailey had hit L.A. with such high hopes, and they'd all been stomped to pieces.

It was a shame because Bailey was a kitchen queen. She'd always loved puttering in the kitchen with their mother, and Cecily could still remember her sister at the age of five, up on a stool, wearing an apron that was way too big for her and rolling out the leftover bits of piecrust Mom had given her. Not content to simply sprinkle them with cinnamon sugar, she'd experimented with everything from jam to taco seasoning. By the time she was in high school she was dreaming up her own cake and cookie recipes. Yes, when it came to creating in the kitchen, her sister was truly talented.

So were a lot of people in L.A., and many of them never made it. Bailey wouldn't either now. At least not down there. But there was no reason she couldn't come home and start a catering business in Icicle Falls. With Samantha and Blake close by to advise her on the business end of things, it was bound to be a success. Cecily decided to suggest that to her once she was done mourning the death of her caterer-to-the-stars dream.

Meanwhile, Cecily needed to choose what to wear. She finally settled on a short-sleeved black top and a black skirt with white polka dots. She put on heels and a pink pearl bracelet—a gift from her first fiancé—and was ready to go.

Her sensible self asked why she was bothering. She shouldn't be making a habit of going out with Todd Black. She decided to ignore her sensible self, especially when Todd showed up at her door, handsome in Dockers and a blue polo shirt. Good Lord, if there was a more handsome man than this one, she didn't know where he was.

"You look great," he said, checking her out. "But then, you always do."

She ignored that blatant flattery and stepped out the door. As they started down the building's stairs to the parking lot, something occurred to her and she stopped. "I should change."

"Don't ever change. I like you just the way you are," he teased.

"I can't ride on a motorcycle in a skirt."

"You won't have to. Mom let me use the car tonight," he joked as he nudged her to begin moving again.

"You have a car?"

"Well, okay, my truck. You okay with that?"

"Of course," she said. What did he think she was, some sort of car snob?

"So," he said as he climbed behind the wheel. "I hope you like action films. That's what's playing at the Falls Cinema."

She preferred romantic comedies but said, "That's fine."

"That's fine," he repeated as he turned the key

in the ignition. "Hmm. Chick speak for, 'It'll have to do.'"

"You sure know a lot about women," she said.

He shot her a grin. "I know a few things." Then he added, "But no man knows everything about women. That's why we're all so fascinated by you. You're a never-ending mystery."

Why did practically everything he said, every look he gave her, make her tingle? It was ridiculous, really, like being in middle school all over again. But the darn tingle was there, and thinking about the trouble it could cause made her nervous.

To cover her nerves, she gave a snort. "Has anyone ever told you you're full of it?"

"A few people."

"Were they all women?" she asked sweetly.

He didn't say anything to that. Instead, he nodded at the radio, where some hip-hop singer was reciting lyrics to the underlying hypnotic pulse of a bass. "Feel free to find something you like."

"I'm surprised you're not listening to country music," she said, searching for a pop station.

"I listen to that, too. I like just about everything."

"Well, that makes you easy to please." The words were barely out of her mouth before she realized she'd handed him yet another opening for a double entendre.

His smile was positively sly. "I am."

"I thought you said you had a serious side."

"I do."

"I'm not convinced. Tell me one thing you can be serious about."

"Taxes. How's that?"

"Impressive. That's it?"

"Death and taxes."

"How about relationships?"

"Those are pretty serious things, too." He pulled up in front of Zelda's, shut off the engine and turned to her. "You think I'm just looking for a hookup, don't you?"

"That did cross my mind."

"I don't know where this is going, but I want to find out. Don't you?"

"I'm not sure," she said honestly. Did she really want to risk a third heartbreak?

"Don't worry. We'll take it one kiss at a time," he said and opened his door. She started to open hers. "Uh-uh," he cautioned, reaching across the seat and stopping her. "My mama raised me to be a gentleman."

"What happened?" Cecily retorted, but she waited for him to walk around and open the door for her.

"See," he said, "I'm not a total Philistine."

"How do you even know what a Philistine is?"

"Hey, I told you. My mama raised me right. I went to Sunday school."

Cecily rolled her eyes and slipped out of the car.

Zelda's was one of the most popular restaurants in Icicle Falls, specializing in Northwest cuisine. As with all the shops and restaurants in town, it boasted hanging baskets overflowing with petunias and geraniums. The glass door had the restaurant's name scrawled across it in gold script and featured the image of a flapper.

Inside, the place was packed with people in town for the weekend to celebrate the Maifest festival, as well as locals. At one table she caught sight of Gerhardt Geissel, who owned Gerhardt's Gasthaus, out with his wife and another couple. The women were dressed in dirndls and the men in lederhosen, an obvious sign that they'd taken part in the late-afternoon performance by their folk-dancing troupe in the town square. Pat Wilder and Ed York occupied another table. It was only a matter of time before those two made their relationship official, and Cecily had a feeling that by Christmas Pat would be sporting a diamond on her left hand. And there, by the window… Her heart rate picked up, and she looked away quickly, trying to pretend she hadn't seen Luke Goodman with his mother and his daughter.

There was no need to feel self-conscious. She'd made it clear to both Luke and herself that she wanted to be only friends.

Still, whenever she ran into him, at the office or anywhere else, she was aware of something between them. She knew it was attraction on his part. What was it for her? Luke didn't hit her zing-o-meter the way Todd did. But she still felt a pull, and that was what bothered her because it wasn't strong enough to encourage him.

It wouldn't be fair. Not when Todd had the effect on her that he had. What she felt for Luke was like the pull of the tide. What she felt when she was with Todd was more like a tidal wave. And she wanted that. She wanted romance with a capital *R*. She wanted to be crazy in love with a man who was crazy in love with her.

But she also wanted someone she could trust. Could she trust Todd Black?

The smile he was giving her as they waited for their table certainly *looked* genuine.

Still, looks could be deceiving. She'd learned that the hard way, and she had two diamond rings to prove it.

Reg, Fiancé Number One, had pursued her with everything from flowers to wine-country jaunts, but six months into their engagement she'd learned that his old girlfriend had come back on the scene. It would have been nice if he'd shared that information with her instead of seeing the other woman on the side. She'd set Reg free to continue stoking the fires with his old flame and dedicated herself to her business.

Then along came Fiancé Number Two, a charming insurance salesman who liked to salsa dance and was an amazingly good listener. This time she was sure she'd made a wise choice. But her insurance salesman, who'd seemed so stable on the outside, turned out to be as stable as a three-legged chair. Marcus had money problems. He was constantly borrowing from Cecily, promising that he'd pay her back and then conveniently forgetting the entire conversation. Marcus finally declared bankruptcy and left for greener pastures, where he found a rich cougar who wanted to buy more than a whole-life policy.

Her matchmaking business hadn't done much for her faith in men, either. It sure would have been refreshing (no, make that a shock) to meet just one man who didn't have specific requests regarding his dream woman's appearance. One man who, instead of asking her to introduce him to a woman with boobs the size of watermelons or a nice, tight ass, had said, "Find me my soul mate."

No wonder that when she returned to Icicle Falls she'd had it with men, lost her confidence in Cupid. But with her sister Samantha a living testimonial for happily-ever-after and Todd Black chipping away at her defenses, here she was, caving and giving the brat with the bow and arrow one last chance. And hoping her famous matchmaking instincts finally kicked in on her own behalf.

Charlene Masters (Charley to her friends), who owned Zelda's, was at her regular post at the reservation podium, greeting her customers. She was another ambassador for true love. After divorcing her cheating husband, who'd then returned, just to bring her more misery, she'd met her Mr. Perfect and was now enjoying newlywed bliss. It could be done.

The question for Cecily was who to do it with. If only she could put Todd Black and Luke Goodman in some giant machine and meld them into one. Todd's sexiness coupled with Luke's dependability—now *that* would be her perfect man.

You don't know that Todd's undependable, she reminded herself. Heck, he owned a business and a house. That required a certain level of dependability. But there was no getting around those bad-boy vibes he gave off. Todd Black, the pirate. Pirates didn't settle down and raise families. And she was ready to get married, wanted to start a family. So, what the heck was she doing going out with him?

Charley greeted her with a surprised "Cec?" then recovered enough to greet Todd. "We've got a nice corner table for you," she told him and led the way to the far end of the dining area.

Which meant they had to pass Luke's table. Cecily was very aware of Todd's hand on her back as they approached, and of Luke's assessing and not-so-happy gaze. She felt an uncomfortable warmth creeping over her cheeks and tried to cool it by telling herself she had nothing to feel awkward about. To prove it, she stopped to say a quick hello and introduced her date. The men shook hands, but it was far from a hearty handshake. They reminded her of boxers touching gloves before a match.

"Todd owns The Man Cave," Cecily said to Luke. He gave Todd a brief nod. "I've seen it."

With the giant Neanderthal in lederhosen painted on the outside, it was hard to miss. "Luke's our production manager at Sweet Dreams," she said to Todd.

"Great place to work," Todd said, giving Cecily one of his killer smiles.

"Yeah, it is," Luke agreed. "The Sterling family means a lot to me." It was said pleasantly enough but, judging by Luke's stiff posture and narrowed eyes, it was a warning of sorts.

Luke's family was already on dessert, wild huckleberry pie for him, coffee for his mom and a strawberry sundae for his daughter. "I was really good today, so I got to go out with Daddy and have ice cream," Serena told Cecily.

"Aren't you glad you were good?" Cecily asked.

Serena nodded vigorously. "Were you good, too?"

"Something like that," Cecily said. She could imagine what Todd would do with that remark.

Before he could even try, Cecily said, "Well, enjoy your evening," and she hurried after Charley.

Luke wasn't hungry anymore. He pushed away his plate.

"Daddy, aren't you going to eat your pie?" Serena asked, obviously shocked by such waste.

"Daddy's had enough," he said.

He'd been trying to convince Cecily Sterling to give him a chance ever since she'd returned to Icicle Falls. And she would have by now if it wasn't for that damn Todd Black. Luke had seen him in Bavarian Brews, putting the moves on her. The guy was slick and good-looking. How did an average man compete with that?

"He who hesitates," his mother said softly.

He could pretend he didn't know what she was talking about, but she wouldn't buy it. "She doesn't think we're a match."

"Well, for heaven's sake, don't take her word for it. From what Muriel has let slip over the last couple of years, the girl wouldn't recognize Prince Charming if he slayed a dragon right in front of her."

"I know who Prince Charming is," Serena piped up. "He dances with the princess at the ball."

Luke had tried that at the Sweet Dreams chocolate ball a couple of years back. He'd probably do better slaying a dragon. "Come on, girls. Let's go home." Zelda's had lost its appeal for him.

Once Cecily and Todd were seated, Charley wished them bon appétit. The look she gave Cecily added, "I expect to hear all about this later." Then she left them alone with their menus.

"Just so you know, you don't have to be good on my account," Todd teased.

Cecily made a face at him. "I figured you wouldn't be able to resist saying something. At least you didn't do it in front of Luke."

"Is he my competition?"

"I don't know." Where had that come from? Of course she knew. She wasn't interested in Luke that way. "Not really."

Todd slung an arm over the back of his chair and regarded her. "So, our heroine is conflicted."

There went her cheeks, warming up again.

"It's okay," Todd said. "I'm not afraid of a little competition. I think I can convince you who the better man is."

And later that night, as they sat in front of her place in his truck, he set about showing her just how superior he was. When she finally got out, her clothes were mussed and her brain was foggy. And she had another date with Todd Black.

Todd drove home wearing a confident smile. Cecily Sterling had kept him dangling like a string of Christmas lights long enough. Now he was done playing games. She was going to be his. Too bad for the Sweet Dreams dude. But in the battle for the babe, that was how it always went, how it had always gone. One guy got the girl and the other one walked away with a big *L* for loser on his forehead.

Todd hadn't become the pro ball player his dad had wanted him to be, but there was one sport he'd excelled at and that was getting girls. (He and his brother both had charm in spades and they'd made good use of it.) And for a teenage boy that kind of success was a lot more gratifying than what his dad had wanted for him.

He'd done other things besides chase girls. By sophomore year in high school he'd decided he needed to work a little harder if he planned to go to college, so he'd pulled up his grades and gotten a 4.0. He'd even turned out for track his junior year (although the old man was not impressed). Still he'd done well, been pretty fast.

But he made his best time with the opposite sex. In college he'd even gotten close to buying a ring, but the nearer he got to hitting the jewelry store for a diamond, the less enthusiastic he became about that relationship. And the more possessive she became. They'd finally had one too many fights and broken up. Just as well. He hadn't been ready. He still wasn't. It would take an exceptional woman to pin him down.

Cecily's perfect features and baby-blue eyes came to mind. Women didn't get any more exceptional than her. Besides being beautiful, she was smart. He liked that. And he liked that she hadn't fallen all over herself to be with him. He appreciated a challenge, liked the fact that she kept the fence high.

But now it was time to jump the fence, time to get this thing moving. She wanted to be with him, even though she'd been trying to hide it ever since they'd met, and God knew he wanted to be with her, more than he'd wanted to be with a woman in a long time.

Flowers always helped fuel a relationship, so Monday morning he went into Lupine Floral.

"Be still, my heart. It's Mr. Gorgeous," Kevin, one of the owners, teased him.

"That's me," Todd said. "Can you guys send some flowers for me today?"

"Of course. Who are we sending to and how much do you want to spend?"

"About fifty bucks, I guess. They need to go to Cecily Sterling over at Sweet Dreams."

"Oh, my. From Mr. Gorgeous to Ms. Beautiful. Are you two an item now?"

"Just hanging out," Todd said.

"Uh-huh," Kevin said with a knowing nod. "Hanging out never gets flowers."

"Sure it does, if you're a nice guy like me. Now, what have you got?"

Kevin led him to the refrigerator case that bloomed with a variety of arrangements. "Come and see."

Todd trailed him over there. Flowers were flowers, as far as he was concerned. But women seemed to like roses. "How about these?" he asked and pointed to a vase of white and pink rosebuds with some kind of greens stuck in with them.

"Oh, boring," Kevin said.

Okay, they were going to stand here all day discussing the artistic merits of flowers. "You pick one."

"Well, if I were you, I'd send this one," Kevin said, reaching in for a gaudy bouquet. "Orange Asiatic lilies, fuchsia carnations, red Peruvian lilies, lavender chrysanthemums and, of course, the requisite greens, all in a glass bubble bowl."

"Works for me," Todd said and got out his credit card. And the sooner it worked, the better he'd like it.

Flowers arrived for Cecily Monday afternoon. The card that came with them was signed, *Thinking about Saturday and smiling, Todd.*

That made her smile, too. It had been a good date, especially that close encounter at the end.

But should she take the risk and allow herself to get serious about him? Was he the get-serious type? She still had her doubts.

She was just leaving to meet Charley for coffee at Bavarian Brews when Luke caught up with her on her way out. "Can I talk to you for a minute?"

Oh, boy. She already knew what he wanted to talk about, and she wasn't looking forward to it. But this was a talk they needed to have. She nodded, and he escorted her around the side of the factory building.

"So, you and that guy—"

"Todd Black," she corrected.

"Are you two serious?"

It was the same question she'd been asking herself since Saturday night. "That was only dinner and a movie." And…she wasn't going to tell Luke about the rest of it.

He propped a hand against the brick wall, bringing himself closer to where she stood. "I like movies. And dinner. And dancing." She knew what he was referring to. She'd danced with him during the chocolate ball at her family's first chocolate festival. The memory spread an unexpected warmth through her body. This was uncomfortable. And confusing.

"Let me take you out," Luke said. "Have dinner with me."

"We work together. It would be awkward."

"I promise not to make it awkward." He leaned in closer, and her nerve endings began to wake up. "All I'm asking is that you give me a chance."

"Oh, I don't—"

"No Sterling woman would pick the first vendor who wanted to do business with Sweet Dreams Chocolates. Don't you think you should be just as discerning when you're doing business of the heart?"

She'd never thought of Luke as a man of many

words, especially poetic words like the ones he'd just uttered.

"A chance—that's all I want," he said. "At least consider it."

She nodded.

Satisfied with that, he pushed away from the wall and let her continue to Bavarian Brews.

Except when she entered her favorite coffee shop she saw Todd inside, waiting in line to order. She did a quick about-face. After her encounter with Luke, she wasn't ready for one with Todd, even if he had sent her flowers. Anyway, she was already feeling jittery. Probably the last thing she needed was caffeine.

No, the last thing she needed was to complicate her life by dating two different men. What on earth was she going to do?

Chapter Four

Cecily was halfway down the street when Charley caught up with her.

"Bavarian Brews is that way," Charley teased.

"Sorry. I was going to call you." Once she got safely away. "I decided I should cut down on my coffee consumption."

"Does that mean I'm going to have to pump you about your love life right here in the middle of the street?"

"There's nothing to pump."

Charley nodded cynically. "Sure. You just happened to run into Todd Black the other night and decided to share a table at my place."

"It was only dinner." Cecily glanced in the direction of the coffee shop. The last thing she wanted was to be standing here when Todd came out. "Give me a rain check on the coffee, okay? I've got to get back to the office."

"Okay." Charley nodded again. "You be careful, buddy. I know he's hot, but I don't want to see you get burned."

"I won't," Cecily said as much to herself as to Charley.

Her friend was right. It was silly to take a chance on getting hurt, especially when a woman could pick a solid, dependable man. Cecily hurried back to Sweet Dreams Chocolates and went straight to Luke's office.

She found him at his desk, frowning in concentration and typing on his computer keyboard with two fingers. He saw her and smiled hopefully. "Hi there. What brings you to my corner of the neighborhood?"

"Dinner. Are you still interested?"

His smile broadened. "Absolutely. How about Friday?"

She didn't want Bailey to spend her first Friday home alone. "Saturday?"

"I can do that. Schwangau?"

That was certainly a more impressive first date than playing pinball in a seedy tavern. Cecily's mind started to wander from the tavern to her first kiss at Todd's house.

She firmly jerked her thoughts off that trail. "Schwangau sounds great."

"Pick you up at six?"

"Sure," she said. And then it seemed there was nothing left to say. She turned to go.

"Cecily."

She turned back.

"Thanks," he said softly.

She nodded.

She'd barely returned to her desk when her cell phone rang. It was Todd, and the very sound of his voice revved her hormones.

"Thanks for the flowers," she said. "They're beautiful."

"Just like the woman I sent them to. When are you

coming back to my cave to play some more pinball?" he asked. Then, before she could answer, he added, "Oh, yeah. That doesn't count as a date. So how about dancing at The Red Barn on Friday night?"

"Isn't Friday a big night at The Man Cave?"

"I'll give myself the night off for bad behavior."

Not interested. Just say it. "My sister's moving back to town, and I'm spending Friday with her."

"Oh? Where's she staying?"

"With me."

"No coming back to your place for a drink after our next date, then," he said. "And, speaking of…if you can't do Friday, how about Saturday?"

"Sorry. I'm busy."

"How long does it take to unpack your sister's suitcase?"

"I'm not busy with her."

There was a long silence before he said, "Oh." Then, "Anyone I know?"

Now the silence was on Cecily's end. She should come right out and tell him it wasn't going to happen between them. She was going in a new, smart direction. With Luke.

"Let me guess. The competition."

Okay, since he asked. "Yes." Luke was a much better candidate for a long-term relationship. And for fatherhood. He was already a family man, which meant he was solid and dependable, not wired for breaking hearts like some people.

"I hope you aren't expecting me to say something inane like 'have a good time,'" Todd said. "You won't have half as much fun as you had with me, you know."

"There's more to life than fun," she said primly.

"Thanks for enlightening me. Seriously, I'm interested in you, Cecily, and I'm not going away just because some other man is, too. Well, unless at some point you want me to. I'm a lot of things, but I'm not a stalker."

"I'm glad to hear it."

"One of my many good qualities," he said. "Talk to you later."

He did have good qualities, Cecily thought as she ended the call. He was smart and funny, and he'd proved he could stay calm in the face of trouble. He was obviously responsible enough to own a business. But was he ready to settle down and have a family? It kept coming back to that. Todd Black was a ladies' man, and she couldn't really see him staying with one woman.

But if he could…

Her thoughts were interrupted by another call, this one from her friend Margo James in L.A. "Hey, you," said Margo. "I'm sitting here in front of a cracker box of a house that's going for a mil, waiting for my client, and figured I'd give you a call. How's life in Small Town, U.S.A.? You ready to come back to the big city yet?"

California had the sun, and when she'd gone down for a visit in January, she'd gotten a big dose of it. But that hadn't been enough to make her want to give up the fresh air and beautiful scenery of Icicle Falls. She'd found her footing in her hometown, made new friends, carved out a life. She still didn't have her *love* life sorted out, but then, she hadn't exactly gotten it sorted out in sunny California, either.

"No. The weather's beautiful up here right now. You should come visit."

"If I did, you'd probably make me go hiking or introduce me to some hairy mountain man. Speaking of men, guess who's engaged."

"Jessica Long."

"Aw, she told you. Or else you're psychic."

It wouldn't have taken any great mental gifts to know that Jessica was on the verge of getting a ring. When Cecily had been down in January, Jessica and her boyfriend hadn't been able to keep their hands off each other. They'd been a pro bono match-up Cecily had arranged, just two friends she'd thought would enjoy each other. And she'd been right.

"Hardly," she said. "Anyone could see where that was heading."

"Well, I'm jealous. When are you going to find me someone perfect?"

"After I find someone for me," Cecily said.

"You've got two men after you. Don't be greedy. By the way, Darby and Ken are pregnant."

Why did it feel as if everyone these days was either getting engaged or getting pregnant? "Well, they've been trying for a year," Cecily reminded both Margo and herself.

"Yeah, I know," Margo said. "Sometimes I wish I hadn't dumped Maurice. He wasn't all that bad."

He'd cheated on her. Twice. "Yeah, he was," Cecily said gently.

"Okay, yeah, he was." Margo sighed. "I don't know why this whole man-woman thing has to be so hard. I think I'm going to become a lesbian."

Cecily laughed. "That won't be happening anytime soon. You like men too much."

"Yeah, though sometimes I wonder why."

"Hey, if it was easy, what would we have to complain about?"

"I could always find something, trust me." There was a moment of silence on the phone, followed by, "Seriously, do you sometimes wonder if you'll ever get it right?"

"All the time," Cecily said.

"Oh, well. If I can't have great sex, I'll have to settle for making a huge commission on this dog of a house I'm about to show. Oh, and this is my client pulling up. I'd better get my game face on."

"Go for it."

"Ciao," Margo said airily.

Cecily went back to writing a product description for their newest chocolate flavors. It would be nice if, for once in her life, she could get those matchmaking instincts that worked so well for everyone else to work on her own behalf.

Bailey looked out the plane window at the lush trees and lawns below. Federal Way was now in view, which meant that within minutes the plane would be landing at Sea-Tac airport outside Seattle. Both her sisters were coming to pick her up, and her mother was home preparing all her favorite foods—mushroom lasagna, chicken Caesar salad and chocolate cake. It was the same chocolate cake her mother had taught her to make when she was twelve, the same recipe she used when she catered parties and needed mini cupcakes.

Those days were now gone. Her business was dead.

So, why had she packed up so many of her kitchen tools and shipped them to Icicle Falls? What a fool. She'd spent a fortune sending home things that would only remind her of her failure.

Well, a girl still needed mini muffin tins and baking sheets and measuring cups and spoons and mixing bowls, for crying out loud. Maybe not a case of cute cupcake holders or tiered serving trays or pastry bags. But still, people would be having birthdays. And baby showers. She'd continue to make fun dishes and treats. She just wouldn't be doing it for a living now.

What *would* she be doing? She blinked hard and told herself not to be a baby. No more crying. She was so done with crying.

"Almost home," said her seatmate, an older man with silver hair.

He was single and lived in Seattle. He'd been a good listener, nodding sympathetically while she told him her woes. He owned a company that distributed seafood, and she'd thought he'd be perfect for her mom. But he hadn't been remotely interested in hearing about her sweet, pretty mother. He'd wanted to know if she ever dated older men. That had been icky and awkward.

She'd told him she had a boyfriend back in Icicle Falls. What a lie! She had no one back in Icicle Falls. She blinked again and wiped at the corner of her eye.

"Is your boyfriend coming to meet you?" asked Mr. Lech.

"No, my sisters will." Her fabulous sisters, who were always there for her. Another tear tried to sneak out of the corner of her eye. She wiped it away and reminded herself that she had much to be grateful for.

And there was a rainbow at the end of this storm. Although her career was over, her love life could take off. There was more than family in Icicle Falls. Brandon Wallace was there. She smiled. Brandon Wallace, ski bum and resident heartbreaker, had been cracking her heart like a jawbreaker off and on since they were kids. In fact, the last time he'd dumped her for another woman had been the final straw. She'd been more than happy to move to L.A.

But that was then. She was a big girl now and more than ready to show Brandon what he'd been missing. Her career might have fizzled, but that didn't mean her love life had to.

The plane landed with a couple of bumps and then taxied to the Jetway. *Okay,* she told herself, *you are now approaching your new life. It will be an adventure.* She only hoped this adventure ended in success.

The plane stopped and everyone hurried to stand up and wait.

"I hope everything works out for you," the older man said. He handed her his business card. "If you ever need anything."

What she really needed was a trip back in time and a chance to turn down catering Samba Barrett's party.

Her suitcase took forever to appear on the baggage carousel, and after seeing her lose her balance trying to grab it and nearly landing on the carousel herself, Bailey's former seatmate came to the rescue and pulled it off. Not an easy feat, considering how big it was and how much she'd crammed into it. He then reminded her...if she needed anything.

She thanked him and hurried off before he could

offer to escort her and her suitcase and carry-ons to her car. Where were Sammy and Cec?

She was about to call when she spotted them. She waved, and they came running to hug her. Oh, those hugs felt good.

"Welcome home," Samantha said.

"I'm so glad to see you guys!" When a girl felt beaten down, there was nothing like family to help her get back on her feet.

"We're glad to see you, too," Cecily told her.

"Mom's home putting the finishing touches on dinner, and we're under strict orders not to get sidetracked shopping in Seattle," Samantha added, "so let's get out of here."

Great idea. She could see her pal from the plane approaching. She gave him a little wave and started for the parking garage at a quick clip.

"Don't tell me. Let me guess," Samantha said. "You picked up a friend?"

"Actually, I thought he'd be perfect for Mom," Bailey began.

"Don't be matching Mom up," Samantha said sternly. "She's not ready for another man."

"I think she is," Bailey insisted. After what Samantha had gone through cleaning up the business mess left behind by their mother's last husband, Bailey understood her sister's reluctance to see their mother find a replacement. Still, Mom deserved to be happy. "What do *you* think?" she asked Cecily. Cec had been a matchmaker. When it came to love, she was an expert. Well, except for when it came to herself. Why her sister was still single was a mystery to Bailey.

"I think it's really good to have you back," Cecily said diplomatically.

"And just in time," Samantha put in. "We could use help in the office."

The office? Was she serious? "I can't type. Remember?" Bailey reminded her. "Anyway, I don't know if I want to work in the office." That probably sounded ungrateful. After all, Samantha had paid for her ticket home. And Sweet Dreams Chocolates was the family business.

They were at Samantha's car now. She turned and stared at Bailey as if she'd announced she was going to run off and join a cult.

Bailey's face sizzled, and she hung her head. She was a terrible ingrate. But she still didn't want to work in the Sweet Dreams office.

Samantha opened the trunk and deposited Bailey's suitcase. "Okay," she said slowly. "What do you want to do?"

Be a caterer. But after what had happened, she was finished with that. "I don't know," she admitted.

"You've got to do something," Samantha said.

"You'll think of something." Cecily gave Bailey another reassuring hug. "You just need some time to find your feet."

Yeah. So there. Gosh, Sammy could be so bossy sometimes.

"You will," Samantha agreed. "And whatever you need, we're there for you."

"I've got what I need—you guys," Bailey said, forgetting her momentary irritation and looking gratefully at her sisters. Even though her older sister was bossy, there was nothing she wouldn't do for her family. And Cecily was always so supportive and sweet. Bailey was lucky to have them both.

Her sisters spent the ride back home filling her in on everything that had been going on in Icicle Falls.

"Bill Will has a new girlfriend," Cecily told her.

"Oh, who?" Bailey asked. Billy Williams, affectionately known as Bill Will, was one of the town's characters. He worked on a nearby guest ranch and spent a lot of time hanging out at Zelda's or The Red Barn. Everyone liked Bill Will, but he wasn't the brightest bulb in the box, so he often got passed over in favor of smarter men.

"Ashley Armstrong," Samantha said in disgust.

"Hey, I hear she's finally getting serious about going back to school," Cecily added from the backseat.

"Yeah, well, with her spousal maintenance about to dry up, she'd better," Samantha said.

"I think she's trying to get her act together," Cecily said. "I hope she does."

"I just hope Bill Will doesn't get hurt." Samantha looked over at Bailey. "Maybe you should go out with him."

Right. Bailey turned around and grinned at Cecily. "Would Bill Will and I be a match?"

Cecily wrinkled her nose. "I don't think so. I have a feeling there's someone better waiting for you."

Brandon Wallace.

"Brandon's not in town," Samantha said as if reading her mind.

Just when her spirits had been lifting. Darn, it was hard to rekindle a romance when one or the other of them was always off somewhere. "Where is he?"

"He moved to Jackson Hole," Samantha said.

"Jackson Hole?" What was there? "Why?"

"Ski resort, of course."

"He's got a girlfriend," Cecily said gently.

"A...girlfriend?" Brandon Wallace, one of the main reasons Bailey had decided she should, indeed, come home, had a girlfriend? "Are you sure?"

Samantha nodded. "I'm sorry."

"How long has he had this girlfriend?" And why hadn't anyone told her?

"According to his mom, they met after he moved there in January."

"That's not very long. Is it serious?" Bailey asked in a small voice. It couldn't be in just a few months.

"Olivia seems to think so," Samantha replied. "She figures they'll be engaged by Christmas."

What did Olivia Wallace know, anyway? Bailey sneaked up a hand to wipe away yet another tear.

"You are way too good for him anyway," Samantha said.

"He was never right for you," Cecily told her.

And what did her sisters know?

Seattle was far behind them now, and the mountains in the distance beckoned. *Welcome home.*

Bailey scowled at them. *Phooey!*

Chapter Five

When Bailey walked into Muriel Sterling's rented cottage, it wasn't hard to see that her mother had gone to a lot of trouble to make her homecoming a celebration. A bouquet of tulips sat in a vase on the counter, along with a batch of peanut butter–chocolate chip cookies divided three ways and wrapped in pink cellophane and tied with pink ribbon—big-girl party favors. There was even a welcome-home present for Bailey, a signed copy of her mother's latest book.

"I thought it might be helpful," she said as Cecily got busy pouring tea.

Bailey read the title, which was in flowing embossed script. *New Beginnings*. Was that what you called this?

She tried to look appreciative. "Thanks, Mama." And then, before her mother could go into one of her soft-spoken pep talks, she changed the subject. "I smell mushroom lasagna."

"And garlic bread," her mother added. "I hope you girls are hungry."

"Of course," Samantha said. "We've been saving our appetites."

"No stop at a Starbucks on the way home?" their mother teased.

"Well, we had to do that," Cecily said with a smile.

The next few minutes were spent companionably in the kitchen, the sisters munching on salmon pâté and crackers while they helped their mother get the food on the table.

Once Muriel had said grace, Samantha raised her mug of chocolate mint tea. "Here's to our sister. We're glad to have you home."

"And to new beginnings," Cecily proclaimed.

Bailey's smile faltered. She'd come home in disgrace, and the romance she'd hoped to rekindle with Brandon was happening with a different woman. How was that a new beginning? But she gamely recovered and passed her plate for her mother to fill.

"I assume your sisters spent the ride over the mountains catching you up on everything that's been going on around here," Mama said.

Bailey nodded, and again, she had trouble keeping the smile on her face. Her mother gave back her plate, and she spent a moment contemplating the food on it. She loved mushroom lasagna, but suddenly she had no appetite.

A soft hand with a slight speckling of age spots covered hers. "Things really are going to work out," her mother said.

Bailey nodded once more. "I know. And I'm so lucky to have all of you. It's good to be home," she said, bursting into tears.

And now, in addition to losing her business and finding out that the man of her dreams had fallen for some other woman, she'd ruined her welcome-home dinner. Her big sister left the table, probably in disgust, probably wondering why she'd bothered to buy such an ingrate a plane ticket home.

But, no, a couple of minutes later Samantha was back. She set a salted caramel on top of the lasagna. "Eat this," she commanded.

As if chocolate fixed everything. But Bailey obeyed and popped it in her mouth. It didn't fix anything, but it did make her feel better.

"Another toast," Samantha proposed. "To the bitches who try to ruin us. May their chocolate supply dry up and their boobs fall off."

Here Bailey was aware of her mother frowning in disapproval, and despite everything she had to smile just a little.

"Amen," she said even as their mother murmured, "Really, Samantha."

Sammy grinned. "It made her smile."

For a moment. Bailey set down her mug with a frown. "I don't know what I'm going to do."

"You'll figure it out," her mother assured her.

She sure hoped Mama was right.

Cecily couldn't help feeling guilty as she got ready for her date with Luke. Her little sister was barely home, and here she was, leaving her. Bailey had a naturally happy disposition, so she'd managed to rally during the dinner at their mother's the night before. She'd been impressed with the changes Cecily had made to the condo after buying it from Samantha, approving the sunny yellow walls and the cream-colored leather sofa and chair. She'd gotten tears in her eyes when she saw the Welcome Home, Bailey sign Cecily had hung on the door, and she'd been delighted with her room.

"This is almost as good as when we shared a room growing up," she'd said with a smile. "I was always kind of sad when Mama and Daddy bought that bigger house and we each got our own room."

Cecily had diplomatically kept her mouth shut on that subject. She'd enjoyed having the privacy.

"This will be fun," Bailey had said, smiling brightly.

But later that night Cecily had heard her crying.

It was hard to come home feeling like a failure, but Cecily hoped that once some of the pain wore off, Bailey would be glad she'd decided to return. Meanwhile, she was going to have to keep working her way through the misery.

"Are you sure you don't mind if I go out?" she asked as she came into the living room.

Bailey was parked on the couch with a can of pop, a bag of veggie chips and a stack of Oreos. She had the TV on and turned to the Food Network. Cecily looked to see what program she was watching, and Bailey quickly aimed the remote and killed it.

But not before Cecily had seen what was playing. "Isn't that *Serve It Up?*"

Bailey pulled a chip out of the bag and studied it. "I was channel surfing."

"Uh-huh." Just what her sister needed—to sit around watching a reality TV show about successful caterers. "Why don't you come out with us," she suggested.

Bailey stared at her in horror. "On your *date?*"

"Luke wouldn't mind." Well, maybe he would, but Cecily was sure he'd understand.

"No," Bailey said with a firm shake of the head. "I'll be fine. Really."

"If you watch that show, it's only going to make you feel worse," Cecily cautioned.

"I don't think anything can make me feel worse."

Cecily remembered how she'd tortured herself watching *The Bachelorette* after breaking up with Fiancé Number Two. "Trust me," she said over her shoulder. "There's always something that can make you feel worse. Come on," she urged. "Come out with us."

"No way," Bailey said stubbornly. "I'll be fine here. Really."

"Okay, then promise me you won't watch *Serve It Up.*"

Bailey heaved a dramatic sigh. "I promise."

The doorbell rang and Cecily went to let Luke in. She opened the door, and there he stood, holding a single red rose and wearing a smile. Luke Goodman wasn't the handsomest man Cecily had ever dated. He certainly didn't have the swarthy good looks of a Todd Black. But he had a strong chin and broad shoulders. Broad enough to cry on. Hmm. Maybe he and Bailey…

"Hi," he said and handed over the flower.

"Thanks," she said. "That was really sweet."

"I figured there was no sense bringing chocolate."

She opened the door wide and invited him in.

He saw Bailey camped out on the couch and gave her a nod and a friendly smile. No chemistry there, Cecily could immediately tell. "Hi, Bailey," he said. "You home visiting?"

"No," she replied. "I'm…home."

"Yeah? Did you come back to work at Sweet Dreams?"

"No. I…" She bit her lip. "I'm…I'm not sure yet what I'm going to do."

He nodded, taking that in. "Well, it's good to see you. Welcome back."

"Thanks," she said and frowned at her can of pop.

"We should get going," Cecily said. "Are you absolutely sure you don't want to come with us?" she asked in one last attempt to get her sister out and having fun. She was aware of Luke next to her, blinking in astonishment.

But he recovered quickly. "Schwangau has a killer new menu."

If she'd had any doubts (which she hadn't), here was proof positive that Luke Goodman was a super nice man. Yes, for once in her life she was being smart about love.

Bailey passed on the offer and shooed them on their way.

"So now we have all the Sterling sisters back in Icicle Falls, huh?" Luke said as they walked to his car.

"It looks like it. Of course, she's not exactly home because she wants to be."

"I know."

She glanced at him in surprise. Although why should she have been surprised? It was a small town, and, for all she knew, Luke had even contributed to Bailey's legal war chest.

"Hey, I check out the magazine covers when I'm waiting in the checkout line, too," he said. Then, as though he'd read her mind, he added, "Yeah, I kicked in a few bucks for the cause."

Once inside the car, which was a hybrid, she smiled. Luke's head practically reached the ceiling. "Do you ever get claustrophobic in this?"

"I did at first," he admitted. "But it's good for the environment and good for the budget, so I adjusted."

It seemed that he'd had to adjust to a lot of things, probably the hardest being the loss of his wife. How did he manage to stay so cheerful? Wired the same as Bailey, obviously. Those two should have been a match.

But there was no understanding the heart. After all, she shouldn't be the least bit interested in Todd Black.

She wasn't, she told herself. Not anymore.

"I think, in the long run, your sister will be glad she came back here," Luke said.

"Now you sound like Samantha. According to her, Icicle Falls is the center of the universe."

He smiled. "Isn't it?"

"Well, there *are* other places in the world," Cecily said.

"But not like this one."

She laughed. "Just how many other places have you seen?"

"Seattle."

"Well, there you go."

"Paris."

The Eiffel Tower, the Louvre, the perfume factories! Paris was a city Cecily had always wanted to visit. "You were in Paris?"

Now his smile wasn't quite so happy. "My wife and I went there for our honeymoon."

"Oh." Cecily tried to think of something else, anything else, to say, but couldn't.

"I have great memories of our time in that city, but it has more to do with her than the spots we visited. I have this theory. Any place can be great if you're with people you care about."

Oh, melt. This man was too good to be true. "So, that's why you like it here?"

He nodded. "All the people I care about are right here in Icicle Falls. Plus, I like rock climbing and hiking and fishing. And chocolate," he said, giving her a wink. "And the family who owns the chocolate company."

"You're sucking up to the wrong woman. Samantha's the one in charge," Cecily pointed out.

"Yeah, but there's only one Sterling woman I'm interested in," he said.

Suddenly, out of nowhere, a tiny zing hit her. Luke Goodman had just hit her zing-o-meter. Maybe not as hard as Todd but she definitely felt it. Maybe, if she gave him a chance, he could hit it even harder.

Okay, Bailey told herself, *you can't sit around all night watching TV and eating junk food.* Well, she could, but if she ate any more Oreos she was going to end up looking like a cookie jar.

So what? Cookie jars were cute. Everyone loved cookie jars. She popped another Oreo in her mouth.

If Mama could see her now, she'd say it was a waste to be eating store-bought cookies when she was such a good baker. Yeah, homemade was better.

"Except nobody ever got food poisoning from an Oreo," she muttered and gobbled down another.

Okay, this really wasn't helping. And it sure wouldn't help to spend money she didn't have on a whole new wardrobe. She shoved away the comfort food and turned off the TV.

Then wondered what to do. Whenever she was stressed or bored, she always found herself in the kitchen. Except the last thing she needed was more food. She'd be right back to the problem of developing cookie-jar hips. Anyway, if she went to the store for supplies, she was bound to run into someone she knew. Not any of her close friends, though, since they'd all moved away, but *someone*.

She thought of her girlfriends Mitsy and Bitsy still living it up in L.A. They were probably getting ready to go dancing at some trendy club while she sat around her sister's place like a bored babysitter. *Only boring people are boring,* she reminded herself, quoting her mother's favorite response when, as a child, she'd complained of being bored.

Quoting her mother made her remember the book she'd tossed on the guest room dresser. Other than cookbooks and *Bon Appétit,* she wasn't a big reader, but her mother had obviously wanted her to read this newest book of hers. Well, she had nothing else to do.

She fetched the book and settled back on the couch with it. She ran her fingers along the gold-embossed script. *New Beginnings.* That was her.

She studied the artsy photograph of a red rose blooming in a blurred black-and-white garden. "Looks like a gardening book," she muttered as she opened it to the first page. But her mother wouldn't have given her this if she didn't think there was something in it for her. She began to read.

Death in Winter, Growth in Spring
A garden is God's constant reminder to us that we

*live in a world of change, a world of birth, death and
rebirth. What happens to us is often exactly like what
happens in our gardens.*

What had happened to her had been nothing like
what happened with the little garden she'd been growing in pots on her apartment patio. She'd lovingly wa-
tered her basil, rosemary and mint, and everything
had thrived. She'd worked hard to grow her business,
and that should have thrived, too.

*Winter comes and the garden dies. But in real-
ity it's not dead. It's merely dormant, waiting for the
warmth of a new spring to bring back to life those pe-
rennials we so enjoyed the year before.*

Bailey frowned. There was no bringing back her
catering career.

*It's often the same with our lives. We plan for cer-
tain things and hope for positive outcomes, dream
big dreams, only to see our plans crumble and our
dreams die.*

Now Bailey felt as though her mother had written
this just for her. Was Mama psychic?

*You may be mourning the death of a dream, but
you don't have to mourn without hope. Like a flower
in winter experiencing a period of dormancy, use this
time to heal and gather strength for spring, when a
new dream will crop up.*

Bailey frowned and tossed the book on the coffee table. She wasn't going to be a caterer again, so
she didn't see how any new dream could "crop up."
Anyway, it was already spring, and she was all dead
and shriveled.

What was on the Food Network now?

* * *

Luke did manage to register higher on the zing-o-meter dial later that night when he kissed Cecily at her door. It started as a soft kiss, with his fingers threading through her hair, and then got a little more adventurous with his tongue teasing the corners of her mouth. Okay, that was nice.

But was it as nice as Todd's kiss?

Todd Black was a practiced seducer. Comparing the two men, Luke, who was Mr. Upright and Noble, and Todd, who was… Well, it was like comparing Superman and Jack Sparrow.

But she liked Jack Sparrow.

You are not going to get your heart broken again she informed herself.

Except she didn't know for sure that Todd was going to break her heart.

This was awful, like choosing between dark and white chocolate.

Oh, now there was a great analogy—comparing an important life choice to picking a favorite candy.

She had to make a decision. *Which man do you want?*

"Both" was not an acceptable answer. *Anyway, you already decided.*

Bailey was still parked on the couch and still vegging out in front of the TV when she came in. Different show but still the Food Network. "Did you guys have a good time?" she asked, using the remote to destroy the evidence.

"We did," Cecily said.

"He's a nice guy."

Yes, he was. And a smart woman would pick the nice guy.

But when she drifted off to sleep, she found herself in a wedding gown, climbing aboard a pirate ship. And there to meet her was Todd Black wearing pirate clothes and guyliner.

"What am I doing here?" she cried, taking in the seedy ship and his equally seedy crew, who looked suspiciously like the regulars at The Man Cave.

"Hey, YOLO," said Todd the pirate.

"You mean, yo-ho-ho," she corrected him.

"I mean YOLO. You only live once," he said and held out a tankard of rum.

The dream went from her drinking rum while Todd's crew sang the same ditty sung by the Pirates in Disneyland's Pirates of the Caribbean ride to doing a wild tango with Todd. He was just making her walk the plank in her bra and panties when she woke up.

Oh, good grief. What was she doing?

Chapter Six

After church the Sterling women gathered at Samantha and Blake's house to celebrate Mother's Day. Blake's parents had come over from Seattle for the occasion, and his grandparents, Tom and Janice Lind, were present, as well. Samantha had prepared a chicken casserole, and Caesar and fruit salads, and Bailey had contributed rosemary scones and a white chocolate cheesecake to round out the menu.

Cecily had made brown sugar facial scrubs for all the women, while Bailey, who was in charge of drinks and had made Bellinis, handed them to guests as they waited for Sunday brunch to make its way to the table.

Samantha was busy dishing up, so Bailey set her drink on the counter. But once they all were seated at the table, Cecily noticed Sam still didn't have hers. The only glass at her place setting was for water. Hmm.

"These scones are delicious," Janice told Bailey.

"I bet she'd give you the recipe in exchange for your banana cake recipe," Samantha teased.

Janice shook a playful finger at her. "You know that's top secret."

And fabulous. Every year Janice's cake won the

Raise the Roof bake-off that collected funds to maintain historic town buildings. She'd been heard to joke that when she died she'd leave her recipe box to Youth Power, her favorite local charity, to be auctioned off.

Cecily was in no hurry to lose Janice, who was a town treasure, but if that recipe box ever came up for auction, she'd definitely bid on it. It would make a great Christmas present for Bailey. Even though she was probably never going to cater again, Cecily felt sure her sister would wind up doing something food-related.

They were just about ready for dessert when Blake tapped on his water glass for everyone's attention. Then he stood. "We're really glad you could all come today, and I want to propose a toast. To our mothers, who do so much for us."

"To our mothers," everyone echoed and clinked glasses.

But Blake was still standing, and Cecily knew why.

"And to our future mothers," he said, raising his glass to Samantha, who was suddenly blushing.

"Oh, my," Mom whispered. "Does this mean what we think it does?"

Blake grinned and nodded. "We're pregnant."

"Oh, sweetie!" Mom jumped up and hurried to hug Samantha, as did all the other women, including Cecily, while the two other men present clapped Blake on the back.

This was followed by a barrage of questions. When was the baby due? Had they picked out names yet? Did they know what they were having? Did they want to know? "In December," Samantha answered. No, they didn't know the sex of the baby yet, but they should be able to tell when Samantha had her twelve-week ultrasound. "We haven't picked out a boy's name yet," Samantha said, "but if it's a girl we're going to name her Rose, after Great-Grandma Rose."

The woman who'd started Sweet Dreams Chocolates. "Perfect," Cecily murmured. Sam deserved to be happy. She'd held their family together when they lost their father and had saved the company from ruin after their stepfather died. Like all proper heroines, she'd been rewarded with a good dose of happily-ever-after, and the baby was the latest installment.

And, of course, they'd all get to enjoy the baby. Cecily could hardly wait to become an aunt.

But she also wanted to become a mother. And a wife. She wanted that happily-ever-after she'd always been so good at helping other people find. She'd hit the snooze button on her biological clock, but now Samantha's announcement had set it off again, and it was ringing loud and clear. Darn it, she didn't want to wait until she was pushing menopause to get pregnant.

You have time, she assured herself. Even if her twenties would be ending this fall, it didn't mean her life was over. And it didn't mean she couldn't get pregnant. Samantha was over thirty, and she'd had no trouble conceiving and her baby was going to be fine. So there was no need to panic…as long as she didn't keep making man mistakes. She had to be smart this time round and choose someone who was truly her perfect match. Not perfect—just perfect for her.

Meanwhile, she would be happy for her sister. "We can have the baby shower at the condo," she offered.

"I'm not sure you'll be able to fit everyone in the

condo," her mother said. "Not with all the people who'll want to come."

"Then we can do it at my house," Janice said. "We have plenty of room."

Talk of the new arrival continued through dessert and coffee, and by the time the party broke up, the child's life had been decided. Of course little Rose—Samantha was convinced the baby would be a girl—would grow up to run Sweet Dreams Chocolates. Naturally, she'd marry a local boy.

"Marrying local is going to become a Sterling woman tradition," Samantha predicted, smiling at Cecily. It wasn't difficult to guess whom her sister was thinking of. Yep, keep the production manager by bringing him into the family. Maybe that wasn't such a bad idea. If she was going to be practical. If she could stop having stupid pirate dreams.

Todd called his mother Sunday afternoon to wish her a happy Mother's Day. He hoped his little brother was taking her out. Or had at least sent flowers. Or a card. Or something.

"Oh, Toddy, the flowers were lovely," she gushed. "And chocolates, too."

"Nothing's too good for you," he said.

"You know, the best Mother's Day would be to have you here."

"I know." His mom lived in Medford, Oregon, now, not exactly close to Icicle Falls. Still, one of these days he needed to hop on his bike and drive out there to see her. "It's hard to get away with the business and all, but count on me for Thanksgiving. So, what are you doing today?"

"Oh, just hanging out."

Which meant his brother wasn't on the job. The turkey was *living* in Medford now. He had no excuse not to go see their mom on Mother's Day.

Todd frowned. "Where's Devon?"

"I haven't heard from him. But I'm sure I will," Mom hurried on, always ready to cover up her younger son's neglect.

"Yeah, I'm sure you will, too," Todd agreed, because as soon as he got off the phone, he was going to call the little twit and give him a verbal boot in the ass.

"I did see him the other day," Mom said. "He came by for dinner."

Oh, yeah, if there was a chance to sucker Mom into cooking for him, Devon would be there. Probably brought a load of wash for her to do, too. Well, that was how it worked when you were the baby of the family, the golden boy.

Devon was Dad's darling, too. And why not? He'd grabbed the brass ring (for about two seconds) and had that pro ball career. If you could call being on a farm team for a couple of years a career. Devon had trashed his shoulder, and that had ended his pitching days, but not before he made it into the family hall of fame. He was still living on the old glory days, drifting from one construction company to the next, getting DUIs and generally living it up. Yep, the darling of the family.

"Do you still have that tavern?"

Mom was getting better at hiding the disgust, but Todd could hear it lurking there. Very low class of him to invest in a tavern. Even if it was a little gold mine, it was a tacky one. "Yeah, I've still got it. I just bought another house."

"A house?"

Now, that interested her. "It's commercially zoned, great location. I'm going to rent it out to someone for a shop."

His mom had been to Icicle Falls to visit, and while she didn't approve of The Man Cave, she did approve of the town with its lovely scenery and intriguing shops.

"Or you could put in a shop yourself," she said.

"It might be hard to run a day business *and* a night business."

"There is that," she admitted. "What sort of shop do you see going in there?"

"I don't know. The house is an old Victorian, lots of gingerbread."

"Oh, how sweet. So, what don't you have up there?"

"Nothing." They had shops for everything a tourist could want, from clothes to specialty soaps and bath items.

"Oh, there has to be something."

"I don't know. I thought maybe a restaurant, but the town has plenty of those."

"It doesn't have a tearoom."

"A what?"

"A fancy little restaurant where ladies can go for tea."

"I don't know," he said again, doubtfully. "A whole restaurant for tea?"

"Like in England, with fancy china, little tea cakes and sandwiches. When I went to London with your aunt for our birthdays, we went to Harrods and had tea. It was lovely. Expensive, too," she added. "They must make a fortune off silly tourists like me and Aunt Sue."

"This isn't exactly London."

"No, but you've got a female population and a lot of visitors. Done right, it could be a real moneymaker."

"Maybe," he said. He'd have to do some research. "Thanks for the tip. I'll think about it."

"I'm sure whatever you put in will be lovely. You've become quite the businessman, sweetie. One of these days you'll be flying down to see me in your own private plane. But don't wait that long," she quickly added.

"Thanksgiving, Mom," he promised again.

They chatted for a few more minutes, and then he hung up and called his brother.

Devon mumbled a sleepy hello.

"You're still in bed?" Todd demanded.

"Hey, I had a late night."

So had Todd. He hadn't gotten home from work until after two, but *he* was awake. "Yeah, well, it's time to get up, Sleeping Ugly. It's Mother's Day."

"What, you want me to send you a bouquet?" joked Devon.

"No. I want you to get your butt out of bed and go over to Mom's and take her out to eat, dickhead."

"Hey, I was going to go over there."

"Don't sucker her into cooking for you, either."

"What do you think I am?"

Selfish, irresponsible.

"I'm gonna go by and surprise her, take her out to dinner."

Now that Todd had called and reminded him. Sheesh.

How could anyone manage to forget Mother's Day? There were ads promoting it everywhere you turned.

"Hey, I'm glad you called," Devon said.

Uh-oh. Todd gritted his teeth. *Here it comes.*

"I'm having kind of a cash-flow problem. I was hoping you could float me a loan for a couple of weeks."

Oh, no. Had he lost his job? "You still working?"

"Yeah, of course. It's just that, well, I had a losing streak at poker, and I owe this guy some money."

"Ask Dad."

"Come on. You know I can't."

Yes, their father would draw the line at paying a gambling debt. "You can be stupid with your money," the old man liked to say, "but I won't give you mine to be stupid with." He'd said as much to Todd when he'd wanted to buy The Man Cave. It had almost killed him later to admit that Todd had made a smart investment.

"How much?" Todd said, resigned to his fate.

"Just a couple hundred. Well, three to be exact."

Todd swore under his breath.

"I'll pay you back, come payday," Devon said immediately.

Todd doubted that. His brother forgot more debts than he remembered. "Okay. I'll wire it to you."

"Hey, thanks."

"But only after I hear from Mom that you took her out for Mother's Day."

"I said I was going to."

"Yeah, well, this will make sure you do."

"You're a real shit sometimes, you know that?" Devon snapped.

"I try," Todd said and ended the call. And there

was another codependent moment to deposit in the old memory bank.

Family ties—they could strangle a guy. In his opinion, romance writers and the movie folks both did their part to keep the propaganda going, convincing people that a happy life meant the house with the white picket fence and the dog crapping in the yard and the kids running around spilling stuff and fighting. And Mom and Dad in the middle of it all like the center of a wheel, stable and content and keeping everyone together. He figured it worked that way for some people, but if you asked him, the whole family thing was the world's biggest crapshoot.

He was in no hurry to throw the dice. It was a lot of grief and hassle all for a cheap tie once a year on Father's Day. Or, in the case of his mom, some flowers and a day spent hoping she'd see one of her sons. Nope, no hurry at all. Maintaining a relationship with a woman that lasted longer than six months was a big enough goal.

And definitely a worthwhile one when it came to Cecily, he thought with a smile. Heck, with her he could even look beyond that six-month marker and still see them together. But the house, the picket fence, the tie, the kids? Okay, he wasn't ready to look quite *that* far into the future yet. Too damned scary.

The next morning Cecily ran into Todd Black at Bavarian Brews. Funny how they both seemed to come in around the same time every morning lately. She wasn't doing this consciously, was she?

"Are you stalking me?" he teased.

"I was just going to ask you the same thing."

"Well, here's to mutual stalking," he said and touched his coffee cup to hers. "So, how was your weekend?" he asked casually.

"Great. My sister's all moved in."

"Good. And how was Saturday?"

"Very nice," she said. The words were barely out of her mouth before a vision of herself on a gangplank in a pink bra and panty set invaded her mind. She could feel her cheeks warming.

Todd gave her a scornful look. "Nice? Wow, you two really lit up the town."

"I guess if I'd been with you, it would have been a night to remember," she scoffed.

"Hey, it would've been more than nice." He moved a step closer. "So, how about hanging out with me next weekend?"

"I'll think about it," she hedged.

"Don't spend too much time thinking," he said and tapped her on the nose.

Even that small contact was enough to shoot an electric charge to her chest. She watched as he sauntered out of the coffee shop. He looked as good from behind as he did from the front. Of course, she was going to get smart and match herself up with Luke, but what could it hurt to play a little pinball on Friday night?

Bailey had logged in TV time with everyone from Rachael Ray to the Barefoot Contessa. She was watching Guy Fieri and thinking how nice it would be to have a cooking show with someone cute like him when the condo door opened and Cecily walked in.

Bailey gave a guilty start and killed the TV. Not

quickly enough, though. Cecily had seen; Bailey could tell by the worried expression on her sister's face.

There was nothing to worry about, really. So what if she was still in her pj's? And so what if the coffee table was littered with evidence of her eating binge? A big bowl with only a couple of unpopped popcorn kernels sat in silent testimony as to what she'd had for lunch, along with three empty soda bottles. If Cecily went looking for her supply of chocolates, she'd find those missing because Bailey had consumed them, too.

"I was just…" She stopped. What was she doing? "Taking a break."

Cecily nodded. "You're allowed."

But Bailey felt guilty. She hopped off the couch. "Would you like me to make dinner?"

"Sure. That'd be great. I've got—"

"Hamburger in the fridge," Bailey finished for her. "I saw it. I'll make us some Nachos Supreme."

Half an hour later they were side by side at the granite-topped eating bar, halfway through a meal of nachos and lemonade, and had exhausted the topic of Cecily's day. They had avoided the subject of Bailey's day. It was all too evident how that had gone.

"So, tomorrow I'm having lunch with Charley, who used to be Charley Albach," Cecily said casually. "Want to join us?"

Charley, the successful restaurant owner? That would be fun. Not! "No, I've actually got some things planned for tomorrow." *To watch the Food Network.*

Unlike their older sister, Cecily wasn't one to pry. She simply nodded and said okay.

The next day, to prove she wasn't a loser, Bailey

showered and got dressed. Then, while Cecily was at lunch, she watched more cooking shows and had a good, long cry.

Okay, this was really bad. She was in a terrible slump. She went to the kitchen and made chocolate-dipped shortbread. There. Now she'd accomplished something.

There were even some cookies left by the time Cecily got home. And Bailey fixed dinner again. "How was lunch with Charley?" she asked.

"Fine," Cecily said. She took a bite of the stuffed pork chops Bailey had made for dinner, then casually added, "Her sous chef just gave notice."

Bailey's forkful of baked potato stopped halfway to her mouth.

"She thought you might be interested."

Suddenly Bailey's heart began to beat faster, and she couldn't quite catch her breath.

"Bailey?" Cecily asked in concern. "Are you okay?"

Bailey swallowed hard and set her fork back down on the plate. "I'm fine." She took a deep breath, then reached for her water glass and gulped half of it. She *was* fine. She wasn't going to allow a little thing like a ruined dream to keep her down.

But what was she going to do? Not work in a restaurant. Ever. Again.

She felt a gentle hand on her arm. "You can't let that woman take your dream from you."

Too late. "I don't want…" Bailey stopped and bit her lip to keep from crying. It didn't help. Sneaky little tears began to creep out of the corners of her eyes.

"It's okay. You don't have to do it," Cecily said, and Bailey nodded and wiped her eyes.

"You could find something different to do for a while," Cecily suggested.

"Like what?" All Bailey knew, all she'd ever breathed, slept and talked, was cooking.

"I don't know. I did see a help-wanted sign in the window of Tina Swift's shop."

"Which one is that?"

"The one that sells lace and china."

Bailey liked nice things. She especially liked china. She'd shipped home two boxes of pretty dishes that she'd used for catering bridal and baby showers. What was she going to do with that stuff now? Maybe she could sell it on consignment.

"It might at least give you something to do while you're figuring out what you *really* want to do," Cecily said, bringing them back to the topic at hand.

Her sister was right. She couldn't sit around forever watching cooking shows and trying to eat away her unhappiness. Her jeans were already uncomfortably tight. She nodded. "I'll go over there tomorrow." And who knew? Maybe it would turn out to be fun. Maybe, someday, she could own a shop here in Icicle Falls, perhaps a kitchen shop. She could be happy owning a kitchen shop. And she could still have fun in the kitchen, cooking for family and friends, maybe even some special man. Although with Brandon gone, she couldn't imagine who that would be.

"I thought I'd try a new chocolate bubble-bath recipe," Cecily said after they'd finished eating. "Want to help me?"

"Sure." She enjoyed doing things with her sister, and it was fun to try a new recipe, whether it was for food or bubble bath.

As they chopped up dark chocolate to heat with soy milk, she found herself comparing her life to her sisters'. Sammy was happy running Sweet Dreams and starting a family with Blake. Cecily now had an important position in the company, handling the marketing and advertising, and she owned her condo and was seeing Luke, who was a great guy. Both her sisters had their acts together, and here she was, with nothing.

It was pretty embarrassing, considering the fact that she'd always believed she'd be the sister to make a big splash in the pool of life. Things had come easy for her growing up—friends, boyfriends, making the cheer squad in high school. She'd even won the junior-baker contest at the Raise the Roof event three years in a row. Her parents had constantly praised her, and her father had predicted she'd become a famous chef. It had never occurred to her that she might fail.

At some point in our lives, failure visits us all, she read in her mother's book later that night. *If you don't fail, you're not reaching high enough.*

Bailey frowned and slumped against the pillows. People should warn you that when you reached too high, you fell and got hurt.

Well, at least working in a shop wouldn't be hard.

Chapter Seven

"This will be a new adventure," Bailey told herself as she entered Tina Swift's Lace and Lovelies shop. And she was ready for a new adventure. Catering was too much work anyway. Nobody really appreciated what you did. You went to the trouble of creating a culinary work of art, and people just snarfed it down and then accused you of making them sick. Selling lace and china would be nothing compared to what she'd been doing. If she got the job.

Insecurity suddenly assailed her. What if Tina wouldn't hire her? Tina was older than Bailey and hung with a different crowd, so Bailey couldn't play the friendship card. What if Tina didn't want the notorious party poisoner working for her?

Don't be silly, she scolded herself. *You can do this.* After all, how hard could it be to sell lace and teacups?

Tina was ringing up a sale. "These lace curtains will look fabulous in your bedroom," she told Hildy Johnson, who owned Johnson's Drugs along with her husband, Nils. "Just the romantic touch you wanted."

"Yes, I think so," Hildy said as she turned her head to see who'd walked into the shop. "Well, Bailey Sterling, I wondered if you'd come back home after that horrible experience in Hollywood."

Great. Now if Tina hasn't already heard, she soon will. Bailey forced herself to smile and shrug.

"You know, if you'd stayed in Icicle Falls, this would never have happened to you," Hildy said. Even though Hildy was old enough to be Bailey's mother, Bailey didn't appreciate the unsolicited advice. Her own mother hadn't said any such thing. But then, Muriel Sterling had ten times the class Hildy had.

"What happened?" Tina asked.

Hildy spoke before Bailey could open her mouth. "You don't know? They started a legal defense fund for her over at the bank. She catered a party for that starlet who got food poisoning."

"She didn't get food poisoning," Bailey said. "At least not from anything I made. It was all a publicity stunt."

"Those Hollywood types," Hildy said in disgust. "Are you suing her?"

"You should," added Tina.

Bailey shook her head. What would be the point? "I just want to move on. In fact, that's why I'm here. My sister told me you're hiring."

"You don't want to work for your family?" Hildy asked, obviously shocked.

Maybe she should've let Sammy find a place for her at Sweet Dreams Chocolates. It was, after all, a family business.

But then she remembered the last time she'd helped with the family business. She'd managed to wreck the important candy sample she'd been delivering in an effort to do her part to save the company. No, it was better for everyone that she wasn't working at Sweet Dreams.

Anyway, she wanted to do her own thing. Well, once upon a time she had. Now she wasn't sure what she wanted or who she was.

"I thought maybe I'd branch out," she said. It sounded better than "I failed."

Tina nodded. "Stick around and we'll talk."

Hildy had been hovering at the counter, probably hoping to assist with the interview. Now she took her cue and said, "Well, I should get back to the drugstore. We're training the Hernandez girl, and I don't like to leave her on her own for too long." She sighed. "It's so hard to find good help."

"Especially when you only pay one penny over minimum wage," Tina said as soon as the door was shut.

"I hope that means you pay more than minimum wage," Bailey said, and she was only half joking.

"At least two pennies over." Tina grinned. "That woman is such a cheapskate. Do you know she wanted me to give her a ten percent discount just because she lives here in town? Like she'd ever give that to anyone who came into the drugstore."

Hildy was notorious for always wanting a bargain. She'd tried a similar stunt when Sweet Dreams Chocolates was struggling. "It's wrong to take advantage of people," Bailey said. She thought of Samba Barrett and frowned.

"I agree," Tina said. "So, tell me about you. I assume you have retail experience?"

Uh-oh. "Um, no," Bailey admitted.

Tina's smile faltered a little. "So you never worked in the shop at your family's company?"

Now Bailey wished she had. She'd spent one summer working in the factory, and after that her father had never been able to get her near the place again. She shook her head. "No, but I had my own business." Oh, no. Why was she reminding Tina about the mess she'd left behind? She bit her lip and waited for Tina to politely tell her to go away.

"Well, it's not that hard to work a cash register. If you want the job, it's yours."

She had a job, a chance for a new beginning! "Great. When can I start?"

"How about tomorrow?"

"Perfect," Bailey said.

"Okay, then. We'll get all the paperwork filled out, and I'll show you a few things, and then you can come in tomorrow at nine. We open at ten."

Bailey ended up staying the rest of the morning, and for the first time since The Incident, she felt hopeful. She could work for Tina, learn the business and then maybe, in a year or two, have a shop of her own.

"That would be almost as good as getting to cook," she told her mother when she called to share her news.

"You'll cook again," her mother assured her.

Of course she would. She'd create culinary treats for her family and friends. It would be enough. She was lucky to be able to come back to a wonderful town like Icicle Falls.

New people had come here to live since she'd moved away, and she saw several unfamiliar faces at Safeway when she stopped in to pick up the makings for dinner. Who was that woman in the jeans and the red blazer?

"Oh, that's Meredith Banks," Linda, the cashier, told her when she asked. "She married Jed Banks, who started the Kid Power program."

"Any new men?" Bailey asked. Probably not. That was one of the benefits of living in the big city. Lots of men.

"Oh, yeah," Linda said. "The town is definitely growing."

Bailey would've loved more specifics, but another customer (yet another woman she didn't recognize) had already unloaded her groceries and was now smiling politely while her fingers did an impatient tap dance on her grocery cart.

Bailey left, thinking that maybe on the weekend Cecily would like to go to The Red Barn and introduce her little sister to some of the new talent in town. Meanwhile, she had a celebratory dinner to make.

By the time Cecily came home, the condo was filled with wonderful aromas. "Oh, my gosh, what do I smell?"

"Three-cheese stuffed chicken. And we have a Mediterranean salad and tiramisu for dessert. We're celebrating."

"Yum. What are we celebrating, besides the fact that I don't have to make dinner?"

"Thanks to you, I got a job," Bailey crowed. "I'm starting at Lace and Lovelies tomorrow."

Cecily broke into a grin. "No way."

"Way," Bailey said, and the two sisters hugged.

"It's probably not what you'll want to do for the rest of your life," Cecily said as she kicked off her shoes.

"It'll be good experience."

As they talked, the sisters drifted into the kitchen, Bailey to put the finishing touches on their dinner and Cecily to open a bottle of Asti Spumante for a toast. "Here's to success," she said, once they sat down to eat. "And to new beginnings."

"To new beginnings," Bailey echoed.

But the next day her new beginning didn't get off to an auspicious start. Even though Tina was nice, Bailey was still nervous, and sometimes when she got nervous, well...things happened.

She was helping Tina with a window display and managed to knock a chintz teapot off its perch and break it. Both she and her employer let out a gasp.

Bailey glanced from the broken china to Tina's face. Tina looked like a woman who'd accidentally dropped a diamond in the ocean.

"I'm so sorry," Bailey said. "Please, take that out of my paycheck."

It took a moment for Tina to reply. "No, that's okay. It could have happened to anyone."

And maybe anyone could have rung up a sale wrong (more nerves). Anyone could have bumped into a display table and knocked over a crystal vase (which went the way of the teapot). Anyone could have gotten flustered and shorted a customer on lace by ten inches. But it didn't happen to anyone. It happened to Bailey.

And by the end of the day, something else happened to Bailey. She got fired.

"Look." Tina's tone of voice said it all before she even finished her sentence. "I don't think this is going to work out."

Who fired someone on her first day at work? "I know today didn't exactly go smoothly," Bailey began.

"Smoothly?" Tina echoed. "That's the understatement of the century."

Okay, that hurt. It wasn't as if Bailey had meant to screw up. "I'm sorry," she said stiffly. "Of course, I'll pay for what I broke."

"No, just forget it."

"No, really. I want to."

Tina waved away Bailey's offer. "I'll write it off."

If she was going to write it off... "Couldn't you give me one more day?" Bailey asked in a small voice.

Tina looked at her in horror. "I can't afford to write off *that* much."

There wasn't anything Bailey could say, other than, "I'll get my purse."

"I'm sorry," Tina said when Bailey returned from the back room. "I hope you find something that's a better fit."

"I'm sure I will," Bailey said. There were all kinds of things she could do. She just had to figure out what they were. She slung her purse onto her shoulder and overturned a pile of lace tablecloths. "Uh, I'll get going."

Tina frowned. "That would be a good idea."

And so Bailey got going...right over to her mother's cottage.

"Hi, sweetie. How was your first day on your new job?"

"I got fired," Bailey said and burst into tears.

Her mother hugged her, then led her to the dining table and seated her with a box of tissues and a cup of chocolate mint tea. "Now, tell me what happened."

It was a short story. Bailey's klutz gene had kicked in, and that had been that.

"Well, I must say, she didn't give you much of a chance," her mother observed.

"I guess I wasn't meant to sell lace," Bailey said. "But I wish she'd given me one more day. I mean, I'm not totally accident prone."

Her mother made no comment, instead saying, "Maybe God has something else in mind for you. Everything happens for a reason—you know that."

Bailey frowned. "I'd sure like to know the reason I got turned into the party poisoner."

"Maybe it was to bring you home to Icicle Falls."

But she'd come back in disgrace. How was that a good thing?

"I think you were meant to come home, and I think something wonderful is waiting for you here," her mother continued. "You just have to discover it."

"I want to, but I have no idea what to do next," Bailey confessed.

"What about working for Olivia?"

Brandon Wallace's mom? "Oh, I don't know," Bailey said. She wasn't sure she wanted to work at the Icicle Creek Lodge, where she could hear firsthand how happy Brandon was with his new girlfriend.

"Olivia was just telling me yesterday that she'd like to hire someone personable to run the front desk."

On the other hand, Bailey liked Olivia Wallace. She and Bailey's mother had been friends since they were girls, and Olivia had been like an adopted aunt to Bailey and her sisters when they were growing up. Bailey had enjoyed many a birthday tea party at Olivia's, and it had been Olivia who'd encouraged her to go after her dream of becoming a caterer.

Working for Olivia would feel more like being with family than clocking in to a job. It might even be fun.

"Let's call her," Mama urged.

Bailey agreed, and a moment later they had Olivia on speakerphone.

"Bailey, I'm glad you're back," Olivia said. "Are you home to stay?"

"I think so." And if her mother was right, she was home for a purpose. What that purpose was, she couldn't imagine.

"She needs a job," Mama put in. "I told her you were looking for someone over at the lodge."

"Oh, Bailey, you'd be perfect!"

"You think so?" Bailey asked hopefully. It would certainly be nice to be perfect for something.

"Absolutely. Come on over and let's talk," Olivia said.

So Bailey left her mother's place and went to the Icicle Creek Lodge.

The lodge was one of the town's most popular B and Bs. Snugged in by fir and cedar trees, it looked like a Bavarian hunting lodge, all stone and timber, with a big front porch and a sweeping lawn. Inside, it was impressive. Its large, elegant reception area had high ceilings and a stone fireplace flanked by big easy chairs. There was also a baby grand piano, and on weekends, evenings and special holidays, the local music teacher came in to serenade the guests. A grand staircase, with an elaborately carved bannister, led to the second-floor landing.

In addition to the family's private quarters, the building had thirty-six guest rooms and a large dining room that Olivia rented out for everything from wedding receptions to high school reunions. It was always booked, but when it wasn't, she partitioned off half, which she kept available as a conference room.

Olivia hired locals to clean the rooms and work in the dining room and kitchen, but she made the breakfasts herself. She was especially fond of baking and, as she liked to say, had the figure to prove it. The lodge rarely had a vacancy, and with the rooms' Victorian decor and beautiful mountain views, it was a popular choice for anniversaries and girlfriend weekends. One thing Bailey knew for sure, she'd have a wonderful working atmosphere.

"I'm so sorry about what happened to you," Olivia said after she'd about smothered Bailey in an enthusiastic, vanilla-scented hug. "But we're all happy you're back home. And having you here will be like having a daughter working with me."

"Sounds like you may be getting one real soon." Maybe her sisters were wrong. She held her breath and hoped Olivia would deny it.

"Well, it does look like it's getting serious between Brandon and Arielle."

How Bailey wished it had gotten serious between Brandon and her. She was positive her mother would say that God had something better planned. It was hard to imagine anything better than Brandon.

"She's a lucky girl," Bailey said.

Now Olivia began fiddling with the blue turquoise ring on her finger. "I know you and Brandon used to be interested in each other."

Interested? There was an understatement. She'd

given her virginity to Brandon Wallace when they were teenagers. All her friends had warned her that he was a heartbreaker, and they'd been right. Still, she'd come home for the first Sweet Dreams chocolate festival, and he'd flirted with her. That had been enough to encourage her to revive the dream of Brandon finally falling hard for her and swearing undying love.

There'd been no falling and no swearing, but when she'd come home for the Fourth, there'd been some hooking up. And that was all it had taken for her to move into his back pocket once again. What a dope she'd been. And now that she was back home for good, he was living in another state.

"But I bet you'll find some wonderful man here, now that you're back," Olivia hurried on to say. "And I agree with your mother. I think you were meant to return to Icicle Falls."

"I don't know what I'm going to do," Bailey confessed. What kind of way was this to conduct a job interview? She felt her face ignite. "Well, I mean, not that I don't want to work for you." Right now she'd clean toilets, dig ditches, anything. She needed money, and she couldn't live off her sisters like a big old leech.

"Oh, honey, I know what you mean. You were born to cook. In fact, I was thinking you might like to help me in the kitchen on weekends once in a while."

That suggestion instantly doused the fire on Bailey's face. She'd just as soon jump off Sleeping Lady Mountain. She shook her head violently. "Oh, no." The very thought of it made her heart pound as if she'd overdosed on caffeine.

"I understand," Olivia said. "But you can't let one bad experience define your whole life."

Sure she could.

"You know what they say," Olivia continued. "When the going gets tough, the tough get going."

"I thought the tough went shopping," Bailey said. Anyway, she liked that saying better than the one Olivia had quoted.

Olivia gave Bailey a hug. "You didn't come home a minute too soon." She released her with an affectionate smile. "Don't worry, honey. We'll get you straightened out."

Bailey would be happy to get straightened out. But one thing she wouldn't get, and that was back in a commercial kitchen. "I'll do anything you ask me to, but, please, don't ask me to do that. Or to handle anything breakable," she added, remembering her experience at Tina's shop. Thank God, Olivia hadn't asked her what she'd been doing since she hit town.

Olivia smiled again. "You'll do fine here."

Bailey needed to do fine somewhere. "I hope so," she said and prayed she'd last at this new job for longer than a day.

Chapter Eight

Cecily's desk phone rang a little after eleven the next morning. It was Luke. "How about lunch?"

They'd had a nice time on their date. So, why not?

Because she didn't know what she was doing or what she wanted—that was why not. It wasn't fair to encourage Luke if she wasn't 100 percent serious.

But she did enjoy his company. And if she was going to be smart about love, he was the logical choice.

"Hello. You still there?"

"I'm thinking," she said.

"You have to think about whether or not you want to eat?" he teased.

"I have to think about whether or not I want to eat with you," she said, trying for the kindest tone of voice possible. "Whether or not I want to string you along."

"Who says you're doing that?"

"Me."

"That was a pretty nice kiss for stringing someone along," he said.

"That was a pretty nice kiss. Period," she admitted.

"Well, there's more where that came from."

She couldn't help smiling. She really did like Luke.

"Come on," he said. "You've got to eat, right?"

"Right."

"And how does a burger at Herman's sound?"

Actually, a fat, juicy cheeseburger and curly fries drenched in chili and melted cheese sounded fabulous. So did a blackberry shake. She hesitated.

"I'll take that as a yes," he said.

"Take it as a yes on one condition."

"Oh? What's that?"

"That I pay for my own lunch." That way it would feel more like friends enjoying a lunch break together than her taking advantage of Luke.

"I can afford to buy you a burger."

"You can, but I don't want you to."

"I tell you what—we'll arm wrestle to see who pays the bill," he said and hung up.

That made her smile again. Luke had been state wrestling champion in high school. There would be no arm wrestling.

She'd barely finished talking to Luke when Todd called. "You hungry?"

"It's not lunchtime yet," she said, prevaricating.

"When it is, I'd like to go someplace with a great view—of a hot blonde sitting across the table from me."

Todd Black made for some very nice scenery himself. But then she remembered that she was being practical. "I can't," she said.

There was a silence on the other end of the line. "Don't tell me—you've got a date."

"Okay, I won't tell you."

"Then go with my blessing, my child. Let me know when you get tired of dating the second string," he added in a low, sexy voice. "I'll take you someplace nice and greasy and lick your fingers clean." His voice alone was enough to make every hormone in her body start shimmying.

She ignored them and said a polite goodbye. Lunch with Luke would be just fine. Lunch with Todd would have been... Her fingers began to tingle. She put them to work typing, but her brain was still stuck on the image of Todd sucking on her index finger. Was it warm in the office today?

A few minutes after noon Cecily and Luke settled in at a corner table with cheeseburgers, Herman's deadly fries and milk shakes. "There's nothing like a Herman's burger," Luke said, taking his first bite. "Well, except for my manly man grilled onion-blue cheeseburger."

"A man who cooks?" She pretended to be impressed.

"No, a man who grills. There's a difference. But I do bake a mean chocolate chip cookie," he added.

"You're full of surprises."

"Good surprises?"

His teasing voice couldn't hide the seriousness behind the question. "What's not good about chocolate chip cookies? You and Bailey will have to swap recipes," she joked, dancing away from the real subject.

Someone new entered Herman's Hamburgers, a someone with dark hair, swarthy skin and chocolate-brown eyes. Oh, no. What was *he* doing here?

Todd caught sight of Cecily and smiled, and she suddenly felt as if she'd just touched a live wire. The physical reaction was quickly doused by a wave of irritation as he started toward their table. He could see she was with someone, but was that stopping him? Noooo.

"Hi there," he said. "Lunchtime in Willy Wonka Land?"

Cecily frowned. Out of the corner of her eye she could see Luke leaning back in his chair, studying their visitor. And he wasn't smiling.

Todd pointed to the fries. "Those look good. Nice and greasy," he added, and Cecily's fingers started tingling again.

"They are good," Luke said. "Too bad you can't join us."

"Uh, yeah. Guess I'll go order my burger before the high school rush begins." Todd flashed Cecily his killer grin. "I'll see you soon."

She hadn't agreed to a date, but he sure made it sound as if she had. The corners of Luke's mouth slipped even farther south, and Cecily could feel a flush of embarrassment race north from her neck to her face. *You have nothing to be embarrassed about.*

"What do you see in that guy?" Luke demanded as Todd walked away.

It seemed shallow to say that Todd turned her burner to high, that every time he was around, she had to fight the urge to glue herself to him. If she wanted to find the perfect man, he was totally the wrong choice. And darn it all, she wanted him anyway.

So instead, she lied, "I don't know." How did you explain chemistry?

Luke shook his head. "Why is it that so many women go for guys like that?"

"Guys like what?" she asked, playing dumb. She

knew exactly what Luke meant. Everything about Todd, from his smart mouth to his gift for flirting, to the very vibes he gave off, said heartbreaker.

"Like...that," Luke said and waved his hand in Todd's general direction.

Todd was now picking up his order. Two teenage girls entered just as he was going out. Both girls' heads swiveled to watch him leave. Todd Black seemed to have the same effect on women of all ages.

"I don't get why women pass up nice guys for creeps like that who never treat their women well."

"Isn't that a rather sweeping generalization? You don't know how he treats his women."

Luke's only concession to her logic was a grunt.

"Your wife didn't pass you up for someone else," she added gently.

Irritation was replaced by sadness. "She was rare."

"You still miss her, don't you?"

He stared at his half-finished hamburger and then shoved it away. "Every day. She was a wonderful woman." He looked up. "But so are you, Cecily. And maybe it's asking too much to think I can have two wonderful women in one lifetime. But that's not going to stop me from trying."

"Do you think a person can be attracted to more than one person?" she mused. At the same time? What she felt for Luke was very different from what she felt for Todd, but there was *something*.

"I know so," he said and took her hand, running his thumb slowly up and down it.

Great. Here she'd been mentally drooling over Todd, and now Luke was sending shivers up her arm. These two men were going to drive her insane.

Luke leaned close. "I've got a few tricks up my sleeve, too. Trust me. I could make you just as happy as he can. In the long run, happier."

What to say to that? "Uh…we should probably get back to work."

He pulled back his hand, sliding it slowly over hers and making her mouth go dry.

She took one last sip of her shake and stood up. It was definitely time to go.

Luke was smart enough not to talk about his rival anymore. Instead, on the way back, he kept the conversation focused on innocuous things, like the new chocolates Sweet Dreams had in the works and Bailey's return home.

"It's great that you're letting her stay with you," he said. It was a very different observation from the one Todd had made. Any woman with half a brain would pick a man like Luke over Todd.

Cecily was beginning to worry that she had only a quarter of a brain.

She was just back in her office when Samantha showed up. "Did I see you walking in with Luke?"

Living in a small town, working with family—the one difference between Icicle Falls and a fishbowl was the lack of water. She shrugged. "We grabbed a hamburger."

Samantha leaned against the doorjamb and cocked an eyebrow. "Yeah?"

"It was just lunch."

"You know it could be more."

"I know."

"I say go for it. Marry him. That way we'll never lose our production manager."

"Well, anything for the company."

Samantha grinned. "You got it," she said and then left.

Cecily leaned back in her desk chair and tapped a fingernail against her teeth. She needed to figure this out, so she decided to play a mental game. She closed her eyes and envisioned herself in a bridal gown, walking down the aisle. Okay, who was at the other end of the aisle?

Todd.

She opened her eyes and sighed. Was this even remotely logical? Of course not. But when did logic and love ever go hand in hand?

Cecily stopped by the bank after work to use the ATM and ran into Lauren Belgado, one of the tellers, who was just leaving.

"Are you ready for the big day?" Cecily asked.

"I hope so. I can't believe it's in sixteen days. I feel like we've been planning this wedding forever."

Lauren and Joe Coyote had gotten engaged on Valentine's Day the year before. Hardly surprising that it felt like forever. Cecily didn't think she'd want to wait that long.

"Well, you're in the final countdown now," she said.

"I can hardly wait," Lauren said, smiling widely. "I'm the luckiest woman in Icicle Falls."

Cecily smiled back. Radiating all that warmth and happiness, people in love were like walking sunbeams. "You got a great guy."

Joe had been the winner of Sweet Dreams' first Mr. Dreamy contest; he'd won because everything he said during the Q and A segment had been so romantic and noble he'd had the audience (mostly women) completely enthralled. Joe wasn't a bad-looking man but he wasn't the most handsome one in town by any means, and due to a construction accident he walked with a limp. But he had the soul of a poet and the heart of a knight in shining armor, and half the women in town would have happily stolen him from Lauren. He was completely dedicated to her, though, which everyone agreed was all he needed to make him a perfect man.

Except there was no such thing as a perfect man, only the man who was perfect for you, Cecily reminded herself as she said goodbye to Lauren.

With that final thought, an image sprang to mind. Two men stood in front of her, one with swarthy skin, dark hair, brown eyes and a wicked grin, the other a big man with a round, earnest face and blue eyes.

Both men wanted her, and she knew which one she *should* pick. But she also knew which one she was going to pick. A woman couldn't stay on the fence forever. Sooner or later she had to jump off and land on one side or the other. The best she could do was hope for a soft landing.

Bailey's first day on the job was going well. So far she'd helped Olivia clean up after that morning's breakfast and had mastered the check-in process. Her nerves had settled down, she hadn't broken anything, and Olivia loved having her around.

It was like being with family, she thought, catching sight of Olivia's older son, Eric.

In addition to being Olivia's bookkeeper, he also doubled as a handyman, taking care of minor repairs and maintaining the grounds. He was several years older than Bailey and a polar opposite of his sexy younger brother, the king of the flirts. Even with a receding hairline he was attractive, though. He was tall and broad-shouldered and wore glasses and a serious expression. Growing up, he'd always seemed like a being from another world—the planet Stuffy.

She'd just given an early check-in to a middle-aged couple who were taking a break on their trip over the mountains to Seattle when Eric came through the lobby, wearing a gray T-shirt, jeans and a tool belt. He didn't look quite so stuffy now. But he still wasn't Brandon.

He gave her a friendly nod as he walked by. "How's it going, Bailey?"

"Great," she said brightly. So what if she wasn't becoming a famous chef? She liked it here at the lodge, liked being around people, liked taking reservations and setting out fresh flowers in the dining room.

He nodded. "Good. It's nice to have you here."

Nice to have you here. That was a balm to her wounded soul. L.A. had spit her out like a piece of overcooked steak. But here under the wing of Olivia, who was the world's best mother hen, she had a feeling she'd be able to rebuild both her broken life and her trampled self-esteem.

That evening at dinner, she had lots to share with her sister. "It's so much fun being at the lodge." She sighed happily. "Everything's working out."

"Everything usually does," Cecily said.

"You sound like Mama," Bailey teased.

"Can you think of anyone you'd rather I sounded like?"

"Nope."

Cecily forked up a piece of trout. "So, have you seen Eric?"

"Yeah." Bailey regarded her sister. "Why are you asking?"

"No reason. Just wondering."

"You're lying. What, do you have…a feeling about him?" Her sister was famous for her instincts when it came to matchmaking. But if she thought there would ever be something between Bailey and Eric, she'd lost her gift.

"No," Cecily admitted. "He's a nice guy. I honestly can't understand why he's still single."

Bailey shrugged. "Maybe he's just…too nice?" She frowned. "That sounds weird, doesn't it?"

"Well, not really," her sister said.

"It makes him seem, I don't know…boring. Gosh, that's kind of mean. But I want to fall in love with someone exciting. I don't want my love life to be one long snooze. Just because we live in a small town doesn't mean our lives have to be small. Right?"

"Right," Cecily agreed.

Boring, Cecily mused Saturday night as she and Bailey drove to her friend Juliet's house for a game night. Was that why Todd pulled her attention away from Luke so easily? He was definitely the more exciting of the two men, and if she wanted to live large, he was the logical choice. And yet here she was, wimping out and choosing an evening with the girls over pinball at The Man Cave. *You have to start living large,* she scolded herself. *Get your cold feet out of the ice bucket and go for it.*

Luke called her the next week. "You in town for the three-day weekend?"

"Yes," she answered cautiously.

"Are you up for a hike on Saturday? Unless, of course, you're planning to do the fun run." He knew her well enough to know that wouldn't be happening. Cecily enjoyed hiking, but running? Not unless she was being chased by a bear.

A hike would be nice, but she couldn't keep doing things with Luke, not unless she was going to start dating him seriously. It wouldn't be fair. "Oh, I don't think so," she began. *I'm about to start living large and that means Todd.*

"Come on," he urged. "The weather's going to be great, and since all the tourists will be busy with the run and the band concert in the park, we'll probably have the trail to ourselves."

Oh, dear. That was the last thing she wanted.

"I'll bring lunch," he added in an effort to sweeten the pot.

"All right," she agreed, only because she couldn't bring herself to say what had to be said on the phone. But somewhere on that hike, they were going to have a conversation about a very different kind of hike—one that Luke would have to take.

"Icicle Creek Lodge," Bailey said, answering the phone.

It was the Thursday before Memorial Day weekend and the last room at the lodge had been booked a week ago, but people kept calling, hoping for a cancellation.

"Bailey?"

She nearly dropped the phone. "Brandon?" She'd

known at some point she'd have to see him, talk to him, but she hadn't been prepared for that moment to sneak up on her.

"What are you doing answering the phone at my mom's place?"

And what are you doing in Jackson Hole with another woman when you should be with me? "I'm working here."

"I thought you were in L.A., becoming a celebrity chef."

He had to be the only person she knew who didn't read the *Star Reporter* while standing in line at the supermarket. Thank God. "That didn't work out." Part of her yearned to keep him on the phone, but fear that he'd ask her why won the day. "Do you want to talk to your mom?"

"No, actually, I want to surprise her. I thought I'd come up for the three-day weekend and bring..." He stopped, like a man hesitating in front of quicksand.

"I heard you met someone down there," Bailey said. It wouldn't help either of them to play dumb.

"Yeah, I... Aw, hell, I didn't plan this. I had a chance for a job in Jackson Hole, and, well, there was Arielle."

There was *Arielle*. And here was Bailey, still wanting the man who'd been leading her on since they were teenagers.

"I'll come down to L.A.," he'd promised, but the New Year came and went, and he never showed up. The texts had faded away, and he'd dropped off Facebook.

He's busy, she'd told herself. She hadn't found out what he was busy with until she came home for good.

"Bails, it just broadsided me," Brandon continued. "I didn't expect to fall in love."

She'd hoped he'd been starting to fall in love with *her.* Of course, Cecily had insisted all along that they weren't a match. She should have listened to her sister. Then maybe she wouldn't have let herself hope, wouldn't have foolishly convinced herself that once she returned home, she and Brandon would pick up where they'd left off and skip happily into the sunset together. What the heck had Arielle done to get Brandon to lay his heart down at her feet?

"But she's incredible. She's an artist."

Bailey was an artist, too. Her medium was food. There was probably no point in mentioning that. In fact, there was no point in saying much of anything. As if sensing her lack of interest, he finally abandoned the topic of Arielle. "Anyway, I wanted to let Eric know. I thought he could take Mom out to Schwangau Saturday night. Then we'll be there waiting. Kind of a belated Mother's Day present."

She guessed that he'd given Olivia only a card. It was Eric who sent flowers or took her out to eat. Of the two sons, Eric was the more considerate, the more responsible. Why couldn't she fall in love with Eric? *I had a chance for a job at the lodge and, well, there was Eric.*

He came in from outside, where he'd been doing some touch-up painting on the trim. He smiled at her as he entered the lobby. It was the same smile he always gave her, a big-brother smile. Eric Wallace would never break a girl's heart. Too bad there was no chemistry there. Maybe chemistry was overrated.

"Your brother's on the phone," she said and held out the receiver.

Eric nodded his thanks and took it. "What's up?"

Bailey tried to look busy, to pretend she wasn't interested in what was being said.

"Yeah. It's a three-day holiday weekend. Where else are we going to be?"

He sounded mildly exasperated, and that made Bailey think of her older sister, who'd been less than happy to hear she didn't want to work in the family business now that she was back home. Samantha carried the responsibility of Sweet Dreams Chocolates on her shoulders just as Eric carried most of the responsibility for the lodge on his. Younger siblings who skipped off to do their own thing were apparently a trial to responsible firstborns, no matter what the business.

"Yeah, yeah. Okay. No, you can't have the Edelweiss Suite. That's been booked for two months. You guys'll have to make do with your old room."

Bailey tried not to think of Brandon and his new love sharing a room, a bed.

"Yeah, fine, I'll have her there. No problem," he said and ended the call. He handed the receiver back to Bailey.

"That'll be a nice surprise for your mom," she said, trying to hide her own feelings behind a screen of politeness.

"Yeah, it will," Eric agreed. "She misses him."

"It's too bad he didn't stay here," Bailey muttered. Then he would never have met the incredible Arielle.

"You still in love with him?"

She was so pathetically obvious. All of Icicle Falls probably knew she was crazy for Brandon.

Eric spoke before she could either confirm or deny. "Sucks to be on the wrong end of love, doesn't it?"

"Yes," she said, "it does." Then she couldn't help but wonder. Who had put him on the wrong side of love?

Saturday did bring lovely weather. The sun painted a golden nimbus above the mountains surrounding town, and the sky was spring blue. It was a perfect day for a hike.

But uneasiness crept over Cecily when she saw where Luke was going to take her. Lost Bride Trail. There was nothing even remotely subtle about his choice. This was the hike almost every couple in Icicle Falls took when things were getting serious. The trail led to a waterfall where the ghost of a long-ago missing bride was rumored to lurk. If a woman saw the lost bride, it was a sure sign she'd be getting engaged.

Crap. She should have gone ahead and had that uncomfortable conversation on the phone.

They parked at the trailhead, and he pulled a backpack, which was bulging with who knew what, out of the trunk.

"Are you planning on running away from home?" she teased.

"Nope. Just planning to eat."

Eat? There was an understatement. Once they reached the falls, they settled at a little picnic table, and he began to empty his backpack. Out came chicken salad sandwiches made with croissants, veggie chips, grapes, chocolate chip cookies and white wine.

"You can pack my lunch anytime," she said, taking it all in. "Did you do this all yourself?"

"Of course. Well, with help from Ginny at the Safeway deli." He pulled out two plastic cups and poured wine into them. "Just because I'm big doesn't mean I'm not in touch with my feminine side."

"Having a little girl probably has something to do with that," she said, accepting the glass.

He nodded, giving her a wry smile. "Last night I had to wear a princess tiara and drink lemonade out of a pink plastic teacup."

Envisioning Luke in a tiara, sipping from a child's teacup, made Cecily smile. "I'm sure it was a great look for you."

"I don't think the pink boa was my color," he said, deadpan.

She giggled. He was such a nice man. She could be happy with him.

But not happy enough. He deserved to find a woman who was crazy about him and melted every time he kissed her. She had to tell him *now*. Her heartbeat broke into an anxious trot. "Luke."

The easy smile on his face began to fade.

This was awful. There was no way she could do this and not hurt him. She tried to soften the blow. "You're a great guy."

"Uh-oh," he said. His tone of voice was light, but she could see in his eyes that he was bracing himself for what was going to come next.

"I don't want to lead you on."

He clenched his jaw. He looked straight ahead and took a sip of his wine.

Oh, this was so not going well. She laid a hand on his arm.

He turned and faced her, shaking his head. "Cecily, what the hell are you doing?"

"I'm trying to pull us back from the edge of a mistake. I don't want to hurt you, and I want to stay friends."

He heaved a deep sigh. "The F-word."

She gave his arm a gentle rub. "You do want to be my friend, don't you?"

He managed a smile. "I've always been your friend, and I always will be."

He was so sweet. Any woman with half a brain would fall instantly in love with him. But, oh, yeah, as she already knew, she had only a quarter of a brain. She sighed and looked away, unable to face him. *You're doing the right thing,* she told herself. *You can't keep stringing this man along.*

This should have been the moment to leave friendship behind and fall into mad, crazy love, and this should have been the man with whom to fall. Instead, here she was, stepping back. She hoped she knew what she was doing, for both their sakes. She sighed and stared out at the waterfall with its miniature rainbows dancing in the sunlight.

Wait. What was that? What was she seeing?

Chapter Nine

Cecily blinked. She was hallucinating, had to be. Opening her eyes again, all she saw was a rushing torrent of water, no shadow of a woman in a white wedding gown. Good. Because the last thing she needed after filing her relationship with Luke under "friends" would've been to see the lost bride.

But what if she had?

"I guess we should start back," he said.

Excellent idea.

Their trip down the trail was a subdued one. Not that Luke was pouting. He'd occasionally point out some wildflower he thought she might have missed on the way up, just to show there were no hard feelings. But after she'd dropped the F-word, there wasn't much to talk about—no discussion of what they could do that night, no plans for future activities. They'd exhausted the topic of their families on the walk up, and Luke had already shared his vacation plans—Disneyland with his daughter and mom. So, that was that. It gave Cecily plenty of time to mull over what she'd done. And what she'd seen.

Catching a glimpse of the lost bride simply meant a person was on the verge of an engagement. That could be with anyone. And if not Luke, there was only one other person it could be.

So there it was. She couldn't have asked for a clearer sign. She was meant to be with Todd.

Bailey wasn't all that interested in nature, so she'd never quite understood the lure of hiking. If you asked her, it just meant a lot of hard work and getting sweaty to see pretty much the same view as you could see from town, only closer and with more bugs. Although she supposed if she was hiking with the right man, maybe she'd like it, especially if they were hiking up to Lost Bride Falls.

She suspected that was where Luke and Cecily had gone. She loved seeing her sister with such a nice man. It was about time.

She was in the middle of folding her laundry when Cecily returned home. "Did you have fun?" Her sister didn't exactly look like a woman who'd had a passionate encounter at the falls.

"We did," Cecily said, then wandered into the kitchen.

"Did you see the lost bride?"

"You know that's a superstition." Cecily pulled a pitcher of lemonade out of the fridge and filled her glass.

"Yeah, but did you see her?" Samantha had before she got together with Blake.

"I don't think so." Cecily took a drink of lemonade.

"So, you're not sure?"

"It's easy to imagine all kinds of things up there," Cecily said with a shrug.

Bailey grinned. "You *did* see the lost bride."

"Well, it would be nice if I had," Cecily admitted. "I'm really ready to find Mr. Right."

"It looks like you have," Bailey said.

"Looks can be deceiving."

That was true. Samba Barrett had looked like a nice person. "So, do you have a date tonight?"

"I'm going to be doing something," Cecily said, her expression guilty. "Will you be okay?"

Bailey nodded vigorously. "Of course. You don't have to babysit me, you know."

"I know. But I don't want to ignore you, either."

She could hardly accuse her sister of that. The other night, Cecily had taught her a new card game.

"You're not ignoring me at all," Bailey said. "Anyway, I have plans for tonight, too." Thank God she wouldn't be sitting at home thinking about Brandon and Arielle whooping it up at Schwangau. "I'm going over to Sammy's for dinner. She invited you, too, but I'll tell her you've got a hot date. Where are you guys going?"

"Just hanging out around town."

Translation: none of your business. Of the three sisters, Cecily was the most private. She was also the most diplomatic; unlike Samantha, she'd never tell someone to butt out of her business. But when she didn't want to share, she didn't want to share. This was clearly one of those moments, so even though Bailey was dying for all the gory details of her sister's upcoming evening with Luke, she knew better than to pry. Opening a clam with her bare hands would be easier than getting her sister to divulge any information on what she was up to if she didn't want to.

"As long as she's out doing something with him,"

Samantha said later when Bailey called her. "Luke's a great guy, and I'm glad she's finally got her head on straight."

"Well, how could she know about those other two guys?" Bailey argued, springing to Cecily's defense. "I mean, they seemed really nice."

"When somebody's asking to borrow money from you, he's not a keeper," Sammy said.

Okay, she had a point. But, "Cec couldn't have known about Number One. No way could she predict he'd go back to his first girlfriend."

"Oh, yeah? You were with them at the restaurant for breakfast when the ex *just happened* to come in, and he invited her to join you guys. Who invites his ex to pull up a chair and have a pancake when he's out with his girlfriend?"

"Yeah, that was a skeezy thing to do," Bailey agreed. "At the time I just thought he was being polite."

"Would *you* want your boyfriend being polite with his ex?"

"No way. You're right. Why didn't I see that? I could have warned her."

"Because, like Cec, you're totally trusting. I think that's why she can match up everybody but herself. When it comes to her own love life, she doesn't see the big picture. Well, didn't," Sammy amended. "Luke is definitely big picture and picture perfect, thank God. I wonder what they're doing tonight."

As soon as Bailey was out the door, Cecily left the condo and made her way over to The Man Cave. It was only seven, but the potholed parking lot was already full of trucks and Jeeps, and the sound of country-rock music was seeping out of the place. The lederhosen-clad Neanderthal painted on the outside seemed to leer at her as she walked past. *Welcome back, sucker.*

Bill Will was there playing pool with Ashley Armstrong, and he called out a friendly greeting. So did a couple of the guys who worked in the warehouse.

That meant Luke would know on Tuesday that she'd been in here, hanging out with Todd. She reminded herself that it didn't matter what Luke knew because now she and Luke were just friends.

Todd was behind the bar, helping Pete distribute beer to his thirsty patrons. At the sight of her, though, he abandoned his post and walked over to meet her. "Well, well, what have we here? And where's the mammoth?"

She frowned in disapproval. "Luke is probably with his family."

Todd smiled. "And that means you're all alone on a Saturday night? What a waste."

"I thought so," she said. "That's why I'm here."

"Come on over to the bar. I'll get you a Coke. No rum," he added. "We can save that for later."

Cocky devil, thinking there'd be a later. Of course, he was right. There would. She followed him to the bar and settled on a stool next to a grizzled older man in coveralls and a hat that said John Deere.

He smiled at her. "Well, hello there."

"Don't be hitting on my girl, Henry," Todd said from the other side of the bar.

Henry pouted. "Are you his girl?"

"He's working on it," Cecily said.

"Hey, until somebody's engaged, she's fair game."

Henry gave Cecily a wink. "These young guys, they don't know how to treat a woman."

"So, you old guys who've been divorced twice have it all figured out, huh, Henry?" Todd teased as he slid a glass of pop in front of Cecily.

"Aw, I just didn't pick too good. It's hard getting it right," Henry explained to Cecily

She couldn't argue with that.

"Want to have another go at the pinball machine?" Todd suggested.

"Sure," she said, and they left Henry to contemplate the mysteries of love.

"I take it he's one of your regulars," Cecily said as they walked away.

"Yep. We got Henry through his divorce a little while ago. Now he's got his eye on Olivia over at Icicle Creek Lodge."

"Olivia?" Cecily said in shock. Surely Olivia could do better than Henry.

Todd nodded. "He's been going over for their Sunday brunches for the last couple of months. He wants a woman who can cook."

"That's romantic," Cecily said in disgust. "And what does Henry bring to the table—so to speak?"

"A lot of money. He owns a packing plant over in Wenatchee. Plus, he's got a stock portfolio I'd kill for."

Cecily looked across the room to where Henry sat nursing a beer and tried to picture him as a successful businessman. "Seriously?"

"Not every rich man wears a suit and drives a Porsche. Didn't you ever read *The Millionaire Next Door?*"

Cecily shook her head.

"There are a lot of guys out there like Henry who've worked hard and been smart with their money."

"If not with their women," Cecily couldn't resist adding.

"Figuring out women is harder than figuring out money," Todd said, making her wonder what exactly had happened to turn him into such a cynic.

"Okay," he said, motioning to the pinball machine. "Let's see if last time was a fluke."

She proved that it wasn't, and, as with her previous visit to The Man Cave, she drew half the men in the place over to watch her.

"Man, you sure can work that thing," Bill Will said when she finally stepped away.

"Where did you learn to do that?" Todd asked.

"A retro place in L.A. that I used to go to with my sister." She'd also gone there with fiancé Number One. She didn't bother to mention that.

"Okay, now *I* get to show off," Todd said and led her over to the dartboard.

There she was, just as pathetic as she'd always been.

"Let's work on that toss." He stepped up behind her, and she was suddenly very aware of all that hard male muscle tucked up against her. He took her hand, but instead of helping her throw the dart, he stood there, his mouth close to her ear. "You smell good," he told her, his breath tickling her ear.

You feel good. "I thought you were going to show me how to throw."

"Yeah, but I like doing this better," he said and nipped playfully at her ear.

Zing!

"Let's get out of here," he whispered.

Great idea.

They were about to leave when the bar had a sudden influx of patrons—Joe Coyote and his pals. "I need to help serve these guys," Todd said. "You mind hanging around for a while?"

No, she didn't. Until she saw Luke trooping in at the tail end of the group. She felt awkward and embarrassed, as if she'd been caught doing something naughty.

There were six other men besides him accompanying Joe, and it wasn't hard to guess why they were there.

Sure enough, Jay Jorgenson, who managed the Safeway produce department, slapped Joe on the back and said to Todd, "Give our boy a Heineken and a shot of sympathy. This is his last weekend as a free man."

"Getting hitched, huh?" Todd said as he complied. "Tough luck, dude."

Tough luck? Cecily supposed Todd was joking around, but maybe he really felt that way about marriage. She could see how broken up Joe was about losing his so-called freedom. If his smile got any bigger, it would split his face in two.

Luke was at the bar now, along with the other members of the bachelor party. He took a seat next to Cecily and said a casual hello, but from the squinty-eyed look he gave Todd and the way he practically strangled his beer bottle, she could tell he wasn't feeling casual.

He turned around and leaned his elbows on the bar, watching the pool game in progress. "So, when we were hiking, you already had plans for tonight."

"No." She didn't have to explain herself to Luke

since they were nothing more than friends, but she explained anyway. "This came up later."

He slugged down some beer, digesting that information. But the expression on his face told her he found it difficult to digest.

Meanwhile Gary Gruber, one of the members of the bachelor party, was filling Todd in on the festivities that lay ahead. "We're hitting Zelda's after this. Gonna give the boy one last look at all the action he'll miss once he's hog-tied. Then we're going back to Willis's place. He's got a keg of Hale's Ale waiting for us." He lowered his voice. "And I got a surprise coming, the kind a guy can't have once he's married, if you get my drift."

Where he'd imported that kind of surprise Cecily couldn't imagine. Certainly not anywhere in town. Next to her, Luke scowled, a sure sign he'd be leaving the party early.

"Another reason to stay single," Todd cracked.

Now Luke wasn't the only one frowning. Really?

Cecily could feel Luke's disapproval swinging in her direction. "Do you know what you're doing?" he asked.

No. "Yes," she said stubbornly.

The bachelor party got louder after a couple of drinks, making Henry and the older patrons glare, so Todd sent the boys on to their next destination. They left, still teasing Joe as they went.

"That poor guy is in for a long night," Todd predicted as they filed out the door.

"But it's his last weekend of freedom," Cecily reminded him, only half joking.

"Guy humor," Todd informed her. "You've got to say that when someone's getting married."

Luke hadn't indulged in guy humor. She nodded slowly. "I...see."

"No, you don't," Todd said with a grin. "Come on. Let's go."

And so Cecily took another ride on Todd's motorcycle, but this time he didn't take her to his house. Instead they wound up at The Red Barn, a popular honky-tonk just outside town. The parking lot was packed, and the old red building practically throbbed with the beat of the music playing inside. Whoever the band was, they were loud.

"Bet you thought I was going to take you back to my place, didn't you?" Todd said as they removed their helmets.

"Actually, I did."

"I did think about it, but I don't want to be accused of trying to cheap out on a date."

"Is that what this is, a date?"

He leaned in close. "It's whatever you want to call it. And the night's not over yet. You might still end up at my place."

The thought gave her a little shiver. Things with Todd could start moving at warp speed. Was she ready for that?

Of course she was. She was tired of her go-nowhere love life.

The Red Barn was an old converted barn, and the inside was decorated appropriately, the lobby occupied by a life-size plastic Jersey cow. Framed photos of barns around eastern Washington hung on the walls. The dance floor was huge, but it was crowded with patrons from neighboring towns like Peshastin and Cashmere, a veritable beehive of dancers and drinkers. Nearly every table between the bar and the dance floor was occupied, if not by people then by the drinks they'd left behind while they hit the dance floor, and there wasn't a seat to be had at the bar. The old hardwood floor was a swirl of denim skirts and jeans as dancers whirled around the floor in a cowboy cha-cha.

Todd attracted other women's attention like a magnet attracted nails, and Cecily was very aware of the glances, the winks and the outright drooling going on as they found their way to the last vacant table in a far corner. Hardly surprising, considering those dark brown eyes, the *let me kiss you senseless* lips and the strong jaw. And then there was that nice set of pecs and the lean torso. He was a fine specimen, all right.

On the outside. She hoped he proved to be as perfect on the inside.

So far, so good. If he was at all aware of the female attention he was garnering, he didn't let on. Instead he focused solely on her as they settled at their table.

"So, how about I go order us a couple of Cokes?"

She cocked her head. "No alcohol?"

"Alcohol makes for sloppy dancing," he said. He ran a hand along her arm. "I did promise to give you a tango lesson a long time ago. Remember?"

She remembered. She'd been on the beat-up leather couch in his shadowy back room, recovering from an encounter with an angry dog, and Todd had been close enough to put her on sensory overload. He seemed to have a gift for doing that.

"This isn't exactly a ballroom," she said, looking

at all the couples now country two-stepping around the old wooden floor.

"No? Wait and see," he said. "Be right back."

She watched as he threaded his way between tables. Women's heads swiveled as he passed, and their men frowned. Cecily realized she was frowning, too. Being with Todd Black would require constant vigilance because there'd always be other women waiting to take him away.

Do you know what you're doing? she asked herself, echoing Luke's question. *Yes,* she answered, *this time I do.*

Her pal Juliet Gerard was out on the floor with her husband, Neil. Once the dance ended and Juliet caught sight of her, she came over with Neil in tow. "You should've told me you were coming here tonight," Juliet scolded. "You could have come with us."

"I didn't know myself until a few minutes ago."

Just then Todd returned with their drinks and Juliet's eyes got big. "Oh."

"Hey, Todd," Neil said, shaking hands with him. "How's it going?"

"Not bad," Todd said.

"You guys wanna join us over at our table?" Neil motioned to a table where Chita, from Cecily's book club, was sitting down with her new husband, Ken Wolfe. "We can always drag up a couple more chairs."

"We're good here," Todd said, "but thanks."

Neil shrugged. "Suit yourself. See you at practice next week."

"Practice?" Cecily asked as the two made their way back to their table.

"He's on my softball team," Todd explained. "The Falls Neanderthals."

"Catchy. Do you all wear caveman jerseys?"

"Now, there's an idea for next year," he said and guzzled down some of his pop. A new song was starting, and he set the glass down. "Come on. Let's two-step."

Once on the dance floor, he showed her that he knew what he was doing, leading her through several fancy moves.

"Okay, that was impressive," she said as they walked off the floor.

"I can be impressive when I want to be," he said.

He could be impressive without even trying. Cecily was well aware of two women at a nearby table eyeing him as though he were the last piece of chocolate on the planet. "How is it you're still single?" she asked.

"I could ask you the same thing," he said.

"I asked you first."

He took a drink of his pop. "I'm cautious."

"And why is that?"

"Don't want to get burned."

"Have you been burned?"

"Once or twice. Okay, now it's your turn."

"Wait a minute," she protested. "You didn't go into very much detail."

He leaned an arm on the table and regarded her. "Why do women always want details about stuff like this? It's kind of ghoulish, doncha think?"

"No."

"Well, then let's go into detail about *your* past. How is it that a beautiful, smart woman like you is still single?"

"Bad choices."

His brows drew together. "Didn't you say you used to own a dating service?"

She should never have started this conversation. "I guess it was easier to match up other people than myself."

"Because?"

"Because?" she repeated. No one had ever asked her that before.

"Yeah, because. Why do you think that was?"

"I don't know," she admitted. She was like the matchmaking equivalent of a doctor who smoked—knew better but still did dumb stuff anyway. She hoped being with Todd wouldn't turn out to be yet another dumb move.

"So, what, were you out there searching for Mr. Perfect?"

"There's no such thing," she scoffed. She'd seen enough to know that.

"You've got that right. There's not," he agreed. "Or a Ms. Perfect, either. Just the one person who's perfect for you."

It was precisely what she'd thought herself, but it seemed like such a non-Todd thing to say. She could feel her mouth dropping.

"Hey, don't look so surprised. I'm not a total Neanderthal." The band had switched to Gloriana's "Good Night," and Todd nodded at the rapidly filling dance floor. "Come on. It's time you learned how to tango."

"To this?"

"Trust me," he said and held out his hand.

She didn't trust him at all. Didn't trust herself, either. What was she doing? She took his hand and took a jolt to the heart.

Out on the floor he pulled her close so they were chest to chest. She was going to ignite here on the dance floor. "Start on your right foot," he said, his breath tickling her ear as he started moving her backward. "Two slow steps. One more and then side and touch," he finished, guiding her through the moves.

She'd done some dancing, so after a couple of missteps it wasn't hard to catch on to what he was doing. Then, just when she'd mastered the first basic step, he brought out a new one, moving back and pulling her against him, reminding her of his muscle and male strength. All her female parts did a happy dance.

"Not bad," he whispered and kissed her ear.

Not bad at all, she thought as he guided her backward again, weaving them through the swaying throng. No one else was doing a ballroom dance, but that didn't faze him. Todd Black obviously liked to go his own way.

And he did it beautifully. With each step she was increasingly aware of his hand on the small of her back, the closeness of his body, the beat of the music like a shared heartbeat between them as they moved in unison. By the time the song was over, her whole body was humming.

And he was still holding her. "You're good on the dance floor, Cecily Sterling," he murmured. He nibbled her neck before turning her loose, and she wandered back to the table, feeling completely off-balance.

She was even more off-balance later that night when he took her to his house and proceeded to show her some more moves, this time on the couch. Her body was having so much fun, it refused to listen to her brain as Todd's seduction special moved her down the track toward utter conquest. Finally, her sensible self pulled the brakes.

She squirmed away before every stitch of clothing she owned could go missing.

"Hey, now," he murmured, "that's not very friendly."

"That's about as friendly as I want to get until I've figured out what this is." She still wasn't sure if he was serious or simply looking for sex.

"How about instead of analyzing this to death, we enjoy the ride," he said, closing the distance between them. He pushed aside her hair and nuzzled her neck.

She shut her eyes and went surfing on the next wave of pleasure. Mouth dry, she swallowed, then said, "We should talk about some things."

"How about you talk and I listen," he said, as his lips began moving south.

"How do you feel about kids?"

Todd's journey stopped. "Kids?"

"Yes, kids."

"They're okay." He tried to kiss her again.

"Spoken like a true family man," she said. Men didn't have biological clocks. Or if they did, theirs were set for a lot later in life.

He sat up and looked at her, his expression serious. "So, is this kid thing some kind of deal breaker?"

"Could be. I don't want to wait forever to have a family, and I don't want to bother with someone who isn't ready for a commitment."

"Hey, I didn't say I wasn't ready for a commitment," he protested. "But usually you take this stuff in steps."

"Okay, how about Step One—marriage?"

"I'm not against it. But I'm not in a hurry, either. There's plenty of time to worry about that after we know where we're going."

"You seemed to have a good idea where you were going a minute ago," she said.

That made him smile. "I sure did, and you didn't seem to mind coming along for the ride."

She pulled away again. "I don't want to get taken for a ride," she told him. "I've been there, done that, and it wasn't fun."

He sobered. "That's not what I meant. I'm not out to hurt you, Cec. I know how that feels. But I also know what it's like to grow up with your parents living in two different homes. I don't want to rush into anything and wind up like my parents. All they did was fight, and it wasn't fun for me or my brother when they finally split."

"My parents loved each other," she said softly. "It can be done."

"I realize that," he said with a nod. "Let's just take this slow, okay?" he added and moved in for another kiss.

She stopped him with a hand to his chest. "Good idea."

"Hey, I didn't mean everything."

"I'm sure you didn't."

"But we're done now, aren't we?"

Not only good-looking, but smart, too. She smiled sweetly at him. "Yes, we are."

Once Cecily was home and in bed she had a lot to think about. She was ready to be in a relationship with Todd, but was he ready to settle down? Would he ever be? She didn't want to wait in limbo with no wedding ring in her future and no family. Todd seemed to be balking at both.

But she'd dumped a lot of heavy stuff on him way too early. She could hardly blame him for balking. He was right; they needed to take it slow.

And if he doesn't want to take this where you do, what then? asked her sensible self. *You know the signs. You've seen them before. The man is allergic to marriage.*

Allergies can be treated, she insisted. *He can change. So can a poopy diaper, but who wants to?*

Still, she and her hormones had taken a vote, and the decision had been unanimous in favor of Todd.

Her sensible self, who hadn't been allowed a vote, now demanded, *What are you doing?*

YOLO, she told that pain-in-the-patootie sensible self. *You only live once, and I'm going to take a gamble on this man. I think it will pay off.*

Okay, but don't come crying to me when you have to deal with the fallout.

This time there'd be no fallout. She hoped.

Bailey had counted on not seeing Brandon. He was in town for only two days. A girl could avoid seeing anyone for two days, even in Icicle Falls.

Not when that girl worked at the Icicle Creek Lodge. She'd left work before the late Friday check-ins and Olivia had given her Saturday and Sunday off, so she came in on Monday hoping against hope that Brandon and the irresistible Arielle had checked out the day before. But, no, here they came just as she was settling in behind the reception desk, the woman carrying nothing but her purse while Brandon lugged a suitcase, a backpack and a shopping bag from Hearth and Home.

Bailey blinked in surprise as she took in the competition who'd walked away with *her* prize. The woman was blonde, and that was about all Bailey could say for her. Well, okay, she had big boobs, but heck, they didn't look that much bigger than Bailey's. She had a hooked nose, a sharp chin that made Bailey think of witches and a haughty smile. She knew how to dress; Bailey would give her that. Her blue sweater was cashmere, and she couldn't have paid less than two hundred dollars for those jeans. Weren't artists supposed to be poor and struggling?

"Bailey," Brandon greeted her as he set the luggage down. "I'm glad we got a chance to see you."

The irresistible Arielle raised a questioning eyebrow.

"Bails and I have known each other since we were kids," Brandon explained and made the introductions.

Arielle was underwhelmed.

"Did you enjoy your visit?" Bailey asked, at a loss for anything else to say.

"It was okay," Arielle said with a shrug.

Had she cast some sort of spell on Brandon? That was the only explanation Bailey could come up with for his fascination with her.

"The place grows on you," Bailey said. Except she hoped it wouldn't grow on this woman. She'd probably kill every flower in the window boxes on the downtown buildings with that vinegary frown of hers.

"I guess," she said. She turned to Brandon, and the vinegar turned to sugar. "We should get going, babe."

"Yeah, you're right," he said and picked up his load again.

"Nice to meet you, Bittie," she said to Bailey and swept off.

"It's Bailey," Bailey called after her, but Arielle wasn't paying any attention.

"She's something else, isn't she?" Brandon said to Bailey.

She was something else, all right.

Eric appeared at that moment, and the two men gave each other a bro hug, complete with slaps on the back.

Arielle had reached the door by now. "Brandon, come on," she demanded irritably.

"I'd better go," he said.

"Yeah, before she tightens the leash any more," his brother agreed.

Brandon just rolled his eyes and smiled good-naturedly. "I'll catch up with you on the Fourth," he said and hurried after Arielle.

"What does he see in her?" Bailey asked as soon as the door had shut behind them.

"Good in bed?" Eric mused, then looked embarrassed, as if he'd somehow insulted Bailey. "Sorry," he said.

"Don't be. I was thinking that myself." It was either that or the witch theory. "It won't last," she decided.

"Don't get your hopes up," he said gently and then left her to stew in her own jealous juices.

Chapter Ten

By Wednesday Bailey was almost resigned to the finality of her romantic loss and was pouring herself into updating the lodge's Facebook page with Muffin, Olivia's cat, perched on the desktop, supervising.

"You have to post more content," she told Olivia.

"Well, honey, that's great, but I'm not sure what else we can put up. We have pictures of the rooms and the mountains and Icicle Creek. And our little furry queen of the lodge," she added, petting Muffin, who purred appreciatively.

"I think it would be great to post pictures of what we serve for breakfast. We can do that on the website and on the Facebook page and call it *What's For Breakfast.*"

Olivia's round face broke into a smile. "That's a lovely idea!"

"Let's start with tomorrow's breakfast," Bailey said. "What are you serving?"

"My egg strata, rhubarb muffins and fruit salad. How does that sound?"

As if Olivia needed *her* seal of approval. "It sounds yummy," Bailey said, and for a wistful moment she wished she could be in the kitchen helping prepare that meal.

No, you're perfectly happy doing what you're doing, she reminded herself. And posting the photographs she took around the lodge was fun. Earlier that morning she'd posted a picture of lupine and gotten lots of likes. Food would get even more.

"Pictures of food will definitely attract attention," she told Olivia.

"Yes, who doesn't love food?" Olivia said and patted her round tummy.

As Bailey had predicted, her post the next day of a plate filled with Olivia's morning offerings drew plenty of likes and comments. One fan posted: *I think I need to come to Icicle Falls for an eat-a-thon.*

Come on up. You'll love it here, Bailey replied.

Icicle Falls was a great place to live, and a woman could be happy here, no matter what kind of work she was doing. But the lingering aroma of bacon drifted out from the dining room to where she sat, making her hungry for something more than food.

So what if she wasn't catering? She was taking pictures of culinary creations, and that was almost as good. She looked at the breakfast picture again and sighed.

"Tough day at work?" said a male voice, making her jump.

She turned to see Eric approaching.

"Hi," she greeted him. "What's the verdict on 308?"

"I should have the toilet fixed by this afternoon, so go ahead and book the room for the weekend."

She nodded and made a note of that, the picture of efficiency.

He cleared his throat. "So, you doing okay?"

"Of course," she said brightly, forgetting her momentary sadness. "Your mom is great to work for."

"Yeah, she is." He hesitated, then asked, "So, uh, the work here, that's okay? You don't miss...your old life?"

Bailey could feel the heat of embarrassment on her face. Of course he knew what had happened in L.A. Everyone in town did.

"No," she said firmly. "Not a bit of it."

He nodded shrewdly. "That's why you're looking at pictures of food and sighing."

She gave a little one-shouldered shrug.

"I guess that's better than sitting around sighing over my idiot brother."

She supposed he'd seen her do that often enough over the years. "He's not the only man in the world," she told both Eric and herself.

"Not by a long shot. The world's full of people. It's stupid to waste time on the ones who don't appreciate you."

That was good advice. In fact, it was downright wise. "Hey, you're pretty smart," she said.

"Getting there."

"So, you know this from personal experience?"

"You could say that."

Had Eric been where she'd been? She was about to ask when his mother entered the lobby. He gave the counter a goodbye tap and moved away.

Bailey watched as he stopped to kiss his mom on the cheek. Eric was a good son. He'd be a good boyfriend, too. She needed an Eric Wallace, someone who wouldn't skip off to Jackson Hole and take up with a snobby artist. Why couldn't his younger brother be more like him?

Because if he was, then he wouldn't be Brandon. Sigh.

You'll find someone, she assured herself. Meanwhile, it was a beautiful, sunny day, and she had a nice job. She had a lot to be thankful for.

"The picture of today's breakfast is getting a whole bunch of likes," she informed Olivia. Olivia had taken off her favorite kitchen apron, but she still had a smudge of flour on the side of her nose.

"That's nice to hear," she said. "I'm ready for a break. Would you like to join me for a cup of tea?"

"But if anyone needs me…" Bailey began.

"Don't worry," Olivia said. "Anyone who needs us will ring the bell, and we can hear it in the kitchen. Anyway, by now our guests are all off shopping or hiking."

They had several remaining: three older couples and two middle-aged sisters who had come up on a whim. Just as Bailey was about to leave her post, the sisters walked through the lobby.

"That was a great breakfast," one, a petite fifty-something brunette, said to Bailey.

As if she'd cooked it. A small part of her wished she had. "Here's the cook," she said, pointing to Olivia.

"We really enjoyed it." The woman smiled. "It's worth staying here just for the food."

Olivia murmured her thanks, and the women went up the floral-carpeted stairs to their room.

"It's always satisfying when people appreciate your hard work," Olivia said as she led the way to the kitchen.

"I'm sure you had plenty of people who appreciated what you made, too."

Bailey had. Every time she'd catered a party people had raved about the food. And she'd always picked up at least one new customer. Still, all those compliments together couldn't stand up to the weight of what had happened with Samba.

Bailey mumbled a yes and hoped Olivia would move on to a new subject.

She was heading over to the little table set up with chairs in a corner of the big commercial kitchen when Olivia said, "You know what would be lovely with our tea? Scones. I think your mother told me you came up with a special scone recipe that uses lavender."

Just because Bailey was no longer catering didn't mean she no longer liked talking about food. "I did. And it's got white chocolate in it, too."

"I have some lavender buds. I use them for my sugar cookies. Let's make some scones."

Baking with Olivia would be like when she was a kid, dusted in flour, rolling out cookies and hanging on Olivia's every word about the secret of not overhandling the dough. Bailey smiled and hurried to wash her hands.

By the time she was finished, Olivia had the ingredients assembled, and in a matter of minutes the treats were ready on the baking sheet.

"I can hardly wait to try these," Olivia said as Bailey slid them into the oven.

"You're going to love them," Bailey promised her. Then, remembering her conversation with Eric and feeling nosy, she asked, "So, does Eric have a girlfriend?" Olivia looked at her hopefully, and she quickly added, "I mean, something he said made me wonder if he did or, um, used to."

Olivia sighed. "There was a girl in Cashmere he liked. It didn't work out, though. He moped around over her for ages."

Bailey could identify with that.

"But I think he's finally put that behind him. At least I hope he has. He's such a good man. I'd like to see him find someone special." She shook her head. "I don't understand why it's so hard for you young people to settle down. When I was your age, we were all getting married at twenty. Young people today are too picky."

"I don't know if it's being picky," Bailey said, "but once you've fallen for someone and it doesn't work out…"

Olivia patted her arm. "Brandon's my baby boy, and I love him dearly, but he's a twit. You'll meet your Mr. Right. He'll come along when you least expect it—mark my words."

Bailey couldn't imagine finding anyone more right than Brandon, but she nodded gamely.

"Now, let's see," Olivia said, "do we want to make some mock Devonshire cream to go with our scones?"

Fifteen minutes later the scones were out of the oven, perfectly formed and golden-brown. Olivia set four on a pretty serving plate and suggested they go enjoy the comfy chairs in the lobby. Once she'd relaxed in a comfy, overstuffed chair, Olivia took one of the scones and bit into it. Bailey watched as her mentor chewed, then closed her eyes. "Delicious," Olivia said. "Lovely taste combination."

Her praise was a balm to Bailey's wounded soul.

Olivia savored another bite, then said, "I hate to see your talents wasted here."

"Oh, they're not," Bailey assured her. A sudden, scary thought occurred. Maybe Olivia was trying to find a nice way to fire her. She launched into a list of everything she was doing right. "I think the website looks really great, especially the food pictures. And I like helping people check in."

"You're doing a wonderful job," Olivia said, and Bailey breathed a sigh of relief. "But I think you're meant for greater things than manning our reception desk."

Once upon a time Bailey, too, had thought she was meant for great things. Maybe she still was. Maybe she'd become a famous food photographer. Except that taking pictures of someone else's culinary creations would be like settling for second best.

"Don't let one bad experience stop you from doing what you're passionate about," Olivia said. "You Sterling women are made of sterner stuff."

Well, her older sister was—that was for sure. Sammy had saved the family company. Sometimes Bailey wished she was more like her.

"I don't think I am," she confessed. Otherwise she'd have stayed in L.A. and fought for her business. She'd have sued Samba Barrett. She'd have…done something. But no matter what she might have done, it would've been too late to save her culinary reputation. So what good did it do to be brave?

"You are," Olivia said. "We all get knocked down at some point in life. And that's where you are right now. You've had a crisis of confidence. But I know you'll pick yourself up and start cooking again. What you end up doing may not look exactly like what you did before, but you'll find your way." Now she pointed a finger at Bailey. "And when you see that path, when you get excited again, don't let fear turn off the spigot. Let the energy flow. That's what I did after my husband died, and look how well we're doing."

"You make it seem so easy," Bailey said.

Olivia chuckled. "Oh, believe me, it's not at first. You were so young back then, you probably don't remember when George died."

"I do." Bailey remembered Olivia seated at her mother's kitchen table, crying, Mama with an arm around her shoulders. They'd all gone to the memorial service, and Bailey had spent a lot of time glancing over at Brandon, who'd been trying not to cry, sending him comforting thoughts.

"I had no head for business, and sometimes I felt like I was drowning. You see, it was a dream we'd shared, something we'd planned on doing together. With him gone…" Olivia picked off a piece of her scone and studied it, then crumbled it between her fingers, watching the broken bits fall onto her plate.

"I can't imagine what that was like," Bailey said. Suddenly her troubles looked as small as the crumbs on Olivia's plate.

"It was hard, but we carried on. And I'm so glad we did. It wasn't the dream I had of running this place with my husband, but it's turned out okay, and it's given me a lot of pleasure." She smiled at Bailey. "The wonderful thing about dreams is that you may wake up from one, but there's always another one waiting. I don't know what God has in mind for you, but I know it's something special."

Bailey nodded and murmured her thanks. She wanted to believe every word Olivia said. Before that awful incident in L.A. she had. She'd skipped through her childhood, enjoying her status as the spoiled baby of the family. Even after losing her father she'd managed to still find joy in life (usually in the kitchen). And when she'd left home she'd gone with a suitcase full of cooking utensils, her small savings, a check from her mother and stepfather and a heart filled with hope. She'd had every expectation that her dreams would come true. Why not? She loved to create in the kitchen; she liked people; she trusted people.

And that, she realized, had been her big mistake. But how could you go through life *not* trusting people?

One of their guests was moving toward the front desk, and that signaled the end of Bailey's chat with Olivia. But it had given her plenty to think about. The wonderful smells from breakfast still haunted the lobby. Now they whispered, "Come back."

But then she thought of all those horrible headlines and plugged her ears.

And she was right to. Morgan Withers, one of the maids, drove that home to her later that day. Morgan had graduated from Icicle Falls High the year before and was still trying to find her direction in life.

"Who was in 201?" she asked Bailey.

"An older guy." He'd been a nice old man. A little doddery, but very sweet.

"That explains it," Morgan said with a frown. "He missed the toilet."

Eeew. Bailey wrinkled her nose. "I could have gone all day without hearing that."

"Well, I could have gone all day without cleaning

that," Morgan said with a scowl. "Sometimes I hate this job."

Okay, so it wasn't fun cleaning up after people, but Olivia paid well, and Bailey found herself mildly incensed on Olivia's behalf. "You don't have to work here," she said.

"Yeah? Well, where am I supposed to work with just a high school diploma?" Morgan growled. "Herman's?"

"I don't know," Bailey said. She was having enough trouble figuring out her own life. "What do you want to do?"

Morgan looked wistful. "I want to be a nurse."

She'd have much bigger messes to deal with as a nurse than she had now, but Bailey decided this wasn't the time to point that out. "That's really noble. You should do it."

"I can't afford to go to school."

"You could save up," Bailey said. She'd saved up to start her catering business.

"I've been trying, but it's really hard."

Especially when you spent all your money on clothes. But Bailey was in no position to judge. She couldn't even begin to count the number of times she'd surrendered to the lure of a cute pair of shoes.

"Well, don't give up," she said. "It's important to go for your dreams."

"Yeah? I saw how well that worked for you," Morgan retorted. The words were barely out of her mouth before her face acquired an instant sunburn. She stared down at her toes. "Sorry. That was mean."

Mean but true, Bailey thought as Morgan slipped off to the kitchen for her break.

And now Morgan wasn't the only one who was grumpy.

That night Bailey returned to her mother's book for more sage advice.

You may be feeling like you are out of options. Trust me, this is never true. We always have options, always have choices. But sometimes, buried under discouragement, they can be hard to see.

Bailey wondered about Morgan the maid. Was she discouraged? Maybe she blew her money because she figured there was no sense in saving it. Maybe she needed to read this book, too. Bailey decided to pass it on when she was done. Even if a girl wasn't lucky enough to have Muriel Sterling for a mother, she could at least have a Muriel Sterling book.

Bailey read on.

Sit down, either on your own or with a close friend or relative, and make a list of all your strengths. Once you've done that, make another list of all the possible ways you can use those strengths.

Hmm. What were her strengths? She padded out to the kitchen and grabbed a piece of paper and a pencil. Book in hand, she knocked on Cecily's bedroom door, and then without waiting for an invitation, she walked in.

Just like when they were teenagers, her sister had her nose in a romance novel. She seemed embarrassed to be caught with it, quickly stuffing it in her nightstand drawer. "What's wrong?" Then she saw what Bailey was carrying. "Oh. You're reading Mom's new book."

"What are my strengths?" Bailey asked, plopping down on the bed.

Cecily snuggled back against the pillows. "Well, you're creative. You've come up with a lot of great recipes."

Bailey nodded and wrote that down. "What else?"

"You're fun and enthusiastic. You're optimistic. Most of the time," Cecily amended.

Okay, the past couple of months she hadn't been so optimistic. But even the sunniest disposition would have trouble breaking through the clouds that had been raining on her. First the catering disaster and then Brandon. Ick.

That had been a Memorial Day to forget. After seeing Brandon and Arielle she'd come home and eaten the chocolate silk pie she'd made the day before to take to the family barbecue at Sammy's, standing over the sink, trying bite by bite to lose the image of Brandon and his new love in his old room, kissing passionately. She'd made a second dessert, a peach cobbler, but after her earlier eating binge she'd felt too sick to do anything, so the peach cobbler had gone off to her sister's without her.

She was past that now. No more feeling sorry for herself and overdosing on chocolate. She was back to being optimistic, and she was going to stay that way even if it killed her.

"What else?" she asked as she wrote *optimistic* and underlined it three times for emphasis.

"You're good with people." Cecily covered a yawn.

Her sister had to work in the morning, and so did she. What was she doing keeping them both up?

"You're loyal," Cecily said drowsily. "You're there when we need you."

"I'm not sure how any of those things are going to

help me find a new career," Bailey said. "How did you know you were supposed to work at Sweet Dreams?"

"I don't know. It just seemed to evolve."

"And you love doing it."

"Actually, I do."

"That's what I want," Bailey said, looking at her list, "to find a career I love. I wish it could be with food. There must be something. Don't you think?"

Cecily didn't say anything, and Bailey glanced up to see that her eyes had dropped shut.

Maybe that was enough list-making for one night. Bailey switched off her sister's light. "Thanks for being such a great sister," she whispered, then started to tiptoe out of the room. Until she stubbed her toe on the corner of the bed. Then the tiptoeing turned to hopping and yelping.

"You okay?" Cecily asked.

"I'm fine," Bailey said between gritted teeth and limped back to her own bed. Or at least she would be fine once her toe stopped throbbing. Once she'd figured out what she wanted to do with the rest of her life.

By the end of the week she was no closer to figuring out her future, but she knew what she'd be doing that Friday night. She was going dancing at The Red Barn with Cecily.

She was just finishing her makeup when her cell phone rang. It was Olivia.

"I need help," she croaked.

"Of course," Bailey said. "What do you need?"

"I need you to come in and cook breakfast tomorrow."

The icy fingers of dread grabbed hold of Bailey, and she swallowed hard. "But what about Betsy?"

Betsy was a retired teacher who loved coming in on weekends and helping Olivia cook.

"She's sick, too."

"Well, then, Lorna?" Lorna Griswald was married and had three kids. She supplemented the family income by working in the kitchen on weekdays. Surely she could step in."

"She went out of town with her family." Now the croak had degenerated into a mere whisper. "I haven't even felt well enough to plan the menu."

"But you plan your menus on Thursdays," Bailey said. And then Olivia bought what she needed for the weekend on Fridays. Olivia had been well enough to go shopping on Thursday. Now Bailey was smelling a rat.

"I think that's when I started feeling bad," Olivia said, sounding as though Death was hovering at her elbow.

Bailey could hardly come right out and tell her boss that she was full of hoo-ha. "Are you sure you feel that bad? Maybe by tomorrow..."

"I can't wait until tomorrow. People will be wanting their breakfast. Oh, honey, I'm sorry to ask, but could you please pitch in just this once? You can make whatever you want."

Whatever she wanted. Her imagination began skipping in circles. Oh, it was so tempting. But... "I can't."

"Yes, you can. Please. I'm depending on you."

Bailey swallowed again. She couldn't do this. Olivia shouldn't ask her.

"Please. For me?"

"What if somebody gets sick?"

"No one will get sick," Olivia promised.

"But if someone does?"

"That's why we have insurance. You'll be fine. I can't talk anymore. I need to sleep. Come on by, and Eric will give you a blank check. Thank you, honey."

And then she was gone, leaving Bailey with a dial tone in her ear and a knot in her stomach.

Chapter Eleven

"You ready to go?" Cecily asked, coming into the bathroom, where Bailey stood staring at her cell phone. "Hey, what's wrong?"

"I have to make breakfast at the lodge tomorrow."

Cecily smiled as if this was good news. "That's great."

"Olivia doesn't have the menu planned," Bailey continued, her voice rising along with her level of panic.

"That's even better. Now you can get creative."

Bailey shook her head. "No, I can't. I…can't do this."

Cecily grabbed her by the arms. "Yes. You can. You really can."

The bad thought wouldn't go away. What if someone got sick?

"No one's going to get sick," said her sister, the mind reader.

Someone was going to get sick right now, as a matter of fact. "I don't feel good," Bailey whimpered and collapsed against the bathroom vanity.

"You'll do great," Cecily assured her.

"But what if—"

Her sister didn't let her finish. "Nothing's going to happen. You can't let one bad experience stop you from doing something you love. Deep down, you know that."

Did she? Maybe. The one thing she did know was that she missed being able to cook for people. It was fine making dinner for her and her sister every night, but that wasn't the same as creating a meal for a large number of people. What she was doing now was the equivalent of an artist hanging her paintings in her closet.

"How many people would you say ate your cooking before the Samba Barrett party?"

She'd had hundreds of catering gigs in L.A. And before she'd moved, she'd been making goodies for everything from friends' birthday parties to church events. "A lot."

"And none of those people ever complained or got sick. Right?"

True.

"And we know Samba Barrett faked her illness for the publicity. Right?"

"Right," Bailey said slowly.

"So, do you really want to let one faker keep lots of other people from enjoying all the yummy things you come up with in the kitchen?" Cecily asked softly.

"No," Bailey decided. Here was an opportunity to do what she loved. She shouldn't run away from it even if she was scared. And Olivia hadn't planned the menu yet (or so she said). Bailey could make whatever she wanted. Well, within limits. She didn't want to get too extravagant. Olivia hadn't mentioned a budget, but Bailey was sure her boss would want her to stick to a reasonable amount. "I could make muffin-tin omelets," she mused. "And Mom's almond puff pastry," she said, getting excited. Add to that a nice fruit salad, and she'd have a lovely menu. "I'd better get over to the lodge. I need to check on how many we'll have for breakfast. Then I've got to make a grocery list and go shopping."

"I guess this means we're not going dancing," Cecily said with a smile.

"Oh, my gosh! I'm sorry. I just wrecked your Friday night."

"Don't worry. I'll find something to do."

Of course she would. She'd call Luke. She'd probably only suggested going dancing because she was worried about Bailey's not having a life. Well, it looked as if she had a life now. She was smiling when she hurried out of the condo.

Bailey had just rushed out the door when Todd called Cecily. "Hey, thought I might sneak away from the old cave and come spin you and your sis around the floor at The Red Barn."

"There'll only be one sister to spin," Cecily said. "Bailey got called in to cook breakfast at the lodge. She just left to plan her menu and go shopping. She'll be busy all night."

"So, you're there all alone? What a shame. I'll be right over."

Not so long ago she would have retorted, "Who says I want you to come over?" They were well beyond that now. "Good idea," she said.

* * *

Eric was behind the reception desk watching a movie on his laptop when Bailey arrived at the lodge. "I hear you're in charge of breakfast," he greeted her.

She nodded. "Is your mom really sick?"

"She's in bed," he said, not actually answering Bailey's question. "So, what are we having?" She told him, and he grinned. "I have to wait until morning for this?"

If the guests reacted half as positively she'd be happy. "Afraid so," she said.

"I don't know if I *can* wait."

"I might be able to find a small piece for a food tester," she said.

"You want me to help you get the groceries?" he asked as he gave her a check.

"No, I can handle it. Anyway, you're busy watching a movie."

"I wouldn't exactly call that 'busy.'"

"It's okay. I can handle it," she repeated.

"Yeah, you can," he said. "Let me know if you need anything."

"Courage?" she joked.

"You've already got that. You just need to tap into it."

She sure hoped he was right.

She double-checked the number of guests and then sat down and did some calculations, figuring out how much food she'd need and how many ingredients she'd have to purchase. Her nerves made it hard to concentrate at first, and she wound up doing her math three times. Then she went into the office and had Eric go through the numbers.

"That's right," he told her. "You know what you're doing."

Yes, she did. Ooh, but what if something went wrong?

That thought trailed her up and down the aisle at the grocery store, but she did her best to ignore it. *You can do this,* she kept telling herself. And once the shopping was done, once she was back in the kitchen at the lodge, whipping up her choux pastry, she almost began to believe herself. She was back on familiar ground, doing work she loved, so she tried not to spoil it with negative thoughts.

Still, she couldn't help praying, *Pleeease, don't let anyone get sick tomorrow.* Although as nervous as she was, there was a good chance someone would. Her!

Twenty minutes after he'd called, Todd was leaning in Cecily's doorway, holding a take-out pizza from Italian Alps and a pack of wine coolers, smiling at her with that wolfish grin of his, making her pulse jump. He also had a DVD.

"I don't want you saying I only came over here to grope you," he said as he sauntered past her.

"Oh? So, no groping tonight?"

"I didn't say that." He set the pizza on the coffee table and made himself at home on the couch. "Hungry?"

Not with the way her sister was feeding her these days, but she had a weakness for pizza, and with the box open, the aroma was wafting over and tickling her nose. "I'll get plates," she said. "What's the movie?"

He held it up and she blinked. It was the latest remake of *Pride and Prejudice.*

"Hey, don't look so shocked. I told you, I'm not a total Philistine."

Now she was suspicious. "You just got that to score points."

"Well, that, too," he admitted. "I thought you'd like it." He walked over to her DVR and put in the movie. "Come on, beautiful. Hurry up and get those plates. Mr. Darby is waiting."

"That's 'Darcy,'" she said as she pulled plates from the cupboard.

"Whatever."

Cecily sneaked a peek in Todd's direction a couple of times during the movie and was surprised to find him actually paying attention. "I can't believe you watched the whole thing," she said as the ending credits began to roll.

He grabbed her remote and switched off the movie. "Things don't always have to be blowing up to get my attention."

He started playing with her hair, and that got *her* attention. "It was sweet of you to pick that movie," she said softly.

"That's me," he said. "Mr. Sweet."

She frowned at him. "Can't you ever be serious?"

"Well, yes. In fact, I'm about to show you how serious I can be." He put an arm around her and drew her close. "I'm serious when I say you're an irresistible woman," he murmured, his lips grazing her ear.

Now she was craving the feel of his lips on hers. She turned her face to him and closed her eyes and Todd took it from there. And, boy, did he know how to take it.

But part of her—darn that sensible self!—wasn't

ready to succumb completely to his charms. "Look at the time," she finally said. "You should be going."

He gave her a mock frown. "Can't *you* ever be serious?" Before she could say anything, he held up a hand. "I know. I know. You are. I should probably pop in at the old cave and see how things are going anyway." He paused. "But are you sure you don't want to watch another movie?" he added and waggled his eyebrows.

She knew what that was code for. She shook her head. "My sister will be home soon."

"And you don't want her to find out you've got a man up here?" he teased.

"Something like that," she said lightly.

In reality, she didn't want to examine her motives for not letting Bailey meet Todd. At least she didn't want to examine them too closely. She suspected that, deep down, she wasn't all that secure about her new relationship with him. Much as she loved her sister, she didn't want to share. There was something about Bailey. Her freckles? Her fresh-faced happiness? Her curves? Whatever it was, Bailey, like Mom, never had trouble attracting men. Cecily might have been considered the family beauty, but if you asked her, Bailey was the true man magnet.

She gave Todd one last kiss and then shooed him out the door. He'd been gone only ten minutes before Bailey rolled back in, all bright eyes and enthusiasm. "Breakfast is going to be fantastic," she predicted. "I'm sorry I ditched you, though." Then she caught sight of the pizza box with a few slices remaining and threw her sister a knowing look. "You had company."

"I did," Cecily admitted and hoped Bailey didn't

ask who that company had been. She probably assumed it was Luke, since Cecily hadn't mentioned that she'd put the brakes on that relationship.

Bailey hugged her. "I'm glad. It's about time you found someone nice."

Cecily wasn't sure *nice* was the right word to use in describing Todd Black. But there were other words that worked just as well—like *sexy* and *exciting* and *addictive.* "I have."

Todd swung by his place and took a nice, cold shower before going to check in on the Neanderthals hanging out at The Man Cave. Cecily was making him crazy. He was more than ready to go beyond what she'd so lovingly referred to as a "grope fest." Groping was all well and good, but it only got the party started, and staying stuck at that sexual level hardly made for a satisfying relationship.

Something was holding her back and it wasn't his technique. She reminded him of a little kid perched at the edge of a pool with her dad in the water urging her to jump. But she couldn't.

It was as if there were parts of herself she kept curtained off. She'd wanted to know all about his past love life, but she hadn't shared much of hers. Had somebody hurt her?

Hard to imagine anyone hurting Cecily Sterling. Who'd want to? She was too nice. So, how had she gone this long without getting engaged? Too picky?

He remembered when he'd met her. She'd been with her sister Samantha, and they'd had a flat tire and pulled into The Man Cave's parking lot. He could still see the look of disdain on her face as she'd taken in his tavern for the first time. She'd hidden it quickly enough, but he'd seen. Maybe she *was* too picky.

But if that was the case, what was she doing with him now?

Dumb question. She wanted him as badly as he wanted her. He could feel the electricity in the air whenever they got together. At some point she was going to let him give her all two hundred and twenty volts. He just had to find a way to reassure her that he wasn't out to hurt her and that she wouldn't get burned.

His bartender, Pete, was holding down the fort and didn't really need him, but he went behind the bar to help out anyway. He liked being here, liked the guys who came in and liked being on top of what was going on in his business. Henry was seated at his regular spot at the bar, Pete keeping him company, wiping up a spill with his bar rag. "What are you doing back here?" he greeted Todd. "Mike said you had a hot date."

"I did."

"Must've cooled off," Henry observed. "What happened? Did the lady lose interest?"

No, she just lost her nerve. "Anybody ever tell you you're a nosy old codger?" Todd said with a frown.

"These younger guys think they're so hot," he said to the old geezer next to him, "but they're not built as well as us."

The other guy chuckled. "Got that right. All flash and no substance."

"Yeah, yeah," Todd said with a grin. "If I need help, I'll be sure to come to you two."

"Vitamins," Henry insisted. "And nuts," he added,

scooping up some cocktail nuts from the bowl in front of him. "Protein keeps the old muscle working."

"You got any muscle at all, Henry?" teased one of the younger men, who'd left the pool table in search of another beer. "Bet it's been a long time since you used it."

That had all the men guffawing and Henry sputtering about his virility.

"So, how's it going with Cecily?" Pete asked as the other men joked with each other.

"Good," Todd said. Even though they were moving more slowly than he would've liked, they were still headed in the right direction. Now, if he could just get Cecily to quit putting on the brakes so they could get there...

At the Icicle Creek Lodge, customers made reservations for when they'd like breakfast—anytime between the hours of seven-thirty and ten in the morning. The lodge was full and most people wanted to eat between eight and nine.

Bailey was ready for them, though. Her Danish puff (which Eric had sampled and heartily approved) had been sliced and arranged on plates, one for each table. In addition to the pastry, she'd also made the salad the night before and grated the cheese for her muffin-tin omelets. Breakfast went out to everyone right on time, and later Misty, the teenage server, returned with more than dirty plates. She had a pile of compliments for the chef.

Bailey felt as if she'd been holding her breath all morning. Now her breathing began to return to normal, and the muscles that had been huddled tightly together in her neck and shoulders relaxed. She'd done it. She'd served up a meal and nobody had gotten sick. Or pretended to. So far.

"Um, everyone's okay out there?"

"Oh, yeah. They haven't left even a crumb. I sure would like to try one of those pastries," Misty said, as she looked longingly at the one remaining plate.

"You will," Bailey promised her. "That plate is for the staff."

Misty's eyes lit up. "Sweet! I can hardly wait."

Bailey smiled. This was why she loved to cook. Eating made people happy. She gazed around the kitchen at the big stove, the griddle, the huge double sink, the Hobart dishwasher, the walk-in cooler. A framed piece of cross-stitch art that read Bless This Kitchen hung on one wall over the stainless-steel storage counters—a gift from Bailey's mom to Olivia years ago. The kitchen had, indeed, been blessed, serving countless guests good food for the past twenty years and giving any number of young cooks their start, including Bailey.

This was where she belonged. Cecily had been right. It would have been stupid to let one bad experience keep her away from this forever. She inhaled deeply. The kitchen smelled of bacon. Tomorrow the menu would change, and it would have a different aroma—maybe cinnamon from Olivia's famous cinnamon rolls or vanilla and brown sugar. Whatever was on the menu, she wanted to be part of it.

Misty had barely left the kitchen when Eric put in an appearance. "Looks like breakfast was a success."

"I think so," Bailey said with a grin.

"I knew you could do it."

"I'm glad you knew. I wasn't so sure."

"Sometimes you have to prove it to yourself."

"I guess you've been there, done that?"

Unlike his charming younger brother, Eric didn't talk much. He certainly didn't talk much about himself. But today he seemed inclined to. "Yeah, I remember my first big lesson when I was doing track in high school. I wiped out on the hurdles, got a ton of dirt embedded in my leg." He shook his head. "Man, getting that cleaned out hurt like the devil. And I felt like a loser. In fact, I wanted to quit."

Bailey nodded. She could identify with that big-time.

"My coach wouldn't let me. He said the only real losers are the ones who go down and never get up again." He smiled at Bailey. "Good for you for getting up."

She smiled back. "Thanks. Can I adopt you as my older brother?"

"Sure. Sisters bake cookies for their brothers, right?"

"Absolutely."

"Welcome to the family, sis. Oh, and by the way, my brother's an idiot."

Considering the woman he'd decided to fall in love with, she couldn't have agreed more.

"I should get to work. Mom's got a to-do list for me a mile long," he said as he started to head out.

"Eric."

He turned, an eyebrow raised in question.

"Thanks for the encouragement."

"Don't thank me. I've got an ulterior motive. I love cookies."

He sauntered off, leaving her with a smile on her

face. Maybe, if Bailey told Olivia she'd changed her mind, Olivia would let her help with the breakfasts every weekend.

She was taking off her apron when Olivia strolled in, looking hale and hearty in jeans and a pink sweatshirt.

"What are you doing here?" Bailey asked in surprise. "Shouldn't you be in bed?"

"I'm feeling so much better. Just thought I'd come in and see how you're doing. How did it go?"

"Great," Bailey crowed.

"I'm glad. You know, I had three guests stop me to rave about breakfast."

Rave reviews. Bailey's lips stretched wider. "I'm so glad."

"Can you do tomorrow's breakfast, too?" Olivia asked.

"But you're okay now," Bailey protested.

"Oh, I'm still too weak to stand up in the kitchen. I realize it's a lot to ask. You'd have to miss church."

"I can go to the evening service," Bailey said quickly. Already her mind was racing with what she could make—waffles with bacon bits in them, served with maple whipped cream. Or maybe oatmeal muffins and quiche.

"That would be lovely," Olivia said. "Thank you, dear."

"My pleasure," Bailey said, and she meant it.

The next morning she got more raves on her waffles, which she'd served with another fruit salad, this one with a yogurt-lime dressing.

"That was wonderful," Olivia said, coming into the kitchen.

Today she looked as hale and hearty as she had the day before. Once more Bailey wondered if Olivia had even been sick. She didn't ask, but she did say, "You look like you're all recovered."

"I am," Olivia said. "There's nothing like having a couple of days off to make you feel like a new woman." She leaned on the counter and took a sip from the coffee mug she was carrying. "You should be doing this full-time, honey. You know that, don't you?"

Bailey focused on wiping down the counter. "I do love to be in the kitchen. I thought maybe you'd let me help out with breakfast once in a while."

"That's what I offered when you first came in," Olivia reminded her. "And, of course, the offer still stands, but I'd love to see you strike out on your own."

"I don't think there's much demand for caterers here in Icicle Falls," Bailey said. It wasn't like L.A., where everyone was either too busy or too important to cook. Anyway, she didn't want to cater. She was done with catering.

"You might consider it anyway. Why not come with me to the chamber-of-commerce meeting this week?"

"Oh, I don't know," Bailey said. Helping Olivia in her kitchen was one thing. Going to the chamber-of-commerce meeting and mingling with all the successful businesspeople in town was quite another.

"You might get some ideas."

Ideas would be good. She still needed to make that list of options her mother had talked about in her book.

"You can come as my guest," Olivia said.

"But who'll watch the front desk?"

"Eric can do it. We won't be gone that long anyway." Olivia checked her watch. "Speaking of guests, we'll have some of them checking out soon. Why don't you go to the front desk, and I'll finish cleaning up in here."

Well, that settled it. It looked as though Bailey was going to the chamber-of-commerce meeting whether she wanted to or not.

Chapter Twelve

The banquet room at Pancake Haus was packed with the town's movers and shakers. Ed York, who owned D'vine Wines, stood visiting with several people, including Sammy and Cecily's friend Charlene Masters. Also in the circle stood longtime family friend Pat Wilder. From the way Ed looked at her when she talked, it was easy to tell he was smitten. And the way she looked back—well, she was smitten, too. All the bed-and-breakfast and motel owners were present, as well as most of the shop owners. Del Stone, the town's mayor, was just finding a seat at the center of the large table next to Dot Morrison, who owned Pancake Haus, and on her other side sat Bubba Swank, who owned The Big Brats, the town's favorite spot for sausages and great German potato salad.

Various people were still filing in. Here came skinny Hildy Johnson, followed by Tina Swift, who sent Bailey an uncomfortable smile and then scooted past her. Samantha entered the room after her, a picture of business casual in dark jeans, a crisp, white blouse and a red leather jacket, her long, brown hair falling loose to her shoulders.

She blinked at the sight of Bailey and hurried over

to give her a hug. "This is a surprise." *As in, what are* you *doing here?*

"Olivia invited me," Bailey said.

Samantha nodded approvingly. "Good idea. You might get inspired."

Before Bailey could ask what, exactly, her big sister thought she'd get inspired to do, Ed York spoke from his end of the banquet room.

"Okay, people," he said, raising his voice to be heard over the hubbub. "Please go ahead and find a seat."

Everyone obliged, and they were almost all seated when one last person slipped into the room.

Saffron, basil and thyme! Who the heck was that? Bailey hadn't seen anyone so beautiful in town since Brandon left. Where had this dark-haired piece of gorgeous been hiding? He should be in Hollywood. He was better-looking than half the aspiring stars down there.

He gave her a sexy smile as he sat down opposite her and Olivia and said, "Hi."

"Hi," she stuttered. Hard to stutter a one-syllable word, but Bailey managed. She also managed to knock over her mug, spilling a river of coffee in his direction. "Oh, sorry." She reached for a napkin to mop it up and knocked over her water glass, as well.

He moved his chair away from the table. "No problem." He grabbed a napkin and mopped up some of it, then disappeared.

Way to drive away a good-looking man, she scolded herself.

"Don't worry. He'll be back," Olivia said.

Sure enough, he was back a moment later with a

handful of napkins. "Olivia, I see you finally found someone as pretty as yourself to hang out with," he teased as he wiped up the mess.

Olivia's plump cheeks turned pink. "You are so full of frijoles," she scolded him. "This is Bailey Sterling."

"Sterling. You're Cecily's sister?"

"Yes. You know her?" Silly question. Everyone in Icicle Falls knew everyone else. So, how come Bailey didn't know *him?*

He nodded. "I do."

Okay. So, how come Cecily hadn't mentioned him?

"Todd Black owns The Man Cave," Olivia explained. "It's a, um…"

"Tavern," Todd supplied.

"Bailey's just returned home from Los Angeles," Olivia said to Todd.

He disposed of the wet napkins, then settled back in his seat, and Bailey kept her hands in her lap, determined not to spill anything else. "What are you doing now that you're here?" he asked.

"I'm working for Olivia."

"Bailey's a caterer. She cooked breakfast for my guests this last weekend and got rave reviews," Olivia said.

The waitress arrived at their end of the table and that stopped conversation for the moment. But once she'd moved on, they picked it up again with Todd asking Bailey about L.A. and where she'd lived.

"I was just outside of L.A.," he said.

"Icicle Falls must seem pretty dull after that," Bailey said. "Why'd you end up here?"

"I came through on a bike trip with my brother.

Saw the for-sale sign on the tavern and decided to buy it."

"Just like that?"

He shrugged. "I had some money saved up. I liked the town, and it looked like a good investment. Things worked out well for me. And I enjoy being here. There's plenty to do—river surfing, fishing, hiking."

All outdoor rough stuff. Obviously she and Todd Black had nothing in common. The way her luck had been going, it figured.

"There's usually a decent band playing at The Red Barn," he continued.

"Do you like to dance?" she asked hopefully.

"I'm not bad on the dance floor," he said with a confident smile.

Yes! A man who liked to dance.

"I hear you bought the Halverson place over on Lavender Lane," Olivia said.

He nodded. "Yep. Good business location, right around the corner from Bavarian Brews. A new coat of paint, and it'll make a nice shop or restaurant."

"Smart," Olivia said. "This man is going places," she told Bailey.

I wouldn't mind going with him, Bailey thought.

Breakfast orders began to arrive, and the chamber members chitchatted as they ate bacon and eggs, pancakes, and Belgian waffles smothered in strawberries and whipped cream, all washed down with juice and Dot's notoriously strong coffee. Everyone was about halfway through when Ed called their meeting to order.

"Before we begin, I'm sure you've all seen that we

have a visitor this morning. Welcome home, Bailey. It's wonderful to have you back in Icicle Falls."

"They can't stay away," Dot cracked. "Once an Icicle, always an Icicle."

Bailey felt her cheeks heating under the warmth of the smiles she saw around the table. Most of these people had seen her grow up. She'd been so excited to leave and make her mark on the world. Now she was back again, a failure, seated amid a crowd of successful people. What was she doing here?

Eric would say she was getting up and getting back in the race. Well, maybe she was.

The business meeting began, starting with a discussion on the upcoming summer wine walk. Then a newcomer who'd recently opened an ice cream and candy shop lobbied to be allowed to put up a larger sign. He was quickly shot down.

"We have a template for the size of our signs and the colors we use," Ed explained, "and we all follow it. That's what keeps Icicle Falls unique, and that's what keeps the visitors coming back. And we all know how important tourism is to our economy."

Everyone nodded. They did, indeed. Tourism had rebuilt their town.

Thanks to the loss of the railroad and the logging industry, by the end of the 1950s Icicle Falls had been on the verge of extinction. The few remaining citizens had taken a look at their mountain setting and concluded that it could be as lovely as any Alpine village. The town had pulled together and remade itself, putting Bavarian facades on the old Western buildings, adding window boxes with flowers and opening shops designed to lure visitors. With the scenery and winter sports working in its favor, Icicle Falls succeeded in turning itself into a charming tourist destination.

But no matter how many visitors came through, it kept its small-town feel, and the people stayed close. Bailey reminded herself that she could have picked a worse place to come and heal her emotional wounds.

"If that's all the business for today, we can adjourn," Ed told the group.

Chairs scraped, people started getting up, and the room was full of voices as everyone began to leave the restaurant and go back to their businesses. Samantha gave Bailey a quick kiss and then was gone, off to run the Sweet Dreams empire. Bailey had planned to follow her out, but that didn't happen.

Ivy Bohn, whose family owned Christmas Haus, a shop that sold Christmas trimmings all year round, caught up to her quickly. "I'm sorry things didn't work out in L.A."

Bailey nodded and said a polite thank-you.

"Have you thought about what you want to do now that you're here?" Ivy asked.

"I'm still trying to figure it out," Bailey said.

"Whatever you do, I hope it'll involve cooking," Ivy said with an encouraging smile. "Let's have coffee sometime."

She and Ivy hadn't been besties in school. In fact, with Ivy a couple of classes ahead of her, they'd moved in different social circles, which made her kindness all the more touching.

"I'd like that," Bailey said.

Everyone here was being so nice to her. It was typical of the people in this town and heartwarming. And yet, so discomfiting. She felt like a caterpillar wandering around loose in a room filled with butterflies.

She was edging toward the door when Ed York caught her arm. "Well," he said cheerfully, "now we have all the Sterling sisters back home again. Have you considered opening a catering business here in Icicle Falls?"

"Oh, no." Bailey shook her head. "I think I need to try something else." She was aware of Todd Black hovering at the edge of their group. Again, she wondered how much he knew about why she was home.

"I keep telling her she was born to cook," Olivia said.

Now Pat Wilder had joined them. "You know what we need?"

This should be interesting. Bailey couldn't imagine another thing the town needed. Icicle Falls had everything from a business supply store to a lingerie shop. And it already had almost every kind of restaurant a person could want. Well, except for a Thai or Chinese restaurant. But even that itch could be scratched thanks to the Safeway deli's offering of pad Thai, General Tso's chicken and egg rolls.

"What?" Olivia asked on Bailey's behalf.

"A tearoom," Pat said. "It would be lovely to have someplace girlie for visitors and for us locals to go with our sisters and daughters and girlfriends."

A feeling came over Bailey that she hadn't experienced since her first year in L.A. Excitement. It rampaged through her brain and down to her heart like a powerful drug.

She could picture it so easily. A cute little cottage. Tables spread with linen tablecloths and decked out with fine china. She could serve scones and cakes and cucumber sandwiches, and she could also sell fancy teas and lovely treats like lemon curd and Devonshire cream. And chocolate, of course, like Sweet Dreams truffles. And pretty teapots and accessories!

But think of the risk. She did and immediately backed away from the precipice of failure.

Todd Black spoke up. "I might have the perfect location for something like that."

"The Halversons' Victorian!" Olivia said. "That would be charming."

And once more Bailey was back at the precipice, enticed by the vision of a sweet Victorian house with lace curtains at the window. It would be the ideal setting for a little tea shop with a tearoom in it.

"Well, there you go," Olivia said as if that settled it all.

Reality stomped onto the scene like an elephant and crushed the vision before it had a chance to grow. "I don't have any start-up money," Bailey said.

"We might be able to work something out," Todd said, taking her arm and walking her out of the room. "Why don't you come take a look at the place, see what you think?"

She glanced over her shoulder at Olivia, who made a shooing gesture. "Go on, honey. It can't hurt to check it out. I'm sure Todd won't mind giving you a lift back to the lodge when you're done."

She was right—what could it hurt? "Okay," Bailey said.

As Todd led her out the door, she could hear Olivia saying to Pat, "Aren't they a cute couple?"

Well, that was embarrassing. She stole a look at

Todd. He was facing straight ahead, pretending not to have heard.

"I really would love to do this," she said. "I can think of so many fabulous things to make and serve. But…" She bit her lip. "It's not just the money." How could she explain that to him?

"Like I said, let's take a look at the place." He led the way to a black truck parked near the restaurant. "If you like it, then we can talk about all your objections."

Once in the truck she couldn't come up with anything to say. Excitement and dread had each taken one end of her tongue and tied it in a giant knot.

"So, you enjoy being back home?" Todd asked in an obvious attempt to put her at ease.

"Yes. It's fun to stay with my sister again. Just like when we were kids."

"Doesn't give either of you much privacy."

She turned to him, puzzled. "For what?"

He cocked an eyebrow. "For entertaining."

"Oh, well, I love to cook, so I'm happy to help Cecily entertain anyone she wants to invite over."

"What if she wants to have a man over?"

Bailey's face felt like a giant flambé. "Oh, *that* kind of entertaining. If she wants to have Luke over, I can always go to Sammy's."

"Sammy? You've found somebody here already?"

"No, I meant my sister Samantha. I call her Sammy."

"And what does she call you?"

"When we were growing up, she called me a pest. So did Cecily." Bailey rolled her eyes. "Sometimes I think they still see me as the baby of the family."

Todd smiled at that. "Well, I still see my brother

that way, too. I've bailed that dude out of half a dozen messes."

Bailey thought of Samantha buying her airline ticket and shipping her home after the Samba Barrett incident. Birth order—and its imperatives—never changed, no matter how old you got.

"Here we are," he said and pulled to a stop in front of a small Victorian. It was a faded white and had equally faded blue shutters at the windows, but it also had a charming front porch and all the gingerbread trim a girl could wish for. Flower beds filled with primroses, and, in keeping with the street name, lavender lined the front walk. The flower beds sported azaleas and rhubarb.

"Look, it's got its own supply of rhubarb and lavender," Bailey said gleefully. She could envision herself making lavender–white chocolate scones, lavender cake and rhubarb muffins. And she could see the place with a new coat of white paint, the shutters painted lavender. She could imagine customers inside, browsing shelves stocked with tea and teapots and pretty table decorations. Oh, yes, it was house lust at first sight.

The house only got better as they walked inside. It had hardwood floors, which would be lovely once they'd been refinished, and the windows let in plenty of light. She'd definitely dress them in lace curtains.

"You could have your tearoom down here and live upstairs," Todd said.

And then she'd have to pay rent on two spaces. She bit her lip.

"You know, there are all kinds of partnerships. In some, one partner puts up the money and the other provides the expertise and creativity. And most of them work," he added with a smile.

What if he risked his money and she failed? She felt her feet suddenly growing very cold. In fact, her toes were starting to get frostbitten. She shook her head violently. "It's a great idea, but I couldn't." She moved toward the front door.

He blocked it. "If you're worrying about whether or not I'm a good business risk, Blake Preston at the bank can vouch for me. He's your brother-in-law, right? He'll give you an honest answer."

She could make a go of this. Correction. She could have *made* a go of it. Now, with all the money that would be involved…she didn't dare try.

"And I know people who can vouch for you," he went on.

"But you don't know what happened before I got here." It was hard to say that and not cry.

"This is a small town. Of course I do."

"I wouldn't be a good investment."

He made a face. "Because you had a setback? Everyone fails at some point. If you don't fail at something, you're not doing much. Hell, I got canned from my first two jobs."

"You did? Why?"

"I had a problem working for stupid people. It turns out I'm better suited to having my own business. At least now when I tell the boss he's making a dumb move, he listens. Come on," he said, taking her by the shoulders and steering her away from the door and back inside. "Let's talk a little about what you'd do with this place."

They talked more than just a little. Another forty

minutes, and they'd discussed everything from where she'd put the till and a glass counter with chocolate truffles for sale, to where she'd position the tables and what she'd use for china.

"I could mix and match," she said excitedly. "A lot of women my age aren't into fine china, and that means their grandmas are dumping it right and left. I could pick up what we need at garage sales and stores like Timeless Treasures here in town." She turned in a slow circle. "Some pretty, old-fashioned pictures on the walls, lace curtains at the windows..."

"There's a shop that sells lace here in town," Todd said. "You know it?"

Tina's Lace and Lovelies. Boy, did she. She nodded.

"The outside of this place needs paint. What color should it be?"

"I think white is fine. Maybe paint the shutters lavender to match the lavender along the front walk. That would complement the lavender theme for the menu. Lavender cake, lavender–white chocolate scones," she said dreamily.

"Sounds good," Todd said. "How about going over to Zelda's and crunching some numbers? Let's see if we can make this work."

Hadn't they just had breakfast? "What time is it?"

He checked his phone. "Twelve-thirty."

Wow! Time flew when you were having fun rebuilding your life. "Okay," she agreed. Why not explore the possibility?

Samantha poked her head inside Cecily's office. "Feel like grabbing something to eat at Zelda's?"

Cecily had half hoped Todd would call to see if

she wanted to meet him at Herman's. That had been a little unrealistic, she decided. Their relationship was still new, and they didn't have to spend every waking minute together.

Except wasn't that what you did when your relationship was new and exciting?

Well, never mind. He was probably busy working. "Sure," she said.

A few minutes later, she and Samantha walked into Zelda's, and she saw what Todd had been busy doing. Suddenly she felt the same way she'd felt when she and Bailey were kids and Bailey had gotten jealous of her blond Barbie doll and cut off its hair.

With a sisterly smile on her face, she started for the table where Todd and Bailey sat deep in lively conversation with only one thought. *I'm going to kill the little brat.*

Chapter Thirteen

Cecily wrestled down the jealous thought that had roared into her brain like an angry beast. Of course there was a simple explanation as to why her sister and Todd were having lunch together and why neither of them had bothered to call her.

Not that they needed to. It was a free country. Bailey could have lunch with anyone she chose. So could Todd. Cecily didn't own him.

But she'd believed things were starting to get serious between them. She'd also believed that about two other men and been wrong. Was she going to be wrong a third time?

Bailey and Todd were so engrossed in their conversation neither one saw her and Samantha approach the table. "Anything good on the menu?" Cecily asked, making Todd jump.

Bailey looked up, her face the picture of delight. "You guys, guess what we're talking about doing?"

Having wild monkey sex on the bar at The Man Cave after hours? Running away to Vegas? "I give up," Cecily said. "What?"

"We're talking about going into business together," Bailey announced.

"Of course, we have a lot to work out," Todd added.

"You don't know each other," Cecily blurted.

"We're working on that," Todd said with a smile.

And doing a darned good job of it from the look of things.

He slid down the banquette and patted the spot where he'd been sitting, inviting Cecily to join him. "Sit down. We'll tell you all about it."

"This is kind of sudden," Samantha said, taking a seat next to Bailey.

"Yeah, but great timing," Todd said.

Maria Gomez came over to take their orders. "The Sterlings have you surrounded," she teased Todd.

"Works for me," he said and grinned at Cecily.

Cecily wasn't so sure it worked for her. Since when had she become so insecure? Oh, yeah. Since Fiancé Number Two.

Samantha and Cecily placed their lunch orders, and Todd returned to the subject of business. "I think we might have a good idea. I recently bought the Halverson house on Lavender Lane. You know it?"

"I do," Samantha said. "Great commercial location, especially for something like a kitchen shop."

"Or a tearoom," Bailey put in, "which is what we're talking about doing."

"You'd be competing with Bavarian Brews," Cecily said. Even as the words paraded out of her mouth, she questioned her motives. Was she being cautious on her sister's behalf or trying to discourage her from working with Todd? Maybe a little of both.

"Not really," he said. "Different retail experience,

probably different clientele, although we'd get some crossover."

"And it won't be just a tearoom," Bailey added. "We'll sell tea and tea accoutrements, cute kitchen items and chocolates. Sweet Dreams chocolates, of course."

"How are you planning to finance this?" Samantha asked.

"I'll put up the money," Todd said. "Bailey can do the work, be in charge of the menu and create the inventory."

"It'll be a while before you see a profit," Samantha mused. "Although you already know that."

He nodded, and the next few minutes were taken up with talking profit and loss, projected growth and a salary draw for Bailey.

Finally Samantha said, "Sounds like a winner to me."

Todd turned to Cecily. "What do you think?"

I think this is a recipe for romantic disaster. "So, basically you'd be a silent partner?" Silent partners didn't get that involved, right?

"Semi-silent," Todd said, "since the place needs some renovation."

How cozy. They'd be working together on the house. "Mmm," Cecily murmured. "So, you'd be both Bailey's partner and her landlord?"

"Of course, we'd want to see some sort of agreement that ensures Bailey's going to profit from this arrangement," Samantha said.

Bailey frowned at her older sister, and Cecily could imagine what she was thinking. Nothing like trying to make an adult decision and having your bossy big sister swoop in and take over. But Samantha did have a point.

"We Sterling women watch out for each other," Cecily said to Todd.

"I can see that," he said. "No worries. I have no intention of screwing your sister."

Cecily cocked an eyebrow, and, realizing what he'd just said, Todd quickly reached for his coffee and took a drink.

Their food arrived, and talk continued. Cecily picked at her salad and argued back and forth with herself as the conversation swirled around her. *This is a great opportunity for your sister.... Is she attracted to Todd?... Good relationships are built on trust.... Can I trust him?... Can I trust her?... Of course I can.*

"I'm excited just thinking about this," Bailey said with a smile. "And I haven't felt that way in months."

And only the rottenest of sisters would try to discourage her new dream.

Talk about great timing. Everything was lining up as if it was meant to be—him getting the Halversons' place for a song and now finding someone who could pull together a tea shop/tearoom. The Man Upstairs was certainly watching over him. Or maybe it was his cosmic reward for contributing to Bailey Sterling's defense fund. Not that she'd needed it. He'd heard her legal fees had been minimal, and, at her insistence, everyone was going to get their money back.

A much easier task than giving the poor kid her confidence back. What had happened to her would've shaken *anyone's* confidence.

But he had a feeling about Bailey Sterling. There

was something special about her. She wasn't drop-dead gorgeous like Cecily, but she was cute in a girl-next-door kind of way, and she had a smile that was nothing short of infectious. Not that he was interested. He was with Cecily, after all, and he was no two-timing weasel. Anyway, only a fool tried to mix business and pleasure.

But a man couldn't help noticing how a woman looked. In fact, he was sure half the men in town had noticed how Bailey Sterling looked. Probably his biggest worry would be whom she married. Maybe Cecily could steer her toward a local guy. The last thing Todd wanted was to start a business and then have his partner get married and go skipping off to some other town.

He doubted she would, though. She was too passionate about food and too fired up about this idea. Like her sisters, she was smart. She obviously had good people skills, since everyone in town appeared to like her. She sure had the connections. The Sterlings were small-town royalty. People would frequent the place simply because of who she was. Oh, yeah. This could be a very good thing.

Or a big pile of shit. He thought of Cecily's lack of enthusiasm as they'd all talked at lunch. He was no dummy himself, and he knew a forced smile when he saw one. Was she jealous of her sister? Untrusting of him? Both? Man, oh, man, he'd better watch where he stepped.

Cecily got in touch with her rotten side later that evening as she and Bailey sat at the kitchen bar in Cecily's condo and ate crab salads, their mother's latest book propped open in front of them.

Previous failures can cast a long shadow. It's important to step out of that shadow. If you don't, you'll never take advantage of new opportunities and you'll never grow.

Bailey tapped on the book. "Mama's right."

"Have you told her about this idea?" Cecily asked.

"Yep, and she thinks it's a good one. She thinks I can do it."

"Of course you can, but maybe you shouldn't rush into doing this with Todd Black. He's got the house, plus a half interest in the business. What are *you* getting?"

"Half the profits. Duh."

Cecily stabbed a piece of crab with her fork and shoved it in her mouth. She looked up to see Bailey eyeing her. "What?"

"I don't understand why you don't want me to do this. Is there something wrong with Todd? Something I don't know about? I asked Sammy about him, and she said he's a good businessman."

"No, there's nothing wrong with him. It's just…"

"Just what?"

"Well, we've been seeing each other. It could get awkward."

"Seeing each other?" Bailey looked at her in surprise. "I thought you were seeing Luke." She frowned. "Except I did wonder why you were sitting so close to Todd."

"That's why. Luke and I are friends—that's all."

Now Bailey studied her salad. "So, you don't want

me to have my tea shop because you don't want me around your boyfriend."

That sounded petty—probably because it was. "No." *Yes.* "Like I said, it could be awkward."

Bailey frowned earnestly. "Cec, this is strictly business. You don't have to worry that I'll steal Todd."

"I know," Cecily lied. She was being silly; they weren't little girls fighting over Barbie dolls. They were grown women.

"You're right," Cecily said. "I'm sorry for being unsupportive. It really is a great plan, and I'm behind you one hundred percent."

Later that night as she and Todd played darts at The Man Cave and she listened to him talking about the tea shop and how smart Bailey's ideas were, she mentally amended her earlier statement to her sister. *I'm behind you 50 percent.* And that was being generous.

No matter how much she was or wasn't behind her sister, the talks continued, and come June the decision had been made. Bailey and Todd were going into business together. Samantha and Blake were consulted, and a contract was drawn up and signed.

The family gathered at Schwangau to celebrate, and Blake raised his wineglass to Bailey. "Here's to success."

"To success," everyone echoed, although Cecily's was a faint one.

"Have you come up with a name yet?" their mother asked.

Cecily remembered the family gathering on Mother's Day, when Samantha and Blake had announced that they were expecting. Another happy event, she thought wistfully. *You're jealous. You bitch!*

"We're going to call it Tea Time," Bailey said.

"Cute." Mom obviously approved. "You could decorate using some cute little clocks around the walls and maybe on the tables."

"Oh, I like that," Bailey said.

"I was just over at Timeless Treasures and saw that Stacy had an anniversary clock in there," Mom said.

"What's an anniversary clock?" Bailey asked.

"It sits under a glass dome, and the pendulum twirls. If you like, I'll get it for you. You could set it by your cash register."

Ideas continued to flow, and as they did even Cecily began to catch the excitement. The tea shop was going to be charming. And she was happy to see her sister excited about life again. *Okay, sis, I'm behind you...60 percent.*

Todd was taking care of the paperwork and necessary permits, which left all the fun to-dos for Bailey, such as planning the decor, the menu and supervising the kitchen remodel.

"We're going to have to turn this into a commercial kitchen," she said to him as they assessed the working space in what would be the future home of Tea Time. "That means we'll need a combination standard and convection stove, a commercial sink and dishwasher, an ice maker, a cooler. I don't think we'll need a walk-in. A French-door reach-in should work, considering the size of the room."

Todd nodded and typed notes in his iPad.

Bailey chewed her lip. "This is going to cost a lot of money."

"Don't worry. I'll make it work. I've already been

over to the bank and talked with Blake Preston. Anyway, you have to spend money to make money."

"I don't mind spending money," Bailey said, smiling. "Well, your money—but I don't want to go over our budget."

"I appreciate that, partner," he said, smiling back.

Partner. She loved the sound of that. It was so nice to have someone right there with her every step of the way. And there'd been quite a few steps—coming up with a business plan, applying for permits so they could remodel the kitchen, talking with contractors, checking out the items she wanted to sell in the shop and looking for china. She'd bought some things from Stacy at Timeless Treasures, and Janice Lind at The Kindness Cupboard had promised to alert her if any useful donations came in.

Bailey had continued to work for Olivia in the mornings, but every spare minute she was at the house, working with Todd and Pete, whom Todd had drafted to help paint the place. Except for the trim, which Bailey had yet to decide on, the outside was now done, and it was time to whip the inside into shape, which would involve painting an accent wall and refinishing the hardwood floors, all of which Todd was doing himself. The kitchen work they'd hire out.

So far he hadn't so much as blinked as she listed the things they'd need. And he was so supportive, so positive. No wonder Cecily was crazy about him.

"Anyway, I have to leave some money in your wallet so you have something to spend on my sister," Bailey teased.

"Good point," he said.

"How long have you guys been going out?" she

asked casually. What did it matter? They were an item. Although when she first got to town, Cecily and Luke had been an item.

"Not long," Todd said. "It took a while to convince her she wanted to be with me."

"That's hard to believe." Okay, that was probably not appropriate.

He grinned. "Yeah? Where were you when I needed somebody to put in a good word for me?"

"What makes you think I would have?" she retorted, matching his tone.

"Hey, I'm not so bad."

You could say that again. For one disloyal moment, Bailey wished she'd met Todd first. *But you didn't,* she told herself, *and he's into Cecily, not you.*

He was sure into her cooking, though. One day she stopped by the house on her lunch break with a plate of chocolate cookies for him to sample while he painted the accent wall.

"Oh, man, these are incredible. You can bake for me anytime."

Just what every baker wanted to hear. "I'm going to make them part of the chocolate tea. We can also serve those white chocolate–lavender scones I made for you last week, along with a chocolate fondue and chocolate mint tea. Oh, and a Sweet Dreams truffle."

He nodded approvingly. "Cross-promotion, a smart idea."

"If I hadn't thought of it, Sammy would have."

"Yeah, but you *did* think of it. You've got a lot of good ideas."

"Only in the kitchen."

He shook his head. "Give yourself some credit.

You've come up with a clever name for this place, figured out a way to double your business by making it both a shop and a restaurant. You've even figured out how to capitalize on the lavender we've got out there along the front walk. All creative ideas. You can't teach that kind of thing. Either a person has it or she doesn't."

She smiled at the accent wall, which would soon be lavender to mimic the lavender growing outside. "It's all coming together nicely," she said.

"Sure is." He took another cookie. "These are addictive."

"They were always a hit when I made them for luncheons or bridal showers." Now that seemed like the ancient past. She groaned at her own foolishness. "I was going to be the caterer to the stars. Sounds pretty silly, doesn't it?"

"It sounds like a pain in the butt," Todd said.

"Actually, it was. People were forever changing their minds about the menu at the last minute or complaining about my prices, even though they were right in line with what other caterers were charging."

"Well, that's people for you. The good thing about having your own place is that you're in charge. People come in, and they pay what you tell them."

"I like that," she said. She liked the whole idea of this new business. It was all she thought about. She'd talked over menu ideas with Olivia and spent every spare minute in the kitchen tweaking old standards into slightly new and different versions. She even dreamed about it. Oh, yes. She was ready for this new adventure. Except… "We need to have plenty of insurance in case…something happens."

"Don't worry. We'll have it. But nothing's going to happen," he assured her. "It's going to be great."

Great. Suddenly shy, she picked at her cookie and confessed, "I always thought I was meant for great things. Does that sound conceited?"

"Nah. Just sounds like you want a lot out of life."

"Sometimes I think it's, I don't know, sort of greedy."

"There's nothing greedy about wanting to experience all life has to offer," Todd said. "Hell, I wanted to own a business empire, be the next Donald Trump." He pointed to her and said, "You're fired," in his best Donald Trump imitation, making her giggle.

"I bet you'll do it," she said. "Start a business empire, I mean."

He nodded and gave a snort. "Yeah."

"No, I'm serious. I bet you will. I mean, look at you. You already have one successful business and now you're investing in another."

He looked out the window, his expression thoughtful. "Yeah, well, my old man's still sure I'll fall on my face. But then, no surprise. Nothing I've ever done has been good enough for him."

What a sad thing to hear. Her own father had always been so supportive. *This is the best cookie I've ever had, Pumpkin.... I'll take another helping of your mac and cheese.... Catering? That's a perfect career choice.*

"Your father sounds like a jerk," Bailey said. "Sorry," she added. "That wasn't very nice of me."

Todd shrugged. "He can be. But then, so can I. Sometimes I think he's just disappointed with his own life. He almost made the majors. If he hadn't blown out his knee, he'd probably have been on a baseball trading card. I guess he hoped I'd do what he couldn't. He's pissed that I didn't have what it took. And then he thought my brother would deliver. Poor Dad. Even Devon let him down."

"We can't always be what our parents want us to be," Bailey said. "Sometimes we can't even be what *we* want to be," she added, remembering her earlier failure. "But that's okay, because things have a way of working out." Now she sounded just like her mother, and the realization made her smile. If she could ever become half as wise, she'd be happy.

"Anyway, everyone here in Icicle Falls thinks you're great," she said, determined to keep them both positive.

"Probably not everyone," he said with a shrug and a cynical smile.

"The ones who count do. Like me. And Cecily," she added hastily.

She thought she saw something in his eyes. Had her mention of Cecily made him uncomfortable? Didn't he want people to know they were together? Or maybe she'd just imagined what she saw.

"I should get back to work," he said. "I want to get this wall done today so I can start sanding the floors on Saturday."

"I need to get going anyway," Bailey said. And the sooner, the better. Todd Black was more tempting than anything she could ever dream up in the kitchen.

Cecily knew Todd was working on the house on Lavender Lane. She decided she'd stop by with lunch. She picked up some chocolate seconds from the Sweet Dreams gift shop, then ducked into Safeway for some deli chicken, potato salad and wine coolers and went to see how the work was coming along.

She was pulling into the street when she saw Bailey and Todd walk out on the front porch. Bailey looked fresh off the rack in a green top that showed off her curves and complemented her chestnut curls. Todd wore a paint-spattered T-shirt and equally spattered jeans. His dark hair was disheveled. Who'd been disheveling it?

Bailey said something, and he laughed. No sarcastic smirk but an actual laugh. What had she said that was so funny? They talked for another minute, and then she left him and went down the front walk wearing a smile.

Cecily frowned. *Oh, no,* she told herself, *Bailey and Todd are not a match.* He was too cynical. She was too naive. He'd tire of her in the blink of an eye. She'd never really understand him. All of that was beside the point anyway. Todd was already taken, and the one who'd taken him wasn't about to give him up. Even if her little sister had said something to make him laugh.

Cecily waited until Todd had gone back inside and Bailey had driven off down the street, and then she gathered her goodies and got out of her car.

He was busy with his paintbrush when she walked in. "Hi. You just missed your sister," he greeted her.

The smile on his face erased her earlier insecurity. She held up her grocery bag. "I thought you might want some lunch."

"Can I have you for dessert?" he teased.

Okay, she'd been imagining things. She caught sight of the plate with a couple of remaining cookies on it and couldn't help frowning. "It looks like you already had dessert."

"You know what they say. Life's uncertain. Eat dessert first. What's in the bag?"

"Just some stuff I picked up from the deli. Want to go sit on the porch and eat?"

He nodded and followed her out, and they settled on the front step.

It was a companionable enough lunch. He asked her how everything was going at the office. She asked if he and Bailey needed any help pulling the house together.

"Nah. I think we've about got it covered. Once I'm done with the floors, we can start moving in the shelves and tables and chairs. We still have to paint the trim, but she can't decide on the color."

He sounded like a husband talking about his wife's decorating ideas and his honey-do list. "You sound so domesticated," she joked. And her sister was the one domesticating him. It was all she could do to keep her smile in place.

"Don't worry. I'm still a wild man," he said and gave her a kiss on the shoulder. Then he grabbed a piece of chicken. "So, you want to bring your sister over to the Cave Saturday night? We've got a darts tournament going. You can watch me in action."

Bring her sister? Hmm. And had she just seen him in action with Bailey? "That'll be a thrill a minute," she said, which he took for a yes.

She wasn't that hungry anymore. She didn't stay much longer.

"Leaving so soon?" he protested, but it seemed halfhearted.

"I've got to get back to the office. I've got some things I need to do."

And one of them involved having a little talk with her sister....

The little talk started out well enough that evening, with Cecily commenting during dinner on the progress Todd was making on the house.

"It's going to be so cute when we're done," Bailey said happily. "When were you by?"

"I went over on my lunch break. I saw you leaving."

Bailey's cheeks turned pink. "I took over some of the cookies I want to serve to see what he thought."

How very innocent. Except pink cheeks didn't lie. "You're blushing," Cecily accused.

"I am?" The pink grew deeper.

"Is that the only reason you took cookies over?"

"Of course! He's my partner. I want him to know what I'm serving. Why else would I bring him cookies?"

"You tell me."

Bailey shoved aside her half-finished plate of enchiladas. "You think I'm trying to steal your boyfriend?"

"Aren't you?" Cecily demanded.

"No!"

Cecily pointed a finger at her sister. "You've always done this. Every time you fall for a guy, you start baking for him."

"But this is different," Bailey protested. "This is business."

"Well, see that you keep it business," Cecily said. She sounded like a bitch. She knew it. But, darn it all, she was tired of losing men, and now that she'd finally given in to the crazy attraction she felt for Todd, she was not going to lose him. And she certainly wasn't going to lose him to her sneaky little sister.

Bailey glared at her. "That wasn't very nice. And don't be bossing me around."

Shades of childhood. *You're not the boss of me.*

"I'm not bossing you around," Cecily insisted. "I'm just expecting you to be a good sister. I'm starting something with Todd, and you should respect that."

"And I'm going into business with him and *you* should respect *that*," Bailey shot back. "And I ought to be able to bring him a sample of something I want to serve without you having a pissy fit."

"I am not having a pissy fit," Cecily said between clenched teeth.

"Yes, you are, and you're getting pissier by the minute, all because you're afraid you can't hang on to your man."

That came painfully close to the truth. Failure in love was even worse than failure in business, and Cecily had failed twice. Which made her twice as insecure about Todd as she would have been if she hadn't been hurt so badly.

Before Cecily could bare her wounded soul to her sister, Bailey said something that really made her mad. "And if you can't hang on to him, it means he wasn't the right one anyway."

Cecily had been in the business of matching people up, and her spoiled little sister had the nerve to lecture her on love? "Oh. Really?"

Bailey's chin lifted a notch. "Yes, really. You don't have a ring on your finger, and you've only just started seeing him."

"How do you know that?" Cecily demanded. She might have been with Todd for a short time, but they'd been dancing toward being a couple for a *long* time. Now that they were, things were heating up fast.

"He told me."

"Told you what?"

"That you'd just started seeing each other."

"When?" Todd was talking to Bailey about their relationship?

"The other day," Bailey replied vaguely. "I don't remember."

They were spending so much time together, it was probably hard to keep all those cozy conversations straight. Why had he told Bailey that, to warn her off or to encourage her? Cecily suddenly felt as if she stood on an icy hill in tennis shoes.

"Anyway, I'm not doing anything wrong, and here you are, accusing me," Bailey said tearfully.

Okay, she was being unreasonable, and after everything her sister had gone through, she should be ashamed.

But before she could open her mouth to apologize, Bailey said, "I don't know if I even want to stay here."

As if Bailey was doing her a favor rather than the other way around. The apology was aborted. "You little ingrate."

"I'm not an ingrate!" Bailey grabbed her plate and marched to the sink. "I just don't want to be yelled at for nothing."

"Nothing! Oh, don't go there."

Bailey scraped her unfinished food into the garbage. "Here I am, cooking for you every night."

"And not having to pay rent," Cecily pointed out.

Bailey whirled around, the picture of outrage. "You'd charge me rent? I'd never charge you rent!"

"I didn't say that."

"You didn't have to. I know when I'm not wanted," Bailey said and stomped out of the kitchen.

Let her go, the little brat. Cecily ignored her half-finished meal, the enchilada sauce turning to acid in her stomach. Why did Bailey have to be such a drama queen?

And why did *she* have to be such a stinker? She'd taken a small thing and blown it out of all proportion. With a sigh Cecily pushed away from the kitchen bar and went to the spare bedroom to make up.

She got to the hallway and heard her sister's tearful voice. "I didn't deserve it, Sammy."

Now Bailey was tattling to Samantha?

"I haven't done anything wrong. And she shouldn't be with Todd anyway. Deep down she knows it."

Bailey, the relationship expert. Cecily ground her teeth.

There was a moment of silence as Bailey listened to whatever Samantha was saying. This was followed by, "No, but if she can't keep his interest, that's not my problem."

The little sneak! She *was* out to get Todd. Cecily strode into the room. "You brat!"

Bailey jumped and let out a squeak and dropped the phone.

"Bailey?" Samantha's tinny voice said. "What in the name of Godiva is going on?"

Cecily grabbed the phone. "Nothing. Except Bailey's tired of staying here. Can she come over to your place?"

"Oh, for crying out loud," Samantha said in disgust.

"That's fine with me," Bailey snapped and grabbed back her cell phone. "I'll be right over," she said and ended the call. "I sure don't want to stay where I'm not wanted."

"Yeah, well, no traitors wanted here," Cecily informed her and left the ingrate to pack. In the kitchen she shoved dishes into the dishwasher, ripped tin foil from the box and covered the remaining enchiladas. Then she threw the pan in the fridge and slammed the door shut after it.

Ten minutes later the front door slammed, too, and Bailey was gone.

Cecily stayed on her barstool. *Good riddance. Let Sam deal with her.*

The condo seemed suddenly very quiet. This was ridiculous. She should call Bailey and apologize, ask her to come back. She picked up her cell phone and fingered the numbers.

Or Bailey could call *her* and apologize. Bailey had been the one who'd escalated their conversation into a full-fledged fight. Bailey had been the one to pull in an ally. Cecily set the phone back down.

But she'd acted like a little girl with her first crush. How pathetic was that? She picked up the phone again. It was wrong to be so suspicious of her sister. She sat there for a few minutes, trying to decide what to say.

"I'm sorry" would be good for starters.

Bailey would be at Sam's house by now. Cecily made the call.

It rolled over to voice mail.

So Bailey wasn't even going to take her call? That was mature.

Well, then. There was no point in leaving a message. She hit End and pushed the phone away.

Chapter Fourteen

"You really should work things out with Cecily," Samantha said once she and Bailey were settled at her kitchen table with mugs of chocolate mint tea.

"How can I? She's being completely unreasonable!"

Samantha studied her baby sister. Bailey could be a bit of a drama queen. "That's out of character for Cec." Cecily usually assumed the role of peacemaker in the family. "Tell me exactly what happened."

"I already told you, Sammy. She just went ballistic on me, accused me of trying to steal Todd."

"Well, are you?"

Bailey's cheeks took on a guilty flush. "We're in business together, for goodness' sake."

"You didn't answer my question."

"Well, I shouldn't have to," Bailey said and frowned at her mug.

"He is gorgeous," Samantha said. And a ladies' man. She'd seen him in action long before Cecily hit town. He had a gift for flirting, and she suspected he was a bit of a bad boy, which was probably why Bailey was attracted to him. Brandon Wallace all over again. If Samantha had known Bailey was going to fall for Todd, she would've done everything she could to discourage her from going into business with him. She should have known. Pregnancy was making her lose her mental edge.

"And he's really nice and really supportive. And I like being around him. But that doesn't mean I'd deliberately steal him from my own sister."

The heck it didn't. Women did crazy things when they were in love.

"Anyway, I didn't even know she was with Todd at first," Bailey continued. "I thought she was with Luke."

So had Samantha. She shook her head. "What's with you two? Todd Black is probably bad news for both of you."

"No, he's not," Bailey insisted, giving herself away. The fresh pink on her face showed that she realized it.

"I have just two words for you," Samantha said. *"Brandon Wallace."*

"He's not like Brandon. He's...more mature."

"An older Brandon," Samantha said.

"You're the one who told me what a good businessman he is," Bailey reminded her.

"Yes, businessman. Not boyfriend. He's a player."

"I don't know why we're having this conversation," Bailey said crossly. "I'm not going to steal him from Cec."

"I believe you," Samantha said. "But I'm warning you...just in case."

"The one you need to be warning is Cec. She's the one who's acting crazy."

"Why don't you call her?" Samantha suggested.

Bailey's expression turned mulish. "No. I'm done talking to her."

"What? You're not going to speak to her for the rest of your lives?"

"No. I'm not going to speak to her until she stops acting crazy."

Cecily acting crazy was hard to imagine. But it was obviously true. Someone was going to have to pull her out of Looney Land, and it looked as though that someone would have to be Samantha.

She put her plan into action later in the week, casually wandering into Cecily's office, where she was busy working on a new Sweet Dreams ad campaign. "Are you past wanting to strangle our sister?"

"For the moment," Cecily said.

"Good. I think the stress of you murdering Bailey would be bad for the baby."

That brought a reluctant smile to Cecily's face.

"How about coming over for dinner Friday night?"

Cecily made a face. "I said I was past strangling her. I didn't say I wanted to eat with her. I need a Bailey break."

"So come and have dinner with Blake and me. I'll send Bailey over to Mom's."

"All right," Cecily said, "on one condition. No lectures about how we need to make up."

Samantha held up both hands. "I wouldn't dream of it. Sisterly mediation is your department."

If Cecily caught the irony of that remark, she didn't let on. Anyway, Samantha wasn't too worried. It wasn't in Cecily's nature to stay mad for long. Bailey's, either. They'd work out this small hiccup after Samantha got Cecily on track with Luke again.

Back in her office, she called down to his.

"What's up?" he asked.

"Dinner Friday at my place," Samantha said. "I'm having an impromptu party."

"Sounds good. What do you want me to bring?"

"Just yourself," Samantha said. "Come on over around six-thirty."

And that took care of that, she thought as she returned to work. Once they got Cecily's confused hormones sorted out, everything would be fine.

After her shift at the lodge, Bailey went to Lace and Lovelies to pick out curtains for her tearoom. It would be a little embarrassing to shop there after the job with Tina hadn't worked out—but, hey, Bailey wasn't going to hold a grudge. Anyway, it was good for business owners to support each other.

The shop door chimed as Bailey entered, catching Tina in the middle of a conversation with Shelley Graves, who worked at Bavarian Brews. "If she doesn't break all the china in that tea shop, it'll be a…" Tina suddenly noticed Bailey and swallowed the rest of her sentence.

Too late. Bailey had heard, and they both knew it. Awkward silence filled the shop, and Bailey could feel her whole face sizzling like a stove top. If she were Samantha, she would've walked on in as if she owned the world. If she were Cecily (well, the old pre–Todd Black Cecily), she'd have smiled and been diplomatic. But she was neither, and she was hurt and humiliated.

She turned and walked right back out. She'd go to Wenatchee, Seattle, the end of the world, anyplace but Tina's shop, to find her lace curtains.

Tina's voice followed her out the door. "Bailey, wait!"

She just kept on walking. People had been mean in the big city, but here, back home in Icicle Falls, she'd expected better. What a dope. People were people, no matter where you lived.

Now she heard footsteps behind her. "Bailey!"

Okay, to keep walking would be rude. *Put on your big-girl panties.* She turned and forced herself to smile pleasantly.

Tina's face was as red as hers probably was. "Bailey."

This was so awkward. Bailey raised one hand. "You're right. I'm a klutz."

And, as Tina had seen, it always got worse when she was nervous. Maybe she *would* break all the china in her tea shop.

"And I'm a bitch. I'm sorry, Bailey. Please come back. Whatever you want, I'll give you fifty percent off."

That wasn't a bargain; it was extortion. "Let's forget it happened," Bailey said. Heck, she'd done her share of gossiping.

"Only if you let me give you a discount."

Bailey wasn't a robber, but she wasn't stupid, either. "Okay. Make it thirty percent, and you've got a deal."

Tina nodded, and they started back to the shop. "I do think the tea shop is a great idea," she said. "I don't know why I was being so catty."

Bailey could sum it up in two words: *Shelley Graves.* Shelley was one of the worst gossips in town. She also didn't like Bailey. No doubt that had something to do with the fact that her boyfriend had dumped her for Bailey way back in high school. Pretty insulting for a senior girl to lose her boyfriend to a lowly freshman. Greg Trotter had gone off to Stanford and forgotten them both, but Shelley had a memory an elephant would envy. She'd probably been happy to talk to anyone who came into Bavarian Brews about the headlines Bailey had made when her business went under.

Of course, Shelley had pretended to have forgiven and forgotten. She was all syrupy smiles whenever Bailey came into Bavarian Brews for a frappé or coffee, but those were about as real as her boobs. (There'd been plenty of women in town more than willing to share the news when she got a boob job after her husband left her and moved to Wyoming. Boy, there was never a shortage of gossip in a small town.) Shelley hadn't done much with her life, so Bailey supposed it made her happy when other people failed.

"It's all right," she said to Tina.

"Is it true you're going into business with Todd Black?"

Bailey nodded.

"Lucky you. That man has half the women in town with their panties on fire."

"He's seeing my sister," Bailey said.

"Oh." That shut Tina up for a moment. "Well, I'm sure the food will be great," she said as they walked into the shop.

"If she doesn't poison anyone," Shelley murmured on her way out. "See you later, Tina."

Better not come into the tea shop, Bailey thought. *Or I might just be tempted to poison* you.

Never mind, she told herself. There would always be people who wanted you to fail. But she wasn't going to, not this time.

* * *

Cecily arrived at Samantha's house on Friday to find the dining room table set for four. Their mother's big crystal vase sat in the center, filled with flowers from Lupine Floral. Okay. This wasn't just for her.

"Who else is coming?" she asked Samantha.

"Um, Luke," Samantha said and skedaddled into the kitchen.

Luke? What was going on here? As if she couldn't guess.

She followed her sister out to the kitchen. "What are you up to?"

Samantha got suddenly busy checking the lasagna in the oven. "Nothing."

"You are such a rotten liar." And an equally bad matchmaker. She should leave right now. Samantha could tell Luke she'd gotten sick.

She was about to announce her departure when she heard male voices drifting into the kitchen from the direction of the front door. Great. He was already here.

She could still go. She should. This little setup looked so...obvious. And Luke would think she was in on it, that she'd changed her mind about their relationship.

"You know, I'm going to have to leave. I'm getting a headache."

Samantha set the lasagna pan on the stove and then turned her stern older-sister gaze on Cecily. "You try to leave, and I'll give you a serious headache."

Then she walked out of the kitchen–family room area and went to the formal dining room, obviously expecting Cecily to follow.

Cecily trailed her, irritation growing with each

step. Samantha had every right to run Sweet Dreams Chocolates, but she sure didn't have the right to run her sisters' lives.

Luke and Blake stood in the dining room chatting while Blake opened a bottle of wine. Luke looked surprised to see Cecily and then pleased. "Hi, Cec."

It would be so incredibly rude to bolt. Anyway, they were still friends. They could have dinner without anyone—namely Luke—getting his hopes up. "Hi," she said. "You're a brave man to come and eat my sister's cooking," she joked.

"Hey, I'm just as good a cook as you," Samantha protested.

"Well, we all know who the real chef in the family is," Blake teased.

Bailey. For a moment Cecily felt guilty that they hadn't made up, but all she had to do to get over that was remind herself what a sneaky brat her sister was.

"Our man's got excellent taste in wine," Blake said, holding up the bottle of merlot, which bore an Icicle Winery label.

"Ed told me it's one of his most popular reds."

Blake began pouring the wine. "I think he says that about half the wines he has at D'vine Wines. But this is a good one, and it's one of our favorites."

"And it's perfect with lasagna," Samantha said

Luke rubbed his hands together. "Lasagna's my favorite."

"Good food, good wine and good friends. It doesn't get any better than that," Samantha said.

"You sound like you're channeling Waldo," Cecily said as Blake handed her a glass of wine. Ironic, considering how crazy their now-deceased stepfather used to make Samantha.

"He couldn't run a business worth squat, but he did have the right attitude about life," Samantha said.

Blake started to hand Luke a glass, but he motioned to Samantha after saying, "Ladies first."

She shook her head. "I'm not much of a wine drinker. Anyway, I'm not drinking these days."

"Not for another six and a half months," added Blake, beaming.

"Wait a minute," Luke said slowly, "are you guys—"

"Yep," Blake said.

"Sweet." Luke slapped him on the back. "Man, you are going to love being a dad."

That was certainly a different reaction to the idea of having kids than Todd had displayed, Cecily thought as Blake and Luke took their wine.

"I wouldn't mind having more myself someday," Luke said, and his glance slipped to Cecily.

Why, oh, why wasn't she in love with him?

"So, babe, you need me to help you carry stuff out from the kitchen?" Blake asked.

"Yes, thanks," Samantha said, and they hurried off, leaving Cecily and Luke alone like two people on a blind date.

Cecily suddenly felt tongue-tied. This was ridiculous. She'd known Luke for years. "We haven't seen your mom and Serena at the gift shop for a while," she said. "What's with that?"

"Serena's on chocolate restriction."

"Chocolate restriction?" Was there any worse punishment? "What did she do?"

"She sneaked into the cookies after my mom told

her she couldn't have any—ate every last one out of the cookie jar. Talk about a sugar high. Then, when Mom got after her, she called Mom a 'doodyhead.'"

Cecily snickered.

"Yeah, it's funny now, but Mom wasn't laughing at the time." Luke let out a long-suffering sigh. "I think the kid's going through chocolate withdrawal. She's a bear to be around."

"I'd be a bear, too, if I couldn't have chocolate."

"Well, maybe," Luke said, "but that's hard to imagine. In fact, it's hard to imagine you ever being anything but nice."

He should have been in her condo a couple of nights ago.

Samantha and Blake were back now with lasagna, tossed salad and French bread, and the four of them sat down to dinner, two couples about to enjoy a meal together.

Except that Cecily and Luke weren't a couple.

But sometimes it felt as though they were. Conversation flowed easily, and it was as if she and Luke had never had their awkward moment on Lost Bride Trail. Later there was plenty of laughter as they played Hearts and ate gingerbread cookies from Cass's bakery.

"Okay," Samantha said. "Cecily's got the lowest score. We need to get her."

"Who's second lowest?" Cecily asked suspiciously.

"That would be Sam," said Blake. She stuck out her tongue at him, and he grinned at her.

"Aha." Luke slipped Samantha the Queen of Spades that hand, giving her thirteen points. He also managed to give Blake, who had the highest score, enough hearts to put him out and end the game with Cecily the winner.

"Oh, fine," Samantha muttered to him. "Turn on your boss."

Luke shrugged. "What can I say? I guess my loyalties are elsewhere."

The smile he gave Cecily felt too intimate. It was time to go home.

"It's Friday night. What's your hurry?" Samantha said, stifling a yawn. Even though she refused to admit it, pregnancy was slowing her down.

Luke rose from his seat the minute Cecily did. "Moms-to-be need their sleep. And you'd better enjoy it now while you can. Both of you," he said.

"You're scaring me," Blake joked.

The sisters hugged, and the men shook hands. Then Luke exited right along with Cecily.

Now things really felt awkward. "Well, see you Monday," she said and started toward her car.

His hand on her arm stopped her.

Oh, no. What's he going to do?

Chapter Fifteen

From the look in his eyes, Cecily could have sworn Luke was going to kiss her. Instead he asked, "Whose idea was that little dinner party, yours or your sister's?"

"Samantha's." *Thanks, sis, for getting his hopes up so I could hurt him all over again.* Feeling she needed to say something, she added, "I had a good time. I hope you did, too."

"Of course I did. I just hoped you'd changed your mind about us."

"I'm sorry, Luke," she said gently. "The chemistry's not there."

"It could be if you gave me half a chance." He must have seen the dread in her face, because he ended the awkward moment, saying, "But I guess you're solid with Black these days."

She nodded.

"Okay, but if he ever doesn't treat you right..."

"You'll be the first man I call," she quipped. And maybe she would. Luke Goodman was the sort of guy a woman could tell her troubles to.

He leaned over and kissed her cheek, surprisingly

setting off butterflies in her stomach. "Good night, Cec," he said, then walked away.

She stood watching him until he turned the corner to his street. What was that she'd just felt?

Nothing compared to what she felt with Todd—*that* was what. She got in her car and drove home, irritation riding shotgun.

The next morning it was time for another little talk—with a different sister.

"Please don't do that again," she said when Samantha answered the phone.

Her sister didn't insult her intelligence by pretending she didn't know what Cecily was talking about. "Why, because you had such a lousy time?"

"No, because it's not fair to Luke. I don't want to be anything more than friends, and your cozy little dinner party only raised false expectations. He's a nice man, and I hated having to shoot him down."

"Yeah, I saw you shooting him down out there on the sidewalk."

"You were watching?" Bad enough that Samantha was interfering but then to spy on her as if…as if she and Luke were lab rats in an experiment! Cecily ground her teeth.

"Of course," Samantha admitted breezily. "Look, I know relationships are your specialty. Your instincts for who should be together are legendary. But you don't seem to be able to apply them to yourself, so why not let the people who care about you help?"

"Because you have no idea what you're doing," Cecily said hotly. "So, stop trying to 'help' me."

"Well, I would if you weren't making such a mess of your love life," Samantha said. "You can't see what's right in front of your face. You're blowing it with Luke, and you're way off the mark with Todd."

"Listen to you! Here you are, talking like Dr. Phil, and you don't have a clue what's going on between Todd and me."

"I'm not sure you do, either," Samantha said. "Otherwise you wouldn't be so insecure. And you'd still be talking to Bailey."

Cecily wanted to protest that she was perfectly secure. Todd had wanted her ever since she'd come back to Icicle Falls. That wasn't the problem. The problem was Bailey and what she was trying to do.

But any protest would be halfhearted. She *was* insecure. There had to be something men found lacking in her and went looking for in other women. And, deep down, she was afraid Todd would spot that missing something.

"I'm sorry I poked my nose in your business," Samantha said. "God knows I shouldn't talk—it took me long enough to see what was right in front of me."

"That's about the most condescending apology I've ever heard," Cecily muttered.

"Well, it's the best I can do on short notice. I'm sorry I made you mad. Really. I think you're nuts to pass up a man like Luke, but I promise I'll butt out. Okay?"

"Okay," Cecily said, somewhat mollified. Although Sam could have left that observation regarding her sanity out of the apology.

"But you and Bailey better resolve things between you before this baby comes. I want both of my sisters at the christening."

Cecily made some noncommittal remark that was

enough to satisfy her sister. Samantha ended the call to go look at cribs with Blake. Cecily set her phone on the kitchen counter and tapped her teeth with her fingernail, mulling over what her sister had said.

Still mulling, she toasted an English muffin, then spread it with some jam and took a thoughtful bite. If Bailey had been there, they would've been having something like eggs Benedict for breakfast. Bailey did like to cook and bake for everyone, not just men with whom she was infatuated. Cecily knew her accusation had been an unfair one. Still, she wasn't ready to call Bailey and make up. She needed to think about it some more.

Which she did as she walked to Bavarian Brews for a latte. By the time she'd purchased her hazelnut mocha, she'd realized Sam was right. She needed to trust her sister, give her the benefit of the doubt. Men might come and go, she told herself, but sisters were forever.

Bailey didn't work at the lodge on Saturdays, so that meant she was probably puttering around at the future home of Tea Time. Cecily decided the best way to extend an olive branch would be to stop over and see how everything was coming along. She purchased another latte and went around the corner to Lavender Lane.

The tea shop's hardwood floors were now refinished, the old oak glowing warm and inviting. The vinyl in the kitchen had cleaned up fine, and the necessary kitchen equipment had been delivered and installed the day before.

"It's perfect," Bailey said to Todd as they surveyed

their new commercial kitchen. "All we need now are tables and chairs, a cash register and shelves for our merchandise. Well, and merchandise."

"What about dishes?"

"I have almost all the dishes. And the linens and glasses and cutlery have been ordered. I'll put up the lace curtains next week."

"I still don't know how you got those for thirty percent off."

"I'm a good negotiator," she said, opting not to tell him about her klutziness or Tina's gossip fest. She was in control of her career again, and she would not be breaking any of her inventory.

"We're making fast progress," Todd said. "We should have no problem being ready for a grand opening in August."

"I can hardly wait." Bailey gave the ice machine a loving pat.

"Do we have ice yet?" he asked.

"We should have."

"Let's see." He reached in and pulled out a handful of cubes. "Well, look at that. We do." He popped one in his mouth. "Want one?"

She smiled and nodded, then opened her mouth. But instead of popping an ice cube in it, he slipped a couple down the back of her blouse, making her squeal from the shock of the cold against her skin.

"This means war," she said and dipped her hand in for some ammunition.

He dodged away from her, and she chased him out of the kitchen into the main part of the house, giggling as she went. She tried unsuccessfully twice to get the ice down his shirt, with him grinning at each failed attempt and goading her to try again. On her third try, she dropped her cubes on the floor. He got to them first, and now it was her turn to run.

But he was quick and caught her, wrapping an arm around her waist and pulling her to him. She laughed and squirmed to escape, but the ice went down her back anyway.

"I guess I'm interrupting something," said a voice from the doorway, and Bailey whirled around to see Cecily, holding a latte to-go cup. The cold of that ice cube was nothing compared to the expression on her face. "I stopped by to say hi and see how things were going," Cecily said, her voice frosty.

Bailey swallowed hard. How to explain this to her sister? "The ice machine came in."

"Hey, Cec, we were just fooling around," Todd added. He came over, put an arm around her and kissed her.

She stood there like an ice sculpture.

"You want to see the kitchen?" Bailey offered.

"No. I can see you're both busy," Cecily said, stepping away from Todd. She set the cup on the floor, then turned and left, Todd following her out the door.

His words echoed back to Bailey. "Come on, Cec. We were just goofing around—that's all."

The screen door banged shut behind them.

Oh, this was not good.

"I'm not sure right now is the time to talk about this," Cecily said stiffly.

The pleading look on Todd's face changed to one of irritation. As if *he* had a right to be irritated? "Okay, fine. I need to get over to The Man Cave and do some paperwork. I'll talk to you later." His tone of voice said he'd rather not.

Who was the injured party here? Cecily shrugged her shoulders as if she couldn't care less where he went. "Fine."

Looking exasperated now, he stepped off the porch and went down the front walk at a brisk clip.

"Cec," Bailey said in a small voice.

Cecily turned to her sister, the traitor, who was standing on the porch. "So, nothing's going on."

Bailey shook her head, tears in her eyes. There she stood in tight jeans and a blouse that was like a billboard for her boobs and wearing full makeup.

"Don't cry. Your makeup will run," Cecily said, her voice as cold as the ice cube Todd had slipped down her sister's back.

Bailey sniffed. "I'm not trying to steal him. I…"

You would if you could. It was hard not to fall for Todd Black; Cecily got that. But her sister wasn't even *trying* to keep their relationship professional. Who had started that ice-cube fight back in the kitchen? Cecily was willing to bet it had been Bailey.

"I would never have done this to you," Cecily said.

"Cec, I didn't mean… I didn't think…"

Oh, she'd thought, all right, but only of her spoiled, baby-of-the-family self. There was no point in taking this conversation any further. Cecily began to walk away.

"Cec, please!" Bailey called.

Cecily kept on going. Even as she walked away, part of her said, *This is wrong, all wrong. She's your sister.*

Yeah, but sisters didn't sabotage each other's love lives.

"Cecily!"

Cecily went on walking, and the next thing she heard was the screen door slamming shut.

Just in time for Mom's birthday party tomorrow, she scolded herself. This would make for a pleasant family get-together.

Well, there'd be lots of people in attendance. She could stay on the far side of the room.

But at some stage she'd have to talk to her sister.

She would—after she and Todd were engaged.

Or…after he and Bailey hooked up. Her steps slowed. Why was she blaming this all on her sister? There had been two people involved in that bit of fun and games she'd witnessed, and Bailey hadn't grabbed Todd. It had been the other way around.

Todd was the one she needed to have that talk with. Cecily started for the edge of town. It wasn't a short walk to The Man Cave, but the day was beautiful and the air fragrant with the scent of roses and peonies warming under the June sun. A couple of white puffy clouds lazed in an azure sky, and the mountains were glorious, the air fresh and clean. In other words, it was a perfect day in Icicle Falls. At least it should have been.

The Man Cave wasn't open for business yet, and Cecily found the door locked when she arrived. She stood in front of it, wondering if she was being insecure and out of control. Maybe the problem wasn't with everyone else but with her. If that was the case, she owed Todd an apology.

Okay, she'd pay up. But first she had to know what

was going on with them. Were they together or weren't they? That wasn't being unreasonable; that was simply wanting to know. *You already know. You've known for a long time.*

No, I don't, she told herself and knocked on the door.

A moment later it opened, and there he stood, looking devilishly handsome. But the sardonic smile was missing. "Don't tell me—let me guess. You killed your sister, and now I'm next."

"I decided to let her live another day," Cecily said and stepped past him into the shadowy interior of the bar. The tables still had the chairs stacked upside down on top of them, and the neon beer signs were off, waiting to come to life when the outside world got dark. "This place always looks kind of sad without people in it," she mused, putting off the conversation they needed to have.

"Most places do."

"Not homes."

"Those can be sad even with people in them," he said.

His comment was a telling one and made her realize how much she still needed to learn about this man.

Before she could say anything, he added, "Not everybody grew up in a perfect family like you and your sister."

"That doesn't mean you can't try to make one," she argued. And speaking of sisters… "So, what's going on with you and Bailey?"

She half hoped he'd take her in his arms and say, "Nothing." Instead he shoved his hands in his pants pockets and said, "You want an honest answer? I don't know."

Well, that was comforting. She tucked her hair behind her ears and tried to look as if her heart hadn't cracked. "Wow, you really make a woman feel special."

"You *are* special. You know that. In fact, you're freakin' amazing."

If she was so amazing, why wasn't he kissing her?

Now he clawed his fingers through his hair, a sure sign of male agitation. "I've wanted you ever since you hit town. I still do."

She raised her eyebrows. If that was true, why wasn't she feeling the love?

She crossed her arms and leaned against the wall. "I can see that."

He frowned. "I was just horsing around with your sister. It was something spontaneous, but I admit I was out of line. Sorry." If he'd left it there, Cecily would have been happy. But he didn't. "She's easy to goof around with. She sends out these happy vibes."

"And I don't?" She was happy. See? She was even smiling. Sort of.

"You've always been a challenge, and I like that. But no man wants to climb the mountain forever. Sooner or later he wants to reach the summit."

"I can guess what that's code for." And he'd come pretty darned close to the summit, closer than he deserved after the way he'd been flirting with Bailey.

He shook his head. "That's not what I'm talking about. I feel there's a lot of you that you keep hidden, that you don't want to share. Sometimes I still don't know where I stand with you."

Was he serious? Did he think she got that close to the summit with every man?

He frowned. "Like right now. I have no idea what you're thinking."

She was thinking they needed a little less talk and a lot more action. She could be just as spontaneous as Bailey. Before he could say any more, she closed the distance between them, took his face in her hands and kissed him like she meant it.

With a growl, he wrapped her in his arms and pulled her close, taking their kiss from sizzling to blazing. Then he pushed her against the wall. "You're driving me crazy," he said as he trailed his mouth down her neck.

He should talk. He had her ready for a straitjacket. "Serves you right," she murmured, running her hands over his shoulders.

It was getting downright steamy in The Man Cave when she realized this wasn't the kind of scenery she wanted around her when she summited. "Todd."

"Mmm?" he said, still busy kissing his way up the trail.

"This isn't working for me." Well, on an emotional level, anyway. On a physical level he was doing fine.

He looked up and blinked. "What?"

"I think we can do better."

"Give me time. I'm working on it."

"That's not what I meant. I mean…" She stopped, suddenly at a loss. She didn't want to insult him by putting down his business. He was a smart businessman, and this tavern was the boozy cornerstone of the financial empire he was building. How to explain that she wanted a nicer setting?

"Oh, I get it. You don't really want to do this now. Here. Well, it's not exactly a beach on Tahiti, is it?"

She hadn't wanted to hurt his feelings, but she knew she had. And did it really matter where they made love? It wasn't as if she was holding out for a ring. Once upon a time she'd believed in doing that, but two fiancés later, she'd changed her belief system.

He turned away from her and started tucking in his shirt.

"That was dumb," she said, setting a hand on his back. "It's about who, not where."

He looked over his shoulder, and she saw a residue of irritation on his face. Then he erased it with the cynical expression he'd perfected. "You'd better pick a more romantic place to put the moves on me next time."

She leaned against the wall, pressing her palms against the wood paneling. "Did you know I was engaged before I came back to Icicle Falls?"

A black eyebrow went up. "That's a detail you hadn't shared with me."

Not that he'd shared many details about *his* romantic past, but she decided not to point that out. Instead, she said, "I was. Twice."

Now both eyebrows went up. "That explains a lot."

"I don't want to screw up a third time."

"Who says you're the one who screwed up?"

She made a face. It would be nice to blame the losers she'd fallen for, but the truth was, she'd picked the wrong men. She'd turned off her instincts.

This time it was Todd who closed the distance between them. He smiled down at her and gently pushed her hair back. "You gotta take a chance, Cec."

She suddenly found it hard to look at him. She nodded and said, "I know."

He tapped her on the nose. "Come over tonight for the darts tournament. Then we'll go to my place, and I'll light some candles."

"Do you even have candles?" she teased.

"I'll buy some."

Just as he drew her to him for a goodbye kiss, they heard the rumble of a motor outside and the crunch of tires on gravel. "Were you expecting company?" she asked.

"No," he said slowly. He opened the tavern door and froze.

From behind him she saw a red truck with jacked-up wheels, and out of it climbed a man who looked so much like Todd he could have been his brother. There was more than one Todd Black in the world?

"Hi, bro," the other man called. He sauntered up to where Todd now leaned in the doorway and gave him a hug.

The man was a little shorter and younger, and his hair was lighter, but the family resemblance was unmistakable. Now he turned to Cecily with an appreciative look and a smile that oozed charm. "Oh, man. Am I in heaven?"

"No, you're in my bar," Todd said irritably.

"Booze and a beautiful woman. I *am* in heaven." The man held out a hand to Cecily. "Hi. I'm Devon Black."

"My pain-in-the-butt younger brother," Todd added, and Cecily noticed he was only half smiling. "What brings you here?"

"I was passing through."

"From Medford."

"Yeah, as a matter of fact. Thought I'd stop in and see how my big brother's doing." To Cecily he said, "He's way older than me. Almost got one foot in the grave."

"I can see that," she said with mock seriousness.

"I, on the other hand, have lots of miles left on me."

"Is it my imagination, or are you already hitting on my girl?"

"Are you really his girl?" Devon demanded.

Cecily smiled and nodded. "Afraid so."

"Why else would she be here?"

"Free beer? Speaking of, it's been a long drive. You gonna give me something to drink? Let's all take a load off."

Cecily figured this was her cue to leave. "I'll let you two catch up."

"You're leaving me alone with this boring dude?" Devon joked.

"Afraid so," she said again. She managed a polite smile even though she was underwhelmed by Todd's brother. While Todd was sardonic and seductive, his brother was slick and ingratiating. And the slightest bit irritating.

Of course, that was only a first impression, and she knew from experience that first impressions weren't always reliable. She certainly hadn't been impressed with Todd the first time she met him.

And she was ridiculously impressed with him now.

"I'll see you this evening," Todd said. She half expected him to kiss her, but he didn't. He just stood there in the doorway with his usual cynical smile, which, she was coming to realize, was a mask.

She'd find out more about his brother later. Meanwhile, she was going to go home, take a bubble bath and shave her legs.

She left The Man Cave smiling. All right. Things were back on track with Todd.

Her cell phone rang, and she saw who it was. She'd had enough of Bailey for one day. She dropped the phone in her purse.

"Not bad," Devon said after Cecily had gone. "Any more like her up here?"

Oh, yeah, that was what he needed, his little brother wreaking havoc with the female population of Icicle Falls. "Don't tell me you've already gone through all the women in Medford."

"All the ones worth going through," Devon said, strolling over to the bar. "How about that beer? Got any Heineken?"

Todd grabbed a bottle for both his brother and himself.

"Cheers," Devon said, clinking bottles.

"Okay, now, you want to tell me what's going on?" Todd asked after they'd both chugged down a healthy swallow.

"What do you mean?"

"You know what I mean."

Devon shrugged.

"You still got a job?"

His brother stalled by taking another long swallow. Bingo. "Okay, what happened?"

"Nothing happened. Shit. Why do you always think something's happened?"

"Because something usually has." Showing up late

for work, getting it on with the boss's daughter and then dumping her, smoking a joint on the job. His brother had been lost for the past seven years, making one bad choice after another.

"Well, not this time. The company went belly-up. Okay?"

"Okay. Sorry."

"So I took my last paycheck and decided to come and see you."

Oh, boy.

"Got any construction companies here in Mountainville?"

"Well, good to see you, too," Todd said. And it was. For a short period of time. His brother for a visit? Okay. His brother here to stay, turning his life upside down? Oh, man, there had to be some other way to help him.

Devon was looking at him expectantly. "There's got to be someone."

"There's Masters Construction. I don't know if they're hiring."

"I'll check it out. Or, hey, you need a bartender?"

Oh, there was another pleasant image, Devon working at The Man Cave, drinking up the inventory. "I don't think so."

Devon frowned. "What, you afraid I'll drink all the beer?"

"It's a possibility." Todd saw that he was practically strangling his bottle. He put it aside and started taking the chairs down from the tables, setting up for the evening crowd.

"Hey, I've done some bartending." Devon started

doing the same with a nearby table. "Come on, Todd. Give me a break. I need some dough."

"I just sent you money."

"Gas ain't cheap."

"You should get rid of that gas-hog truck," Todd said and set down a chair with a little more force than necessary.

"I need it for my tools. So, how about it? Want some help around here? Just until I can get on my feet."

"I have help." Damn it all, the last thing he needed was Devon up here, making him crazy.

"I know. You're afraid I'll cut in on your action."

What? Were they back in high school? "Yeah, that's it."

Devon's smile fell away. "Oh, wait, I get it. That's right. You're Mr. Super Businessman now, big man in town. It'll mess up your image if your screw-up brother's around, won't it?"

Todd could feel the muscles in his jaw tightening. "I didn't say that."

"You didn't have to. I just thought it might be kind of fun living in the same town, but, hey, my bad." Devon gave a chair an angry shove and made for the door.

Shit. "Dev, don't be a jerk. Come on back."

His brother turned and glared at him. "I know when I'm not wanted."

"You don't know squat." Todd pulled out a chair and sat down, kicking another one to the side. "Sit."

Devon walked over and fell onto the chair, looking sullen.

"It's not that I don't want to see you. But, yeah, I don't want you screwing up around here. I like this place and I like the people and I don't need you doing stuff to embarrass me."

Devon's face grew red, and he dropped his gaze. "You used to be a lot more fun," he muttered.

"We're not kids tearing up the town anymore, Dev. We're adults. If you can act like one, then you're welcome to stay."

"Jeez, you sound like Dad."

"Even the old man's getting fed up, huh?" That was saying something, since Devon was his favorite of the two brothers.

"Tough love and all that shit."

Todd gave a mirthless laugh. Oh, yeah, their dad was good at that.

"That's why I moved to Medford. But, hey, with no job, it's time to move on." He paused. "So, can you use some help around here?"

Todd shrugged. "Yeah, I guess I can. And I could use some help on a place I just bought. If you want to paint the trim."

"Sure. Can I bunk with you for a while?"

Cecily...candles...romance... And Devon. "No." His brother's face fell, and he quickly added, "You can sleep on the sofa in the office, though. It's pretty comfortable. And there's a bathroom."

"Has it got a shower?"

"What does this look like? Motel 6? You can shower at my place. But not tonight."

Devon nodded sagely. "The blonde, right?"

"Yeah, the blonde. And she's off-limits."

"Got it."

"Good."

Devon leaned across the table and punched Todd playfully on the arm. "Hey, this is gonna be fun."

Yeah, fun.

Bailey's call to her sister went to the wasteland of voice mail. Cecily was still mad and in no mood to talk.

Bailey couldn't blame her. Much as she denied it, deep down (okay, not so deep) she wanted Todd. And even though she'd been trying not to steal her sister's boyfriend (she could try harder), what Cec had witnessed back in the tea shop hadn't exactly been professional.

How would *she* have felt if she'd been in her sister's shoes and stumbled on that scene? She needed to find Cecily now and promise she wouldn't do anything with Todd. Ever.

She finished up at the tea shop, then drove to the condo. Cecily's car wasn't in the garage, but Bailey still had a key, so she let herself in. Everything was neat and tidy now that she wasn't staying there, leaving a trail of tissues and coffee mugs everywhere she went.

She wandered into the kitchen. More neatness. It could have been a model-home kitchen. Cecily probably hadn't cooked anything since she'd left. She opened the fridge and saw half a rotisserie chicken from the Safeway deli, along with a covered bowl of carrot salad. This was how Cecily kept her curves under control, Bailey thought, conscious of the ten extra pounds she'd put on in the past couple of months.

She glanced over at the little tablet of paper sitting on the far end of the counter. She should leave a note.

But that seemed so impersonal. For now she'd go back to Sammy's and bake her mother's birthday cake for the party the following day. Then tonight she'd look for her sister. She knew exactly where Cecily would be.

Cecily wasn't at The Man Cave when Bailey came in around seven. In fact, there were only two women. A pretty blonde in tight jeans and a tank top was playing pool with Bill Will, everyone's favorite cowboy. The other woman, in jeans, flip-flops and a T-shirt, was playing darts with half a dozen men. Someone new, who resembled Todd, was behind the bar with Pete. Was Todd's brother in town visiting? Had to be. He looked so much like him.

But Todd was still the best-looking guy there, wearing the same jeans and T-shirt he'd had on earlier in the day and still looking just as sexy. He was leaning against the bar, watching the proceedings and wearing an easy smile. One of the men said something to him and nodded in Bailey's direction, and suddenly the smile didn't seem quite so easy.

He wasn't happy to see her. The incident at the house had ruined things. What had started as a promising partnership and growing friendship was now about as good as a fallen soufflé.

But you could always make a new soufflé. She'd find Cec and straighten everything out. And she and Todd would be strictly partners. Well, partners and friends, but not friends with benefits.

Todd left the group at the dartboard and came across the room to meet her. "Hey there," he greeted her. "I'm glad to see your sister hasn't murdered you."

"Or you," she said. "I'm really sorry I messed things up between you and Cec."

"You didn't."

She should have said, "Good," or "I'm glad," but she couldn't quite nudge the words out of her mouth. Instead, she said, "At least we know the ice machine works."

He smiled and nodded.

Now the new guy joined them. "Well, hello," he said, giving Bailey an appreciative once-over. "What have we got here?"

"My business partner," Todd said sternly.

If that was meant to put the newcomer in his place, it didn't. "You sure can pick 'em, bro."

"So, you're Todd's brother. It's nice to meet you," Bailey said.

"It's even nicer to know me," the newcomer said with a wink. "I'm Devon. Everyone calls me Dev."

"I'm Bailey."

"And everyone calls you 'gorgeous,'" said Devon, making her blush. Man, Todd's brother was sure full of hoo-ha.

"This is the first I've heard of you having a partner in this place," Devon said to his brother.

"Oh, we're not in business here," Bailey explained. "We're opening a tea shop."

From the look Devon gave his brother, it was clear Todd was going to get teased about that later.

"Come on and have a beer," Todd said, ignoring his brother.

"Actually, I'm looking for Cec. I thought she might be here."

The mention of her sister's name made him shoot

a glance toward the door. Was he nervous about Cec finding them together? As if they had something to be ashamed of?

"She should be here any minute," he said.

Bailey didn't want to get him (or herself) in trouble with Cec. "I'll wait out in the parking lot," she offered.

"No need to do that."

"And why would you want to when you can have a beer and play darts?" his brother threw in.

Good point. "I don't know how to play darts."

"We'll teach you. Right, Todd?"

"Absolutely," said Todd, moving her away from his brother. "Get Bailey a Hale's pale ale."

Well, why not? She had to do something while she waited for her sister.

Heart pumping with nervous excitement, Cecily walked carefully across the potholed parking lot of The Man Cave through trucks, Jeeps and motorcycles. The Neanderthal in lederhosen painted on the outside wall seemed to leer at her as she passed him.

This place was no Zelda's, but she'd better get used to it. She'd be spending a lot of time here. Maybe, once they were engaged, Todd would even want her to help out behind the bar. If he did ask her to help, she would, since it would be a while before she could convince him he even wanted a family.

The thought of plodding her way to having kids was frustrating. After two false starts, she was more than ready to follow Samantha into the land of married bliss and parenthood and not excited about the prospect of waiting indefinitely. But a woman had to make sacrifices for the man she loved. One step at a time, she told herself as she opened the door.

The usual gang was present—the grizzled old guys at the bar, the pool players, the token woman or two and, over in the corner…her sister!

Chapter Sixteen

Cecily watched her sister throwing darts. Two barely caught the outside of the dartboard, and the last throw missed entirely, lodging in the wall. Todd said something, and she gave him a playful slap on the arm.

Cecily's eyes narrowed. All right, he would not be reaching the summit tonight—at least not with her.

As she stormed back across the parking lot, she could almost hear the Neanderthal in lederhosen snickering. *Modern woman not too bright.*

That was for sure.

She returned to the condo and dug out the ice cream. Then she found a movie on Netflix and stared at the TV, seeing Bailey flirting with Todd and him eating it up like the dog he was.

Her cell phone rang around nine, and Todd's name appeared on the screen. She didn't pick up. He called again at nine-thirty, and then at quarter to ten he was pounding on her door. She turned off the lights and went to bed. Alone. Under the circumstances, that was best. She was in no mood to get romantic with Todd, no matter how many candles he lit.

What the hell was happening here? What the hell was happening to his life? One minute everything was going smoothly, and the next it was a mess. Todd banged on Cecily's door one last time, waited one more frustrating minute and then gave up. What had gone wrong between the promise of candlelit romance with hot sex and now?

His brother, for one thing, but that wasn't what had kept Cecily away. Had she come to the bar and seen her sister hanging out there? Todd frowned. That was the only explanation that made sense. That on top of the ice-machine fiasco—man, no wonder she wasn't answering her door. He wouldn't let himself in, either. *You deserve this,* he told himself. *You're being a jerk.* Only a jerk of the first order would be flirting with his business partner when he was seeing another woman. And sisters? Did he have to be doing this with sisters?

He returned to the tavern, where he knew Bailey would be waiting, still hoping her sister would show up, and he didn't return in a happy mood. The mood got even less happy when he saw that his brother had abandoned the bar, where he was supposed to be helping out, to play darts with Bailey.

He could tell her heart wasn't in it, though. She was looking hopefully toward the door, but at the sight of Todd coming in alone, the hope faded.

"I still haven't seen my sister," she told him.

"I don't think she's coming in," Todd said, and Bailey bit her lip, her expression anxious.

"Hey, we can still have fun," Devon insisted. "How about another beer, Bailey?"

"Hard to serve her when you're not behind the bar," Todd said between gritted teeth.

Devon shrugged. "Not that much going on right now."

Todd glanced over to where Pete was busy pulling pints of draft. "Yeah?"

"Guess we got a couple of thirsty ones in the last couple of minutes," Devon said and went behind the bar.

"I think I'll go home," Bailey said.

Todd nodded in agreement. The sooner she got away from his womanizing brother, the better he'd like it.

"If she does come in, will you tell her I was here?"

Todd nodded again, even though he knew Cecily wouldn't be coming in. Bailey wasn't the only one she wasn't talking to right now.

She left, and Todd went to sit at the end of the bar next to Henry.

"You look like the end of the world, son," Henry said to him. "Woman troubles?"

"That's what happens when you're greedy," said his brother, giving Henry a refill on his beer.

Todd scowled at Devon.

"I'll take one of those two off your hands," Devon offered with a smirk. "Which one do you want, Bailey or that Cecily?"

"Cecily's sister?" Henry said in surprise.

"Sister?" echoed Devon.

"I'm not seeing Bailey," Todd told Henry.

"Then I guess I can," Devon said.

Todd pointed a finger at him. "No. You can't."

Devon frowned. "You just said you're not seeing her."

"That doesn't mean *you* can."

"Hey, you don't own every girl in town. In fact, you don't own this town."

"Don't push me, Dev," Todd growled. "I'm not in the mood."

"Yeah? Well, me neither. Anyway, I kinda like her."

"Stay away from her."

Devon planted both hands on the bar and leaned toward Todd. "Who's gonna make me?"

Todd stood and planted his hands on the bar, too. "Who do you think?"

Henry scuttled off farther down the bar, taking his beer with him.

"Oh, big man," Devon said scornfully.

Todd jabbed a finger at his brother. "Just stop it, Dev. Like I said, I'm not in the mood." Damn it all, he should have been at his place with Cecily, making use of those stupid candles he'd bought at Johnson's Drugs.

But, of course, Devon didn't stop. How many beers had he had? Enough to make him contentious. He came around the bar. "Just because you've made some money, it doesn't make you better than me. You never had a ball career."

"Yeah? Neither did you." Okay, that was a rotten thing to say. He knew it the second the words were out of his mouth. He'd been there for his brother during that big disappointment, telling him he would've been great if it hadn't been for his trashed pitching arm. He'd been there for Dev when he talked about going back to school, had even lent him money. And now, with one sentence, he'd erased all the good-brother points he'd ever scored.

He started to apologize but didn't get any further than "Dev" before his brother socked him in the jaw.

He reeled backward into a table, knocking booze

onto the floor and making the table rock. "Whoa, there," Bill Will said, trying to steady him.

Meanwhile, here was Dev, motioning for him to bring it on. Great. He was in a tavern brawl in his own bar.

Feeling the eyes of every man present on him, he mustered as much dignity as he could and got up to walk past Devon. "I'm not going to fight with you. This is stupid."

"You bastard! I'm sick of hearing about what a success you are, how you've made something of your life. You've got a tavern. Big deal!"

Who'd been talking about what a success he was? Surely not his old man. There was no time to process that remark since his brother was shoving him.

"Cut it out!" he yelled and shoved back.

Devon cut it out by shoving him again, and that was when he snapped. With a primal snarl, he rushed his brother, plummeting them both into the wall, parting customers like the Red Sea and nearly knocking over the Budweiser sign.

"Call the cops!" one of the women screeched.

Todd turned and held out a hand. "No—no cops."

Then something crashed down on his head, and he saw stars. And the Red Sea closed in on him. And it smelled like beer.

When he came to, he had a knot on his head, and Tilda Morrison and Jamal Lincoln were hauling his brother away, Dev's words floating back to him: "Man, even the cops here are hot."

Oh, great. Just great. He staggered after them. "Tilda!"

She stopped and looked at him sternly, one eyebrow raised.

"Uh, that's my brother."

"Not anymore," Dev muttered, his jaw stuck out.

"I never would have guessed," Tilda said.

Yeah, the resemblance was pretty obvious.

"Did you know I was a pro ball player?" Dev asked her, trying to keep his balance.

"Uh-huh. Come on, A-Rod," she said and started moving Devon toward the door again.

"Where are you taking him?" Well, duh. Where did he think?

"Drunk and disorderly. Witnesses say he assaulted you," Tilda said. "You want to press charges?"

"No! Here, just give him to me. I'll take care of him."

"We can see how well that's working for you," Jamal said. "He can cool off in a cell tonight."

"Want to keep me company?" Devon asked, leering at Tilda.

She gave his arm a jerk and really got him moving. "You have the right to remain silent. Use it."

"Get someone to look at that bump on your head," Jamal advised. "You might have a concussion."

And then they were gone. The enthralled silence in The Man Cave lasted another moment, after which the patrons went back to their business, or rather discussing Todd's business.

"Why don't you go on home? I can close up." Pete handed him a bag of ice; he set it on the small mountain growing on top of his head and winced.

Home. *There's no place like home. Home is where the heart is. Yeah, right.* He went back to his empty house. The candles in the bedroom mocked him. He picked one up and threw it against the wall. And then another. And another. That made him feel good…for about a second. He dug some aspirin out of the medicine cabinet and swallowed a couple of pills dry. That should help the headache.

But nothing was going to help the ache he felt deep in his chest. He fell onto his bed and shut his eyes and saw the faces of Cecily, Bailey and Devon. They all kept whirling around like a carousel.

"When did you get so messed up?" he mumbled.

He was still trying to figure that out when he finally drifted off to sleep. He woke up the next morning feeling as if someone had planted an ax in his forehead and went in search of more aspirin. Then he went in search of his brother.

He didn't have to look far. Devon was just checking out of the Icicle Falls B and B for miscreants. He greeted Todd with a stony glare.

"I'll take you to the house."

"No, thanks," Devon said. "Take me back to my truck, and I'm out of here."

"Don't you have to go to court?"

"Do you care?"

Todd sighed. "Yeah, I do. I said some shitty stuff last night. I'm sorry."

Devon suddenly became fascinated with the view of Sleeping Lady Mountain. "Yeah, well, I don't remember much of what you said. Except that it pissed me off." He shrugged. "I was a shit, too. I've been a shit for a long time now." He turned his gaze back to Todd, offering a close-up view of unhealed pain and regret.

Put a plunger on my head and crown me king of the shits. How hard it must have been to think you had a dream securely held in your hands, only to have it slip through your fingers.

Todd clapped a hand on his brother's back and started them toward his truck. "Come on over to the house. We both need coffee."

Three mugs of coffee, two bowls of cornflakes and an hour later, they were brothers again and hovering somewhere near friendship.

"I've gotta get my act together," Devon said, staring into his mug. "Dad's right. I've become a total loser."

"Dad isn't always right about everything," Todd said.

"Yeah, but he was about me. It's just that, damn, for so many years—all through high school and then the minors—I was a baseball player. That's who I was. And now I don't know who I am. I guess I came here to find out. It seemed to work for you."

Todd nodded. He'd figured out who he was long before he hit Icicle Falls, but there was no sense saying that to his brother. "You're good with your hands."

Devon smirked. "That's what all the women say."

"Now, look," Todd said, "you can't be playing fast and loose with the women up here."

Devon shook his head. "I know. I know. Man, you never used to be such a priss."

"And you never used to be…" Oh, no. He wasn't going to start that again. "What happened with Gina?"

Devon's brows drew into an angry V.

"You guys were serious. What happened?"

"My career ended—that's what happened."

Todd nodded slowly. "Okay, I get it. She was a bitch

to you after your career fell apart, and now you're going to make every woman you meet pay for it."

"No," Devon protested. "I like women."

"You mean you like to use women."

"Hey, who doesn't want to get laid? And don't tell me you've never used a woman."

Todd couldn't tell him any such thing. And at one time, that hadn't bothered him. His girlfriends had never had any reason to complain when he was with them. He treated them well...except when the relationship began to get serious. Then he'd always bolted. Had he been planning to bolt with Cecily? And what about Bailey? Oh, man, life had been so simple only a few months ago.

"Speaking of women, what's with you and the sisters?"

Todd dropped his head in his hands. "I don't know."

"Man, you're even more screwed up than me."

"That's not possible," Todd retorted, and Devon grinned and punched him on the arm.

He chewed his lip a moment, then said, "I, uh, don't suppose you want me to help out at The Man Cave anymore."

"You, me and beer? Until we both get our heads on straight, maybe not. You can paint the trim on the tea shop."

Devon nodded, resigned.

"And I'll put in a good word for you with Dan Masters."

"Thanks, Todd."

Todd pulled a spare key out of the junk drawer. "Here. You may as well move in. I think my love life is toast."

* * *

Cecily was in no mood to see her sister at her mother's birthday party the next day. She played hooky from church even though Bailey was probably busy in Samantha's kitchen, making appetizers for the party. Cecily knew how to put on a smiling mask and pretend everything was fine, but she didn't want to wear the darned thing all day.

She made herself some French toast—she, too, could make fancy breakfasts—and spent some time surfing the internet and checking out what her friends on Facebook were up to.

Half of them had posts about their kids. *Guess who's walking!... Here's the picture of our new baby girl. Isn't she the cutest?*

Okay, that was enough time on the internet. She wrapped up the rose-scented bath salts she'd made for her mother and then headed for the shower.

She was at Samantha's house by one-thirty to help with the last-minute details before the guests arrived at two. Samantha met her at the door wearing a white knit dress that showed off her baby bump.

She took in Cecily's pink floral sundress. "Your dress…"

Cecily smiled and smoothed the skirt. It was the dress's debut. She'd gotten it at Gilded Lily's, and the moment she'd put it on she'd felt as if she could rule the world. "I bought it last week. It was on sale," she said as she stepped inside.

"Crap," Samantha muttered.

"What?" Cecily asked.

Now their mother came out from the great room. "Cecily, darling, you look lovely," she greeted her daughter, giving Cecily a kiss on the cheek. "And how sweet. You and Bailey decided to dress alike."

Before Cecily could say anything, Bailey appeared, bearing a platter of prosciutto-wrapped dates and wearing the exact same dress. She stopped short and blinked in surprise, then blushed.

Oh, no. Seriously? If Cecily's friend Ella had still been running the shop, this never would have happened. Cecily could feel her smile tipping down at the edges.

"I'll change," Bailey said.

"Don't bother," Cecily told her, trying her best not to sound snippy. The effort failed.

What the heck? They could pretend they were in middle school again, when Bailey had made a habit of copying her style. As the middle daughter, she'd been trying to establish her own identity, and it had been a constant source of aggravation every time her younger sister came home with the same color top or brand of jeans.

But they were beyond that now. Now her sister went after her man.

The best present she could give her mother would be not to pull every long, curly hair from Bailey's head, so she turned to Samantha and asked, "What do you want me to do?"

"Help us get the food on the table," Samantha said.

Cecily nodded and followed Bailey back into the kitchen, where she'd laid out several platters of appetizers. Here her sister's creative genius was on beautiful display—phyllo cups with some sort of cream cheese filling, veggies and a curry dip, stuffed mushrooms and mini quiches, all beautifully garnished.

And on the kitchen table was the birthday cake, no doubt carrot cake, which was their mother's favorite. It sat on a cut-glass pedestal plate and was decorated with delicate orange slices. Next to it sat two trays of cookies with dabs of chocolate frosting or dusted with powdered sugar.

Bailey had really outdone herself, and even though she was still on Cecily's most unwanted list, Cecily couldn't help being impressed.

"Are you still mad at me?" Bailey asked in a small voice.

Their mother's birthday party was hardly the arena for a catfight. "Let's not talk about it now," Cecily said.

She picked up a couple of platters and left for the dining room, where her mother and Samantha were talking in low voices. They fell silent at the sight of her, and Mom asked Samantha, "Which plates do you want to use, dear?"

Great. They'd been talking about her. "Setting up for your own birthday party?" Cecily teased, pretending she hadn't noticed.

"There's no stopping her," Samantha said.

"As if there's anything left to do," Mom said. "You girls are far too efficient."

"We learned from the best," Cecily said and kissed her on the cheek.

Bailey came out with two more platters and placed them on the table, then scurried back into the kitchen.

Their little sister was normally the chattiest of them all. Anyone, especially a mother, could tell that something was wrong, so it was hardly surprising to see a thoughtful frown appear on Mom's face.

Cecily returned to the kitchen, where Bailey was making their mother's favorite punch, a sweet concoction of lemonade, orange sherbet and lime soda. "I'd appreciate it if you'd drop the martyr act," Cecily said in a low voice.

"I'm not acting like a martyr," Bailey protested, scowling as she scooped the last of the sherbet into the punch bowl.

"Yes, you are, and you've got no reason to. You're the one who…" *Caused all this trouble.* She bit her lip. She was *not* going there, not on their mother's birthday.

Bailey set aside the scoop and the empty sherbet container. "I'm the one who what?" she demanded.

The doorbell rang, announcing the arrival of the first guests. It was time to act like grown-ups. "Never mind." Cecily picked up the punch bowl to take it out.

"I can do it," Bailey said in a huffy voice and grabbed it back.

That was a mistake. The sea of calories inside the big glass bowl sloshed up over the edge, spilling onto her.

She let out a yelp as the wave of punch drenched the front of her dress. This was followed by a hybrid sound of disgust that came out as "Eeewk." She set down the punch bowl and looked forlornly at her sopping bodice. Then she glared at Cecily. "You did that on purpose."

"Who grabbed the punch bowl?" Cecily retorted.

Now their mother and sister entered the kitchen, followed by Mom's friend Dot Morrison.

"Is everything all right?" Mom asked.

"My dress," Bailey wailed as if the copycat garment had been ruined for life.

"It wasn't your color anyway, kiddo," Dot said.

"I'll go change," Bailey muttered, making an attempt at dignity, and flounced out of the kitchen.

"That kid always was a klutz," Dot said after she was gone.

Cecily decided not to enlighten Dot as to the real reason for the spill. She tried to wipe the bitchy smile off her face as she deposited the punch on the dining room table, but it kept sneaking back.

Fortunately, more guests were arriving, so bitchy was easily mistaken for friendly. After bringing out the coffee, Cecily helped Samantha collect sweaters and purses and piled presents on the coffee table. As the guests settled in, she delivered punch and fetched coffee and generally made herself useful.

Bailey came back downstairs wearing white capris and a green blouse that accented her chestnut hair. As Dot had implied, it was a much more flattering color for her than what she'd been wearing. If they'd been on better terms, Cecily would have pointed that out. Of course, if they'd been on better terms, Bailey would never have wound up wearing orange sherbet punch in the first place.

She, too, started mingling, taking presents, offering punch and coffee, but keeping as far from Cecily as possible.

Meanwhile, their mother chatted with her friends, accepted a birthday kiss on the cheek from Arnie Amundsen, her longtime admirer, and watched her two feuding daughters. Gracious as always, she opened presents and gushed over each one. She raved over Bailey's carrot orange cake and bragged about Cecily's creativity after the "This is your life" DVD Cecily had put together from old pictures and home movies. Finally, she smiled and hugged each departing guest.

But when Cecily tried to escape, Mom said, "Stay another minute, darling. I want to talk to you."

Uh-oh, Cecily thought.

"Samantha, would you ask Bailey if she could join us?"

There was no hiding from a motherly lecture, not even in the kitchen.

"Okay," Samantha said. "Then I think baby and I will go have another piece of cake." She sent Cecily a look that said *good luck,* then disappeared into the kitchen, and Cecily sat down on the couch, bracing herself for what was to come.

A moment later Bailey entered the living room, clearly chagrined. She, too, knew what was coming. She sat down on the far end of the couch from Cecily. "Did you enjoy your party?" she asked Mom.

Ah, the old distraction technique. It wouldn't work, but Cecily admired the effort.

Now their mother looked at them with the *I'm so disappointed* expression that had worked so well ever since they were small. "This is not like my girls."

There was no point in pretending they didn't know what she was talking about. Cecily found it difficult to look her mother in the eye and wound up staring at her lap instead. The view of her pink floral dress wasn't any better. It only served to remind her of her earlier childish reaction to Bailey's dress.

"Would you like to tell me what's going on?" Mom asked quietly.

Actually, no. It was all so painful and humiliating. Cecily glanced over at Bailey, who was gnawing her lip and obviously not planning to volunteer any information.

How to explain this to their mother without sounding as if she were thirteen?

"This has something to do with a man," Muriel said. It wasn't a question.

"Mama, how did you know?" Bailey asked in astonishment.

The frosty incident at the front door had to be a big tip-off.

"I asked your sister, and she told me you two were having a misunderstanding."

There was an epic understatement.

"It wasn't too difficult to figure out what kind of misunderstanding. There's nothing else that could come between sisters," their mother said. "Love is a strong emotion. It pulls out the best in us and the worst."

Cecily knew what it had pulled out in her. Bailey squirmed down on her end of the couch.

"You're not the first women to fight over a man," Mom said gently. "You know, Pat Wilder and I nearly lost our friendship over one."

"You, Mama?" Bailey asked, sounding as shocked as Cecily felt.

It was hard to imagine their mother, sweet-tempered and kind, fighting with anyone.

"It was over your father. We both wanted him."

"How did you resolve that?" Cecily asked. When it came right down to it, she didn't want to lose her sister. But she didn't want to lose her man, either.

"It resolved itself," Mom said simply. "And it will with you girls, too. One of you will get the man and one of you won't. But whichever one of you doesn't, you're going to have to trust that the right one for you is still making his way to you. You're both lovely girls, and I know you'll both find someone who's right for you, so there's no need to break a lifetime bond over this person."

But what about that feeling of betrayal? "What if it's more than that?" Cecily asked.

"You need to work it out," her mother said firmly. "Don't let your love life ruin your family life. Men will come and go, but sisters are forever. Now I'm going to visit with Samantha so you two can have some privacy."

Yes, they were back full circle to childhood. *You girls go to your room, and don't come down until you're friends again.*

Their mother left, and an uncomfortable silence settled on the room.

Bailey was the first to break it. "What are we going to do?"

"Arm wrestle for him," Cecily said with a faint smile. Except this wasn't funny. "You know, it's not just about who gets Todd. It's about the way you set out to undermine my relationship with him from the start."

"No," Bailey corrected her. "It's about the way you accused me of doing that."

Okay, they were going to talk in circles. The old *go to your room* method of conflict resolution wasn't going to work this time. "Fine," Cecily said stiffly, getting up from the couch.

"Where are you going?" Bailey demanded.

"Home."

"Mom wants us to work this out."

"Mom isn't the one who has to deal with you," Cecily retorted. She collected her purse from the kitchen, then went to where her mother and Samantha sat in the family room and said goodbye.

"Are you girls okay?" Mom asked after Cecily had kissed her.

"We will be," Cecily assured her. But it was going to take more than a conversation on the couch. "Happy birthday."

"It is, now that you girls have made up," Mom said.

Cecily left her mother in happy ignorance. As she passed the living room on her way out the door, she saw that Bailey had abandoned the couch. She was probably upstairs, pouting in the future nursery, where she'd been sleeping. How appropriate: the baby of the family was in the nursery, acting like a baby.

Cecily remembered what a spoiled brat her sister had been as a preschooler, always carrying on until she got her way. *Well, not this time, baby sister. Not this time.*

Chapter Seventeen

Cecily had a lot to think about. Such serious thinking required the aid of mint chocolate chip ice cream, so she stopped by Safeway on her way home.

She was standing in front of the freezer, trying to decide if Ben & Jerry's Cherry Garcia would be a better choice, when a little girl called her name from the end of the aisle. She turned to see Serena Goodman, dolled up in pink shorts and a Hello Kitty top, skipping toward her, Luke walking behind carrying a produce container of strawberries and a head of lettuce.

"Hi, Miss Cecily," Serena greeted her. "I learned how to skip. See?" She skipped in a circle to demonstrate, her blond curls bobbing.

"That's impressive," Cecily said. "Who taught you that?"

"My daddy," Serena said as Luke joined them.

Cecily couldn't help smiling at the image of Luke Goodman, gentle giant, skipping down the sidewalk next to his daughter.

"I'm a man of many talents," he said. "How was your mom's birthday party?" he asked as Serena practiced her new skill.

"I think she had a good time," Cecily said. "The entire older generation of Icicle Falls showed up."

"No surprise. Everyone loves Muriel." He studied her. "You've been planning this for two weeks. Shouldn't you be looking more pleased with yourself?"

How had he seen past the pleasant face she'd put on? "I *am* pleased with myself," she lied.

"And that's why you're standing in front of the ice cream."

"You've seen too many movies," she said. "Not every woman gets depressed and dives into the ice cream."

"My wife's choice was always Rocky Road," he said, refusing to be fooled. "So, what's wrong?"

"My sister," she blurted.

"Bailey?"

"I have two sisters. What makes you think it's her?"

"Educated guess. Am I right?"

"I love her dearly," Cecily began. It was true. She did. Maybe that was why she felt so angry, so betrayed.

"But?" he prompted.

"But we're having…some problems."

Serena was back now. "Daddy, are we getting ice cream?"

"Not today, princess. We're going to help Miss Cecily pick some out, though. What kind should she get, chocolate or vanilla?"

"Chocolate!" Serena crowed.

"How about mint chocolate chip?" Cecily said, and Serena nodded enthusiastically. "Do you want to come over to my house and help eat it?" It seemed only right to offer.

"Can we, Daddy?"

"Sure," Luke said, smiling at Cecily.

She found herself smiling back. After her turbulent weekend, running into Luke was the equivalent of surviving a shipwreck and discovering a warm, sandy beach with a restaurant that served piña coladas.

They followed her back to the condo. Luke sat on a barstool at the kitchen counter while Serena joined Cecily, watching eagerly as she got out bowls and spoons and dished up the ice cream.

"You can take that one to your daddy," Cecily said, handing Serena the bowl with the biggest helping.

Serena nodded knowingly. "Daddy always gets the biggest bowl."

"That's something my mom does," Luke explained, his face turning red.

"My mom always did that with my dad," Cecily said.

Her parents had enjoyed a happy marriage. All her life, she'd assumed she'd follow in their footsteps. So far those footsteps were proving hard to find.

She gave Serena her ice cream, and the child climbed up on a stool next to her father and dug in. There they sat, a family in waiting, the family she could have if she chose Luke and let Bailey have Todd.

"Your ice cream's melting," he said.

She blinked.

"Where were you?"

She shook her head. "Nowhere. Just thinking."

"Yeah? About what?"

She busied herself with putting away the ice cream container. "Why can't love be easy?"

"Who says it can't? All you need is to be with the right person." Now he sounded like her mother.

"I love my daddy," Serena said around a mouthful of ice cream.

"Your daddy's a very special man."

Who was she talking to, Serena or herself? Serena, of course, but she shouldn't have said that. It was completely inappropriate, considering the fact that she was with Todd. In theory, anyway.

No, not just in theory. They *should* be together. They'd been moving in that direction for the past two years. They were meant to be together.

And yet Luke looked so right sitting at her kitchen counter....

"It'll work out," he said.

Was he reading her mind?

"Whatever's going on with you and Bailey," he added, even though they both knew she was no longer talking about Bailey.

"It will," she agreed. Like Mom had said, the situation would resolve itself. But what if it didn't resolve in the way she hoped? She set aside her bowl of ice cream. It wasn't helping.

"You must have had to go pick the strawberries," Bernadette Goodman teased her son when he dropped off the items he'd bought for her at the store.

"Got sidetracked," he said, hoping to leave it at that.

"We had ice cream with Miss Cecily," Serena piped up.

"You did?" his mom said to Serena as she looked at him.

"Don't get excited, Mom. It was no big deal." He

sure wished it could be the beginning of a big deal, though. There had to be some way he could get her to see that falling from friendship into love made for a nice, soft landing.

Serena wandered off to the spare room, which his mother had turned into a playroom for her, and Bernadette took advantage of her departure to launch into a motherly lecture. "Maybe not, but it opened the door. If you don't get a little more aggressive, some other man is going to steal her away right from under your nose."

He made a face. "She's not mine to steal, Ma. And anyway, she's with Todd Black."

"Who's that?" She might as well have said, "Who could possibly be more worthy than my son?"

"He owns The Man Cave." And if you asked Luke, he sure wasn't more worthy.

Bernadette frowned. "*That* place."

Luke shrugged and started for the playroom. "I need to get Serena home."

"No man ever got the woman he wanted by giving up," Bernadette called after him.

"Thanks for the advice." He wasn't giving up— not really. Still, what did his mom expect him to do, grab Cecily by the hair and haul her back to his place? Damn, if only it were that easy.

On Monday Devon showed up at the tea shop to paint the outside trim and ended up getting drafted to help Bailey hang curtains.

"Oh, yes," she said as they surveyed their work. "Those antique white curtain rods were a good choice.

They look exactly as I'd imagined they would with the curtains."

"They're sure…lacy," Devon said.

She giggled. "That's the idea. Our clientele is going to be women."

He nodded. "Yeah, chicks will love this place."

"I hope so. I want it to do well. I want this to be a solid investment for your brother." Although lately she'd been wondering if it would've been better if they'd never met. Then her sister would still be speaking to her. She'd still be working at the Icicle Creek Lodge, happily cooking breakfast for the guests. That would have been a good life.

Not as good as having a tea shop and making fancy treats and cute little tea cakes, though. But the situation had taken an ugly turn, and now it seemed as if every happy moment was salted with some unhappy thought.

"Hey, you worried?" Devon asked.

"What? No. Everything's great."

"It's gonna be," he said. "My brother's smart when it comes to business." He studied her a moment. "Not always so smart when it comes to…other things."

She got the message loud and clear. *Don't count on him for love.*

Well, she wasn't going to. He wasn't hers to count on, and she was going to lose these inappropriate feelings. She concentrated on a mental image of grabbing a fistful of little pink hearts with the initials B.S. + T.B. and dumping them in a giant chintz teapot. *There. All gone.*

If only it were that easy.

"Well, I'd better go outside and start on that trim

before my brother gets here and chews my ass off for not working."

"Hanging curtains is work, too," Bailey assured him.

"No, that was fun," he said, flashing her a killer smile.

She wished she could fall in love with Devon. A brother for each sister; that would solve everything. Why couldn't love be simple? A couple of the little hearts tried to climb out of the teapot, and she pushed them back in. *Now, stay there!*

The chairs and tables for the tearoom were being delivered, and his brother had most of the trim done when Todd arrived at Tea Time. Bailey had decided on lavender, and it had been the right choice. It pulled everything together.

"Lookin' good," he said to Devon.

Devon grinned. "Hey, I do good work."

"And fast."

"Gotta get this done. I've got an interview with Dan Masters later this afternoon. Thanks for putting in a word for me."

"No problem." It had taken only a couple of minutes this morning, and Todd had been glad to do it. Maybe this town was what his brother needed to pull his life together.

He hoped one of them could.

He went inside just as the delivery guys were going out the door, leaving behind the furniture equivalent of a logjam. "Can't you set the tables over there?" Bailey was pleading.

"Sorry, lady. Not in our job description," said one

of the men. He looked big enough to lift an entire table with one finger.

Jerk, Todd thought. "Hey, not to worry," he told Bailey. "I'm here."

The way her face lit up at the sight of him hit him like a shot of tequila. Was he developing a split personality, each one pursuing a different sister? Oh, man. He was in deep shit.

He began moving chairs. Anything to keep from dealing with this.

"Now it really looks like something in here," Bailey said after she and Todd had set the last table by one of the front windows.

It did. With the tables and chairs in place and the curtains on the windows, the dream was coming to life.

"I can hardly wait until we have people in here," she said.

He surveyed the room and nodded. "Come August, this place will be packed."

"It's like waiting to have a baby," she said.

"I think starting a business is easier."

"Me, too," she agreed. "But you know what I mean. It's exciting to start something new. After all the budgeting, the planning and the work, now we can see it coming together."

"You're a born entrepreneur," he said, and the admiration in his voice warmed her heart.

Simmer down, she told herself. *Concentrate on the business.* "I am excited to be working on my own dreams instead of for someone else."

She'd enjoyed planning her menu, poring over

countless restaurant supply websites with Todd and choosing her cooking utensils and cutlery and glass-ware. It had been serious work but at the same time fun, with him cracking jokes and making her laugh.

There was nothing wrong with having fun. It proved you worked well together.

But that was all this was going to be. Work. She wasn't going to steal Todd. Still, she couldn't help remembering how good it had felt when he'd put his arm around her during their impromptu ice fight, and her thoughts did like to sneak off, wondering how it would feel to kiss him. Darn. Where was that giant teapot when you needed it?

He gave her an elbow nudge. "Hey, where are you?"

"Just thinking." *About you and me and what could have been but won't.* "About how great our tea shop is going to be."

He nodded. "It's the second biggest buzz in the world, starting a new business."

"What's the first biggest?"

"I'm a guy. Can't you guess?"

Oh, yes, and guessing sent a guilty flush to her face.

He grinned and shook his head. "You know, that's one of the things I like about you. You're such an in-nocent."

"I'm not that innocent," she protested, and that made him laugh.

But then the laughing stopped and the expression on his face changed to something more serious. She turned a little more in his direction; he moved a little closer to her. He looked at her lips and moved closer still.

Her mother had said things would work out, that she and Cecily would both end up with the man they were supposed to be with. Couldn't *he* be the man she was meant to be with? It would be so easy to kiss Todd right now. Everything in her wanted to.

"Hey, I'm done with the trim," Devon called, poking his head in the door. "Am I interrupting something?"

Face flaming, she took a step back, and Todd frowned and did the same.

He ran his fingers through his hair. "Uh, no." To Bailey he said, "If you don't need any more help here, I'd better get going. I need to pick up some stuff for the Cave."

"I'm good," she said. Boy, was she, considering what she could have just done.

"I've gotten in some messes with women," Devon said, falling into step with Todd as he hurried down the walkway, "but you're out-messing 'em all."

As if he needed his brother to tell him that? "Did you say you have to be somewhere?"

Devon held up both hands. "Just sayin'."

"I already know," Todd growled.

"That Bailey's pretty nice. If you're not gonna be with her..."

Todd whipped around to face him. "No."

Both his brother's eyebrows went up. "So, that's how it is."

"I don't know how it is," Todd snapped.

Devon chuckled. "Man, have you got it bad, you poor slob. Glad I'm not you." He picked up his empty paint bucket. "I'll get this cleaned up."

"Good idea," Todd said grumpily. He had some cleaning up to do, too.

Cecily had barely gotten home from work when she heard the sound of a motorcycle pulling into her parking lot. Todd. He was back, coming to make up.

She was more than ready. They'd forget all those missteps they'd taken recently and move on from here.

She darted to the bathroom, did a five-second tooth brushing, applied lip gloss and then spritzed on perfume. She was still wearing her work clothes, a black skirt and cream-colored sleeveless blouse, coupled with a pink cardigan. Not very sexy. She shed the sweater and undid the top couple of buttons on the blouse. There, that was better. Anyway, it was all she had time for. He was knocking on the door.

As she went to answer it, she rethought her dinner menu. Okay, forget leftovers. She'd broil some chicken, serve it with wild rice and a Caesar salad. She could make brownies for dessert.

The tavern was closed on Mondays. They'd have all evening together. She smiled as she opened the door. "Perfect timing. I was just trying to decide what to make for dinner."

He didn't return her *all is forgiven* smile. Something she'd sensed for one dangerous moment when she first saw her sister with Todd poked its ugly head out from the cubbyhole in her mind where she'd stuffed it. She pushed it back.

"We need to talk," he said.

"You're right." She led the way to the couch where he'd kissed her so passionately. "I need to apologize for my behavior this weekend." He was about to speak but she hurried on, hoping that if she talked fast enough and long enough he wouldn't say what she knew he was going to say. "I was being insecure and bitchy. That's not me, really."

"I understand that," he said.

She motioned for him to sit on the couch and joined him, sitting close, as if her physical nearness would keep him emotionally tied to her.

"Cec, this isn't about anything you've done."

She pulled away. "It's my sister." Bitterness was bleeding into her voice, making her sound small and petty.

He let out his breath in a hiss. "Yeah, it is. But this isn't working between us. You know that."

No, she didn't. "It was working fine," she insisted.

He shook his head "It just looked like it. Hell, I wanted it to work. But there's something happening with Bailey, something different from what was going on with us. She and I are alike in a lot of ways. I think..." He hesitated as if afraid to continue.

"Go on," Cecily said. *Don't stop now. You're on a roll.*

"I think she could end up being my best friend."

And *she* couldn't? Cecily pressed her lips together and blinked back tears. Her throat was suddenly too tight for words to squeeze through. All she could do was nod. Rejected again. *The third time's the charm? Three strikes and you're out?*

"I hate like hell to hurt you." He let out his breath. "But I'd hurt you more in the long run if I kept trying to make this work. I want to stop the direction we're going in while there's still time to come out of this as friends."

Friends, but not best friends. Certainly not friends with benefits. She'd had her chance for benefits, and she hadn't taken it. If she had, they'd be solidly together now. Wouldn't they?

She looked out her living room window, not seeing the pine and fir trees or the silhouette of Sleeping Lady Mountain. Instead, she saw herself alone again, still searching for her perfect man.

"I'm sorry, Cec. I really am," Todd said, and she heard something in his voice she'd rarely heard—sincerity. Then he kissed her on the cheek and walked out the door.

So, just as her mother had predicted, the situation had resolved itself.

They should have left Bailey in L.A.

Todd had really stepped in it, falling for one sister and hurting another.

How had this happened? He'd wanted Cecily; he was crazy about Cecily.

But he had the terrifying suspicion that he was falling in love with Bailey. There was a connection building there that he couldn't deny and an attraction that he was finding increasingly impossible to resist.

Yeah, Cecily had turned his crank, and he enjoyed being with her, liked letting his sarcastic side run rampant. But it was different with Bailey. Somehow, with her, he found himself being so much more genuine.

Whoa, there was a revelation. But it was true. Bailey admired his business acumen, appreciated the fact that he wanted to succeed. She didn't look down on his seedy little tavern. In fact, when she was there, she fit with the place, the people. Whenever Cecily had come in, she'd always given the subtle impression that she was slumming—underestimating Henry's financial worth, thinking the place sad when there weren't any people in it. Okay, it wasn't Zelda's, but it wasn't supposed to be. It was a guy hangout, no frills, no fuss. Just beer and pool, a game or two of darts—a place for locals. For guys who couldn't afford an addition to their houses but still wanted a man cave to retreat to. He supposed he could have explained that to her, and yet, even if he had, he wasn't sure she would've understood.

She was pissed at him now, but he'd done her a favor. He'd done them both a favor. They weren't a fit. He should have realized it months ago, and if he hadn't been so busy trying to prove to himself that he could get her, he would have seen that.

He remembered something his old man had once said. *Being with the wrong woman is like swallowing hot pepper sauce. It may taste good at first, but you'll feel it later and it won't be good coming out the other end.*

He didn't want that kind of misery for either of them.

And what if he'd been wrong about Bailey? What if he was misreading her? What if Cecily stayed pissed...at both of them? He had a sneaking suspicion that, even though he'd stepped away from the hot sauce, there was still misery in his future.

Chapter Eighteen

Devon sat bolt upright in the futon bed where he'd been sleeping in his brother's spare room. What time was it? He grabbed his cell phone and saw that he'd slept right through the clock alarm. This was his first day of work at Masters Construction, and he was due at seven. It was now ten to seven. *Shit, shit, shit!*

He threw off the covers and dressed in under a minute. He brushed his teeth in record time, too, and pulled on his boots. Meanwhile, his brother was sleeping the sleep of the dead. Man, it had to be nice to set your own schedule.

He could have set his own schedule, had some sweet business investments, if he'd managed his money instead of burning through it. Not that he'd made a lot as an AAA player, but he'd made enough that he could have saved something. What a dumb shit. And now here he was, with a chance to start over, and he was friggin' late. Double dumb. He raced out the door. Pedal to the metal and maybe he'd be only five minutes late to the construction site.

He put the address in his GPS and roared off down the street. He could make it. He hit Icicle Creek Road, a nice open stretch, and really floored it. And that was when the patrol car hidden behind a Willkommen in Icicle Falls sign came after him like the Batmobile and put on the flashing red light.

He swore and pulled over. Oh, yeah, this was what he needed, another run-in with the local cops.

He watched his rearview mirror and saw the same lady cop who'd hauled his ass off to jail after his fight with Todd get out of the patrol car and approach his truck. Oh, great.

He lowered the window and laid his head back against the headrest, awaiting his doom.

Now she was at his window. "Do you know how fast you were going?"

"Sixty."

"And are you aware, sir, that the speed limit on this road is fifty?"

"I am now," he said. "And can you please not call me 'sir'? It's not like we haven't met. Or maybe you forgot."

"I remember," she said, stone-faced. "License and registration, please."

He got both and passed them to her. "Fine. Just write me the ticket. Then maybe you can give me a police escort to work and tell Dan Masters that I tried to get to the site on time."

"You're working for Dan Masters?"

"This is my first day. My alarm didn't go off."

"You know that's no excuse for speeding. You could have killed someone."

"Yeah, there's so many people on this road. Or I might have hit a squirrel."

Her eyes narrowed. "Are you giving me lip?"

"I could think of a lot of things I'd like to give you,

pretty lady, but lip isn't one of them. Not when you're in that uniform, anyway. Look, I deserve the ticket. Just hand it over."

She nodded and went back to her patrol car, and Devon sat in his truck, seething. Of all the places to be patrolling, she had to pick this road. Why couldn't she have been in town somewhere eating a doughnut?

Judging from that tight ass of hers, she didn't eat doughnuts. Did she have a boyfriend? Probably. And he was probably even bigger and tougher than her.

Now she was back. "I'm giving you a warning this time, since you're new in town. Don't let me catch you speeding again."

"No, ma'am," he said. She started to walk away "Hey, Officer Friendly. You got a boyfriend?"

She frowned. "You been watching *Raising Arizona?*"

He grinned at her. "Nicolas Cage. I remember that movie."

"This isn't the movies," she said and marched back to her patrol car.

Devon grinned. *She likes me.*

Yeah, he thought later, once he was settled in at the building site and swinging a hammer. Maybe he'd stick around Icicle Falls for a while.

It was nearly noon, and Bailey was stocking shelves with exotic teas and jams when Todd walked in. "I see our merchandise made it," he said.

"Yep." All except the chocolate. The cash register and glass display case sat on the other side of the room. When they had their grand opening, that case would hold all manner of Sweet Dreams truffles, from their white chocolate rose truffle to the newest flavor, dark chocolate ginger.

She stepped back to admire her handiwork. Yes, it was starting to look like a real business. "Wait till I get my teapots and china mugs set out."

"Then there'll be way too much estrogen in the air for me," he joked.

Today he was wearing jeans and a brown T-shirt decorated with a likeness of the Neanderthal that lurched across the outside of his tavern. Proud to Be a Neanderthal the shirt bragged. Todd could drag her back to his cave anytime and do whatever he wanted.

Stop that, she scolded herself. *He's not yours, and you're going to be nothing but professional from now on.*

She smiled a professional smile without an ounce of flirting in it. "It'll work for our customers, though."

"You're doing a great job of pulling this together," he said.

"I can hardly wait to see it filled with people." She could already envision shoppers browsing through the fancy food items and picking out the perfect teapot, could see mothers and their little girls at those tables, enjoying a tea party, imagine girlfriends indulging in the chocolate tea she planned to serve or sisters meeting to sample her white chocolate–lavender scones.

Sisters. The pleasant vision curdled. Cec was still mad at her.

She'd get over it once she and Todd were engaged, but Bailey wasn't sure how *she'd* feel. Her sister's animosity still stung like a bad burn, and even though she wanted to patch things up, she didn't know if they'd ever be able to regain what they'd lost.

And the idea of Todd with another woman was painful. She was so drawn to him, more strongly than she'd ever been drawn to Brandon. (Who would have thought that was possible?) How was she going to run a business with this man, go through the years watching him build a life with someone else, especially when that someone was her own sister? Pretty hard to avoid the happy couple when they'd all be sharing a table during the holidays.

She'd have to find a way, though. If Todd and her sister were meant to be, then that was that. She'd simply have to deal with it.

"So, you going to the street dance?" he asked casually.

The Fourth of July was only a few days away. The residents of Icicle Falls celebrated with parades and picnics and fireworks on the Wenatchee River at night. But the festivities started on the third with the street dance. People of all ages turned out to visit with each other, show off their dance moves and eat everything from hamburgers and corn on the cob to cotton candy. There'd been a lot Bailey had missed when she moved to L.A., and the street dance was right near the top of that list.

"I don't know." The last thing she wanted to do was hang around on the edge of the crowd and watch Todd and Cec swaying together to some romantic love song. "Are you and Cec going?"

His easy smile was replaced by the serious expression he wore when they were talking about budgets and profit margins. "Cec and I aren't together anymore."

Oh, no. Oh, yes! Oh, crud. A tin of jasmine tea

slipped from her hands and landed on the floor. She knelt to pick it up. "You're not?"

He knelt, too. And the look he gave her was hot enough to boil a tea bag. "I think you can guess why."

She wanted to throw her arms around him and kiss him. No, she wanted to throw up. "I thought you might want to go," he said, bringing them back to the subject of the dance.

She stood and took a step back. "You just broke up with my sister." How could she go to the street dance with Todd when he'd just dumped Cecily?

This is what you've wanted, she reminded herself. Except now that she had it, she didn't want it so much. Guilt had erected an enormous wall between her and him.

He stood, too, and pulled her toward him. "I like your sister, but I think I'm falling in love with you."

They'd been moving toward this like a leaf on the Wenatchee River being pulled along by the current. She'd felt drawn to him from the first time she saw him at Pancake Haus. Yet all she could say was "Poor Cec."

"Poor all of us if I'd kept seeing her when I could feel the situation changing between you and me," Todd said. "I may be a lot of things, but I'm not a hypocrite. I wanted Cec, but I'm not the right man for her. I can see that now. And I'm not going to ruin our lives by being with the wrong person. Growing up, I saw first-hand what happens when you do that. I wouldn't wish that on anybody, especially her."

Everything he said made sense. Still, she hesitated.

"You think seeing us together is going to come as some big surprise to her?"

But Bailey continued to hesitate.

"Come on, Bailey," he said gently. "I know this is awkward."

Awkward? This was more than awkward. It was grand theft boyfriend. Cec would kill her.

"I really think something's happening between us," he said. "Let's not screw it up."

She looked into his eyes and thought, *Soul mate,* and the walls of resistance crumbled. "Okay," she said. "Let's go." Fear of an ugly sisterly encounter encouraged her to add, "But can we wait until dark?"

"Are you doing the seven-layer dip for the Fourth again?" Samantha asked Cecily as they left Sweet Dreams Chocolates for lunch at Zelda's.

The Sterling family gathered together for a barbecue to celebrate Independence Day every year. Since their mother had downsized, the location had been switched to Samantha and Blake's house. The family would go to the parade in the morning, then explore the arts and crafts booths, returning midafternoon for a big meal and croquet on the lawn. This would be followed in the evening with snacks on the riverbank as they watched their fellow residents set off fireworks. Cecily had always been part of this family event. Even when she lived in L.A., she'd come home to spend the Fourth in Icicle Falls.

This year she had no desire to do that. Todd had dumped her and was probably making plans with Bailey. No way was she going to stay around for that. She'd already booked a flight to L.A.

"Actually, I'm not going to be here," she said.

Samantha looked at her in shock. "You're kidding."

"A friend in L.A. invited me to come down there." The truth was, she'd invited herself, but she preferred not to share that information.

Samantha frowned.

Cecily cut her off before she could say anything. "Right now I need some time away." She could feel her sister's assessing gaze. Humiliation infused her skin, heating her face.

"You and Todd broke up," Samantha guessed.

"You could say that," Cecily said, trying to keep her tone light. Darkness crept in, and she added, "Or you could say he dumped me."

Samantha let out a long breath. "I think we need to start lunch with a Chocolate Kiss."

Two Chocolate Kisses and a few bites of salad later, Cecily didn't feel any better. Samantha had tried to keep the conversation on business, the latest book Cecily's book club was reading, what she thought of the movie Cass had picked for their next girls' movie night, anything but the subject of Cecily's love life. It didn't help.

"Tell me again why I came back here?" Cecily asked miserably.

"Because your life in L.A. sucked."

"Oh, yeah. Now it sucks here, too. How special."

At that moment Luke walked in with his mom and daughter.

"Cecily!" cried Serena, even as her grandmother admonished her to use her inside voice.

"I'm betting it doesn't have to," Samantha said in a low voice, and Cecily made a face at her.

Serena was the first to reach the table. "Miss Cecily, you know what? Grandma took me over to where Daddy works, but we didn't get chocolate."

"Well, we'll have to fix that," Cecily said.

Luke and his mother had arrived at the table now. "I think she likes coming to see you as much as she does getting chocolate samples," Bernadette Goodman said to Cecily.

"When I grow up I'm going to work for you," Serena informed her.

"What are you going to do?" Cecily asked.

"Sell chocolate."

"You might want to run the company, like Samantha does," Cecily said.

Serena cocked her head and studied Samantha, considering.

"Then you can eat all the chocolate you want," Samantha told her.

"Okay," Serena said, nodding. "I'll do that."

"Well, that settles that," Samantha said. "Now we know who to leave the company to."

"I get ice cream for dessert," Serena confided. "And if I'm really good, Daddy's going to take me to the street dance. Are you going to the street dance?"

"Not this time," Cecily said, keeping her voice neutral.

"Other plans?" Luke asked casually.

"I'm going to see some friends in L.A.," she said, not quite meeting his eyes.

"Oh," he said, taking that in. It probably wasn't hard to put two and two together.

Now Serena was tugging on her father's arm. "Come on, Daddy. Let's go eat."

"Always lovely to see you," Bernadette said to the sisters and led Serena away.

Luke lingered a moment longer. "So, you're not going to be around for the Fourth," he said, as if still trying to wrap his mind around this bit of information.

She shook her head.

"I need to...talk to Charley," Samantha improvised, and she, too, scrammed, leaving Luke and Cecily on their own.

"Are things over with you and Black?" Luke asked.

She nodded. "It didn't work out."

"Cec," he began.

"Don't. Let's not go there. Okay?"

He released a long, frustrated breath. "Fine. See you when you get back."

She felt sure she wouldn't see him around the office now that she'd shot him down again. But all she could think about was how much she still wanted Todd. God only knew why. And God only knew why she kept pushing away a man who cared about her. A man who was more than willing to give her that family she wanted.

"You're an idiot," she told herself. Why, oh, why couldn't she feel the same electricity with Luke that she felt with Todd?

Maria came over to see if she wanted anything else.

"Yeah," she said, shoving away her salad. "Another Chocolate Kiss." It looked as if that was the only kind she was going to get for a very long time.

Damn it all, Luke was done trying with Cecily. Life was too short to waste on a woman who wasn't interested. So what if she liked his kid—and he felt the earth shift under his feet when he kissed her? So what if they were the best match she'd ever make? She couldn't see it. Or refused to. And if she wanted to be stubborn and stupid, then he was done.

His mother's hopeful smile fell away at the sight of his angry face. "Rome wasn't built in a day," she said gently as he slid into his seat.

"Yeah, and 'He who hesitates…'" Luke quoted back to her. "Anyway, nothing's getting built—not now."

"What were you building, Daddy?" Serena asked.

A new life. At least he'd been hoping to. He didn't want to stay single forever, and his daughter needed a mother. Cecily was his dream woman—kindhearted, funny, great with kids. She'd been giving Serena a birthday present every year ever since her first birthday. Even when she'd lived in L.A. she never forgot, always sent something.

Well, there were other women out there who could remember a birthday, other women with blond hair. None as beautiful as Cecily Sterling, but, hey, he didn't need drop-dead gorgeous. He didn't have to have the prettiest girl in town.

But he wanted her like a fish wanted water. What was he going to do?

"Daddy, what were you building?" Serena persisted.

"Nothing, princess."

"Timing," his mother said.

"What's that supposed to mean?" he said irritably.

"Maybe the timing isn't right."

He picked up his menu and glared at his options. The timing never seemed to be right for them. It probably never would be.

* * *

Devon stopped by The Man Cave on his way home from work.

"How was the first day on the job?" Todd asked.

"It was okay," Devon said with a shrug. "It's money."

"Not the same as pitching a no-hitter," Todd said and handed him a beer.

"Not the same as having your own business, being in charge of your own life."

"Not as much responsibility, either," Todd pointed out. "You collect your paycheck, you go home and you forget about work."

"Until you get laid off."

"A lot less hassle than losing your shirt."

His brother was right about that. Still, someday he wanted some kind of business of his own. He wanted to be successful. And he didn't want to have to worry about getting fired over being late for work. Masters had been decent about it when Devon explained, but Devon knew he wouldn't like him making a habit of it.

"Everything went okay, right?"

"Oh, yeah. Once I got there. My alarm didn't go off."

"I heard it."

"You did? Why didn't you come wake me up?" Devon demanded.

"What, do I look like Mom? Anyway, I figured you heard it, and I rolled over and went back to sleep."

"Guess I'll have to turn the volume up higher," Devon said. "The lady cop stopped me on Icicle Creek Road."

Todd shook his head over his brother's bad luck. "She give you a ticket?"

"Let me off with a warning."

"Tilda? You're kidding."

"Nope."

"She never lets anyone off with a warning."

Devon took a slug of beer and digested that information. "She got a boyfriend?"

Todd shook his head again. "She was going out with one of our local firefighters for a while, but they broke up." He looked suspiciously at Devon. "Why are you asking?"

"I'm thinking maybe I'll take her to that street dance that's coming up."

"You and the cop?" Todd scoffed. "Does she know how many DUIs you've had?"

"That's ancient history."

"Not *that* ancient."

"But it's in the past." He'd treated his trashed shoulder with alcohol. Driven buzzed more than once. Got caught more than once. That was the old Devon, though. He was done with that stuff. New town, new start, new Devon.

Todd raised a hand. "Just sayin'. And it wasn't too long ago that you hit me over the head with a beer bottle."

"But I didn't drive."

"Thanks to the Icicle Falls Police giving you a ride to the station."

Devon frowned. "You gonna bring up every mistake I ever made?"

"No, just the ones that prove my point. Tilda's not your type. Anyway, the cops will all be working the street dance."

"Maybe I'll work on her while she's working the dance," Devon said with a grin.

"And maybe you're nuts," Todd said. "But go ahead. Be my guest."

"You think I can't get her."

"I'm thinking, why would you want her? They don't come any tougher than Tilda."

"Tough on the outside, soft on the inside. Anyway, if I stick around, I'm not planning on staying celibate."

His brother chuckled. "On second thought, go ahead. It's about time you met your match. Try and mess with Tilda, and she'll cut your heart out and eat it for breakfast."

Okay, maybe not. Devon wanted some female attention, but he didn't want to get pistol-whipped.

Still, Tilda the cop was pretty hot, and different from any other woman he'd ever met.

"I think she likes me," he said. Yeah, he decided, he'd show up at the street dance and see what happened.

The night of the street dance arrived, and with her sister out of town, Bailey felt free to actually show up in the light of day. Strolling along the edge of the crowd, holding hands with Todd, she felt like the luckiest woman in the world. Well, until she'd see one or other of her sister's friends. Then she felt as if she should have a big, red *R,* for rat, on her chest.

"Hey, what's with the frown?" Todd asked.

"Nothing," Bailey said, trying to sound cheery.

"You're feeling guilty," he said. "Cut it out."

"I can't help it."

He pulled her to him. "Yeah, you can. Think about

how good we are together, think about how great your tea shop is going to be."

She managed a smile.

"That's better," he said. "Now stop worrying about your sister."

That was the wrong thing to say. It started her brooding about her sister all over again. "She didn't even say goodbye."

"She's pissed. Give her time."

How much time? At the rate they were going, it would be years before they spoke again. If she and Todd ever got married, would Cec even come to the wedding?

Oh, no, there was Cecily's best bud, Charley, with her husband, Dan Masters.

Bailey gave Todd's arm a tug. "Let's go get some shaved ice."

But it was too late. Dan was already calling hello to Todd. Trapped.

"Hey, your brother's working out great," Dan greeted him.

"Glad to hear it," Todd said. "Hi, Charley."

"Hi," Bailey said, too.

"Hi," Charley said in return. Her voice was as full of warmth as a freezer.

Oh, this was uncomfortable. Beyond uncomfortable. This was awful. Under different circumstances, Charley would have asked how the tea shop was coming along, but now she just stood next to her husband, tight-lipped and unfriendly. *Get me out of here,* thought Bailey.

At that moment Todd's brother, Devon, sauntered up. "This is some show," he said, looking around.

"It's a town tradition," Dan told him. "You can't live in Icicle Falls and not come to the street dance."

"Oh, there's Chita," Charley said. "I need to talk to her about book club." And with that she moved away, leaving her husband to say a quick goodbye and follow her.

"She hates me," Bailey said miserably.

"Who could hate you?" Devon asked.

"Lots of people," Bailey responded with a sigh.

"I don't believe it," Devon said.

"This'll blow over," Todd assured her with a hug.

Just then Tilda the cop strolled by. She was in uniform and looking stern as usual.

Devon stopped her with a wave. "Hey, lady cop, I've got a problem."

"I'm sure you do."

"I don't have anybody to dance with."

"I'm not surprised," she said and started to walk on.

He took a step backward. "I'd love to know what you look like out of that uniform."

"Yeah?"

"Yeah."

"Well, don't get your hopes up," she said, then strode off.

Devon gave a cocky nod. "She's into me."

"I can tell," Todd said.

Devon's attempt to flirt with Tilda had been a great diversion, and for a moment Bailey forgot that she was a rotten sister and actually smiled. Until she glanced across the crowd and saw Charley and Chita, Cecily's posse, staring daggers at her.

"I want to go home," she said to Todd.

He followed her gaze and frowned. "Never mind them."

The band was an eighties revival group, and now they were playing "What a Feeling."

"Come on," Todd said. "Let's dance."

They did, and they kept right on dancing through "Kiss on My List," and by the time the band started playing "I Wanna Dance with Somebody," Bailey was enjoying herself.

There was nobody else she wanted to dance with. Todd knew how to move a girl. He twirled her like a puppet master, and when he drew her close so she could feel the hard, muscled planes of his body and smiled at her as if she were the only woman in the world, it got her endorphins dancing, too. Every move felt choreographed, as if they'd been dance partners for years instead of a few short minutes.

"That was fantastic," she said as they finally went in search of shaved ice to cool off.

"I try," he said, not really sounding humble.

"Bailey!" called a male voice.

She turned to see Brandon moving her way through the crowd. No girlfriend, though. Where was Arielle the Amazing?

He'd caught up to them now. "Thought I'd find you here somewhere," he said.

Todd put an arm around her shoulders as if to remind her of his presence.

"Hi, Brandon," she said. "Have you met Todd Black?"

Brandon's gaze slipped from the hand holding her possessively to Todd's face. "You own the tavern, right?"

"That's right," Todd said, and his hand caressed

Bailey's upper arm. "Where's Arielle?" Bailey asked. "Didn't she come with you?"

Brandon frowned. "She had some stuff going on. We're... I'm not sure things are working out between us."

Only a couple of months ago, Bailey would have heard that and felt she'd won the love lotto. After years of on-again, off-again idiocy, all she felt now was sorry for him.

"Gosh, I'm sorry," she said.

He shrugged. "I guess it wasn't meant to be." He looked at her wistfully. "I guess I should have..."

"Yeah, you should have," Todd said, taking up the slack. "You snooze, you lose, pal." And with that he started moving toward the shaved-ice booth, drawing Bailey along with him.

"'Bye," she called over her shoulder. Then to Todd, "That was kind of rude. I mean, we weren't done talking."

"Oh, yeah, we were. I know that trick. Play on a woman's sympathy. It's a sure way to get laid."

Bailey scowled at him. "We've known each other for years."

"And you never got together."

Define "got together." Bailey nibbled her lower lip.

Todd's shrewd look made her blush. "So, you were his booty-call babe."

That sounded terrible. "No," she protested.

He shook his head. "What a jerk."

"You've never made a booty call?"

"Okay, I've been a jerk, too. But it's not right. It's never right to use someone. And if he'd really appreciated you, he'd have done something about it long before this." Todd leaned down and kissed her. "Anyway, you were meant to be with me."

He said it as though it were an irrefutable fact. That was fine with her.

Until they ran into Cass Wilkes. "I don't see your sister anywhere," Cass said.

"She went to L.A. to visit friends," Bailey explained. *And to get away from me.*

Bailey could tell the moment Cass put two and two together and realized that three must have been a crowd. "Oh, well, um, have fun," she said and hurried off.

How could she have fun now? What was her sister doing tonight? Was she wishing she was back in Icicle Falls? Was she wishing her sister, the man-stealer, had never come to town?

Bailey lost her appetite for shaved ice and, after a few bites, tossed the rest in the garbage.

"Let's go dance again," Todd said.

Now the band began to play "You Give Love a Bad Name," and suddenly Bailey didn't want to dance anymore. Stealing her sister's boyfriend. Did it get any badder than that?

"This was so not a good idea," she said as Todd followed her down the street, away from the revelers. "I'm a terrible sister," she added and burst into tears.

He caught her by the arm and pulled her to him. "You're a bad sister for falling in love? You *are* falling in love, aren't you?" he asked softly and put a finger under her chin, lifting her face so she could look at him.

She nodded. There was no sense denying it. He

could see it in her eyes. He'd probably seen it in her eyes right from the start.

"I can promise you that things will work out for your sister."

"How do you know?" she demanded miserably.

"I'm observant. Trust me. She's going to be okay, and so are we." And to prove it, he kissed her.

It was better than anything she'd imagined. He turned her into a human flambé. She was going to melt right here in his arms.

"Want to see some fireworks?" he whispered.

"Where?"

"Back at my place," he said with a grin.

Fireworks with Todd. She should feel guilty. She should feel bad for Cecily.

Cecily who?

Chapter Nineteen

"Spend tomorrow with me," Todd urged when he dropped Bailey off at Samantha's house.

She'd happily spend not only the next day but also the rest of her life with him. "We always have a family barbecue on the Fourth, and then we go watch the fireworks together."

"Oh, that's right," he said, pulling away a little. "The perfect family."

"We are," Bailey insisted. At least they had been until she and Cecily started fighting. If Cec had been in town, it would have been impossible for her to bring Todd.

"Babe, there's no such thing."

"Why don't you come over for the barbecue and see for yourself?" she suggested.

"Okay, I will. I want to see a so-called perfect family close up."

"You can bring your brother, too."

"What, so you guys can see an *im*perfect family close up?"

"You're not all that imperfect, are you?" she teased.

"Yeah, we are. And my brother's a royal pain in the ass. But I love the guy," he said with a shrug.

"So, what time and how much beer do you want me to bring?"

She told him, then indulged herself with one last kiss. But once she left him, she couldn't help remembering his cynical comment. Maybe there *was* no such thing as a perfect family.

Hers came close, though. They'd always enjoyed each other and been there for each other.

Except now they weren't. Well, two of them weren't, anyway. She was getting together with a great guy, but this current situation with her sister sure took the shine off of her newfound joy.

Samantha was already in bed when Bailey slipped in the front door. These days Sammy never stayed awake past ten. Blake was in the family room, watching TV. Bailey could have joined him, but she opted for going up to her room.

She was now sharing space with a crib and a baby dresser. She'd have to move out in a few months. Once the tea shop was open, she could fix up the top story of the house to live in. She smiled, envisioning herself living there with Todd someday. Or maybe in his house... The corners of her mouth turned down. If only her sister would forgive her.

She should. After all, a girl couldn't help whom she fell in love with. And it wasn't like Cec to hold a grudge. Yes, they'd had their moments growing up, but in spite of that, they'd always been close.

It was Cecily who'd listened to her teenage woes when Brandon Wallace had broken her heart, Cecily who'd told her he wasn't right for her when he raised her hopes again once they were grown-ups. And, as kids, whenever Samantha had gone on a big-sister rampage over Bailey getting into her things, Cecily had stepped in as mediator. Samantha had told Bailey there was no Santa Claus. Cecily had told her that of course there was, allowing her to believe for another couple of years.

But Bailey had done her part for her sister, too. In high school she'd baked cookies for Cecily when her boyfriends came over, and when they lived in L.A. she'd catered different events for Cecily's business, charging her only the cost of food. She'd been happy to help her sister. And Cec had been happy to help *her*, sending business her way whenever possible.

How could they erase that history? They couldn't. Her sister was angry now, but eventually she'd forgive her.

"She will, won't she?" Bailey asked her mother the next day as she and her mother and sister sat on Samantha's deck drinking lemonade. Blake and Todd and his brother were setting up the croquet course in the backyard with Blake's father supervising.

"Of course she will," Muriel said. "It's going to take some time, but she'll come around."

"I wanted her to be at the grand opening," Bailey said. They were always there for each other in big, momentous things. Heck, they'd all pulled together to plan the town's first chocolate festival. Her sisters had brought her home when her catering business failed. Surely Cecily would come to give moral support when she launched this new business.

That was an unrealistic expectation, she thought sadly. She'd ruined her sister's love life. Why should she come?

"She'll be there," Samantha said in a tone of voice that implied much sisterly bullying.

"I don't know if she's ever going to forgive me," Bailey said. What if she didn't? What would happen to their family then?

"You're not the one who dumped her," Samantha said.

That made Todd sound like a jerk. "It wasn't working between them," Bailey said in his defense. Or was it hers?

Her mother patted her arm. "Let's give the dust a chance to settle."

When Todd kissed her, she could convince herself that what they had was all that mattered in the world, but here with her family, seeing one of them missing and knowing why—well, it put a whole different color on the situation, sucking out the sunshine and turning her new relationship a dingy gray.

Blake's mother, who'd been in the house, joined them now, and that ended the conversation. Not that there was anything left to say.

"We're ready," Blake called. "Come on down here and take your beating."

As far as Bailey was concerned, she'd already taken a beating.

But later that evening as she and Todd sat on a blanket on the banks of the Wenatchee River, watching the fireworks explode overhead, his arm draped over her shoulder, she decided any beating she had to take from her sister was worth it. Anyway, Cecily had been in the business of love. Deep down, she understood. She had to.

* * *

"If you don't need me, I think I'm going to stay down here a little longer," Cecily said to Samantha on the phone.

"We can manage. How long?"

"A couple of weeks or so," Cecily said vaguely as she poured herself a glass of orange juice and went out onto her friend Margo's apartment balcony to soak up some rays.

Silence reigned on the other end of the call. Then her sister asked cautiously, "You're not thinking of moving back there, are you?"

It had crossed her mind. But, "No," she said. She'd fallen in love with Icicle Falls all over again, and, really, there was no place else she wanted to live. She just had to figure out how she was going to live there and watch her sister and Todd build a life together.

"Well, that's a relief. We need you."

"You could find anyone to run the chocolate festival and do your advertising," Cecily said.

"I wasn't talking about Sweet Dreams. I was talking about our family. You're coming back for Bailey's grand opening next month, aren't you?"

"I'll try," Cecily said diplomatically.

"You'd better do more than try," said Samantha, now in bossy big-sister mode. "I don't want to have to deal with the fallout if you don't. This kind of stuff isn't good for expectant mothers."

"Playing that card again?" Cecily teased.

"It's the only one I've got. Seriously, I know you want to bitch-slap Bailey right now."

"Oh, that's too kind," Cecily said lightly. "I was thinking more in terms of murder."

"Bad idea. Mom would get mad."

"Yeah, that's probably true."

"It's on the tenth."

"I know," Cecily assured her. Bailey had talked about the date often enough.

"Okay," Samantha said, and her tone of voice added, "Don't let me down." They chatted a few more minutes, then Samantha said, "I've got to go. I need to talk with Luke about boosting production on our chocolate garden set."

Luke. If she'd picked him instead of Todd, both she and Bailey would be happy now. And why was it she hadn't chosen Luke? Oh, yeah, that pesky chemistry thing. *This is what you get for being picky,* she told herself as she looked out at a sea of buildings baking under sun-drenched smog. *Oh, yeah, I'm having fun. Wish I wasn't here.*

It was tea party time at Muriel Sterling-Wittman's house with Olivia Wallace, Dot Morrison, Pat Wilder, Janice Lind and Bailey in attendance. All the goodies being served were in the running for the Tea Time menu, and Bailey had called in the town experts for advice.

"You have to serve this lavender cake," Olivia said. "It's heavenly."

Dot shook her head. "I'm partial to the carrot cake, myself."

"Maybe I should serve both," Bailey said.

"Don't make your menu too extensive," Olivia cautioned.

"And remember, you can always change your menu,

make substitutions, if you feel like you're getting tired of the same thing," Janice said.

"Except people will develop favorites and expect to see them when they come in," Dot pointed out. "Do the two cakes, the scones and those chocolate cookies. You need the chocolate cookies for the chocolate tea."

"I agree," Muriel said.

"But what about the lavender sugar cookies?" Bailey asked.

"I think you've got enough lavender items without them," Dot replied.

"No, but she needs those cookies for her afternoon-tea plate," Olivia said, and Dot capitulated with a shrug.

"I think you could eliminate the ham sandwiches," Pat suggested.

"I wondered if I should have them because they're sort of English," Bailey said.

"Go with the salmon instead. More of a fit for this area," Dot advised.

Olivia took another bite of cake. "Really, I could eat an entire lavender cake in one sitting." She smiled at Bailey. "You're going to have a success on your hands."

Bailey certainly hoped so. She thought of all the time and energy and money that had gone into this business. If it failed...

"That sister of yours better come back for the grand opening," Dot said sternly, looking at Muriel as if she could still control her grown daughter.

The other women seemed as uncomfortable as Bailey felt, but her mother smiled serenely and said, "I'm sure she'll be here. The Sterlings always stick together."

Correction: the Sterlings always *had* stuck together. Bailey had called her sister several times, but Cecily never picked up. What if Cecily never talked to her again? Sudden tears stung her eyes.

"Now look what you've done," Olivia scolded Dot. She patted Bailey's hand. "Everything will be fine, honey. You'll see."

"And your tea shop is going to be a smashing success, kiddo," Dot added. "Sorry I even mentioned your sister, even if she is being a brat."

"These situations have a way of working out," Pat said in a comforting voice.

She smiled at Mama, and Bailey remembered the story about how Pat and her mother had fallen out over a man. They'd patched things up. Could she and Cecily do that, too?

Bailey and Todd sat at a table in Pancake Haus going over their to-do lists. "The Facebook page is great," he said. "I got hungry looking at all those pictures of food."

"And you saw how many likes we've got. I think everyone in Icicle Falls has liked us." All except for one sister, who was still in California...

"Yeah, not a bad start. So, you're done hiring?" he asked, pulling back her thoughts before they could wander any further into the bog of misery.

She swallowed a mouthful of pancake and nodded. "Yep. I actually lured Ginny away from the deli. She was looking for a change and wants to maybe have a shop of her own someday, so she figured this would be a good learning experience. She'll help me in the kitchen before we open and then ring up sales. I've also hired a full-time server, and Amber Wilkes will come in to help on Saturdays."

"How about a dishwasher? Oh, yeah. That's going to be me."

Bailey laughed. "You did say we needed to stay on budget."

"Me and my big mouth," he joked as Dot Morrison came over to greet them.

"Are you two all ready for your grand opening?"

"We're getting there," Bailey said.

"Well, put me down as a yes. I'm coming with Olivia."

Bailey brought up her guest list on her iPad and checked off Dot's name.

"I've got to hand it to you Sterling girls. You're a clever bunch." Dot pointed a finger at Todd. "And you, Mr. Hot Stuff, are lucky to get one of them."

Todd shrugged. "I had to settle, Dot, since you wouldn't go out with me."

"Didn't want to wear you out, kid," Dot cracked. "You'd never have been able to keep up."

"Hey, she's right," Todd said as Dot sauntered off in the direction of the kitchen. "I hope I have half as much energy at her age."

"She's inspiring," Bailey agreed. "And she's sure had a lot of good advice. Everyone at the chamber has been helpful."

"They know the importance of sticking together."

That made Bailey think of Cecily all over again. Samantha had promised her that Cec was coming back in time for their gala opening. She hoped Sammy knew what she was talking about.

* * *

It hadn't been all smog and misery for Cecily. She'd had a good time. Yes, indeed. Days at the beach lying on a towel reading romance novels and flirting with surfers, dancing at trendy clubs, seeing friends, paying for dinners out with friends (which had about broken the bank).

Oh, who was she kidding? Reading about fictional happy endings was getting old, and none of the surfers held her interest. She sweltered in the heat and missed the fresh mountain air. She'd go out to a restaurant and speculate about who was at Zelda's. Or go dancing and wish she was two-stepping at The Red Barn or, even worse, remember what a good dancer Todd was. Every man she met was only interested in hooking up, and the only topic of conversation at parties was who was seeing whom and which men had the most money. Oh, and what movie project had been greenlighted. She was living at the shallow end of the pool. Still, L.A. was an exciting place, full of energy. Not everyone here was shallow. What was wrong with her? Why was she just seeing the negatives?

Any place can be great if you're with people you care about. Where had she heard that before? Oh, yeah, Luke. It looked as though he was right. No wonder she was feeling restless. The people she cared about most weren't here. They were in Icicle Falls. No matter what, heartbreak or happiness, that was where she belonged.

"The chocolates are boxed up for the tea shop," Luke reported to Samantha. "I'm sending Jimmy over there with them this morning."

"Thanks," Samantha said. "Bailey wants to have everything in place by this afternoon."

"So, she's all ready for the big unveiling tomorrow."

"Yes, and it looks wonderful. You'll have to come and bring your mom and Serena."

"Oh, yeah," he said. "I have a feeling Serena's going to be a regular customer." Then he casually added, "I assume Cecily's coming back for this."

"She'll be there," Samantha said, and he could hear the steel in her voice.

Cecily's sudden vacation had come as a surprise to a lot of the Sweet Dreams staff but not to Luke. He knew exactly why she'd left town. He understood her need to lick her wounds, but enough was enough. It was time to come home.

It was also time to settle what should have been settled long ago. He'd been a wimp and let her dangle him like a fish on a hook. Of course, he had no one to blame for that but himself. He'd taken the bait. He could have looked around for another woman.

And yet, although he'd tried to convince himself otherwise, he didn't want another woman—not when he knew that he and Cecily would be good together. He had no idea why she didn't see that. She was supposed to be the expert in these things. As far as he was concerned, he was through with trusting the expert.

"You should have stayed longer," Cecily's friend Margo said as Cecily followed her out to the car, pulling her suitcase behind. "How am I going to find my perfect match without you here to guide me?"

Margo never listened to her when it came to men, so Cecily considered that a moot question.

"I mean, when's the last time you had a vacation?"

Cecily hadn't felt the need for one. She'd enjoyed

working at the Sweet Dreams office, and the days had run smoothly together. "A while, but this visit has been like three vacations. I need to go home to recover. Anyway, I have to get back for the opening of my sister's tea shop."

Much as she wanted to stay away, she knew she couldn't. She was far from excited about seeing Bailey and Todd together, but family solidarity was important, and if she didn't show up her mother would not be happy. That was the main reason she was doing this. She didn't want to disappoint Mom. After losing two husbands, her daughters were all she had, and regardless of what Cecily felt about her sister, she was determined to keep up appearances for Mom's sake.

And she needed to catch this flight. She should have booked an earlier one. This would be cutting it close, and if she missed the opening, it would really be ugly.

"Let's just hope she doesn't poison anyone this time around," Margo said callously as they got in her convertible. She gave her long, blond hair a flip and started the car, and Cecily surreptitiously checked the time on her cell phone. They should have left an hour ago, but it had been hard to get Margo moving after their late night out.

Margo must have seen her because she said, "Don't worry. You'll make your flight."

Who was she kidding? Freeway traffic was constipated, even this early on a Saturday morning, and they crawled along. "You're gonna make it," Margo said again half an hour later as they inched forward.

How many miles had they gone? Two? Cecily pressed her lips together and stared out the window. Why hadn't she arranged different transportation to the airport?

By the time they got to LAX, she had ten minutes to clear security and reach her gate.

"You'll be fine," Margo said as they air-kissed goodbye. "Call me when you need a break from Small Town, U.S.A."

Cecily thanked her and hurried to the nearest curbside check-in.

That ate up six of her precious minutes. And she still had to get through airport security. She looked at the line. She'd never make it. No way was she going to get back to Icicle Falls in time for Bailey's grand opening.

With a sigh she pulled out her driver's license and her e-ticket and went to the end of the line. If she got any flight out that would get her to Seattle in time, it would be a miracle. She should probably call Samantha and let her know.

Except she didn't want to have to tell Sam, Ms. Organized, that she'd missed her flight. She sure didn't want to tell her mother. The very idea of having to hear the disappointment in her mother's voice made her queasy. And what made her even sicker was the suspicion that she'd actually *wanted* to miss this flight, that she wanted, in some small, spiteful way, to rain on Bailey's parade.

She moved slowly behind a young family returning from Disneyland (the mouse ears on the two little boys were a big clue) and prayed that somewhere in this huge airport there would be an airline that could get her out of here.

Two women came up behind her. "Look at this line," one said in disgust.

Cecily's sentiments exactly.

"I'll be glad when we get to Seattle," said the other. "Poor Linda."

"Awful to lose someone like that."

Like what?

"It just goes to show, you never know when it's your time."

"But to have her die so suddenly, and them not speaking. God, I bet she feels guilty."

"I'm dying for an iced coffee," said one of the women, and that turned the subject in a whole new direction.

Cecily never got to hear any more about Linda and the sudden death of the mysterious person with whom she'd been on the outs, but she got the underlying message loud and clear. She really needed to make that flight.

Chapter Twenty

WELCOME TO TEA TIME

We hope you'll come often to enjoy our specially chosen selection of teas and accompanying goodies, all made with love. Here's what you'll find on the menu.

Afternoon Teas:

Lavender Tea:
   Lavender-white chocolate scones with Devonshire cream & lavender honey
   Lavender sugar cookies
   Chocolate cookies
   Tea sandwiches

Chocolate Tea:
   Chocolate delight cookies
   Chocolate cake
   Lavender-white chocolate scones

Chocolate fondue, featuring seasonal fruits

À la Carte:
Chicken curry sandwich
Salmon salad sandwich
Smoked salmon quiche

Chocolate cake
Lavender cake
Carrot orange cake
Blackberry scones
Lavender–white chocolate scones

Teas:
Lady Grey
Lavender Earl Grey
Orange Pekoe
Mixed Berry
Jasmine
Green
Chamomile
Chocolate Mint

By Saturday at one-thirty, everything was ready for the grand opening, which was really going to be more of an open house. People would be able to purchase items, but today the eats were on Bailey and Todd. They'd be offering samples from the menu, as well as a list of the teas and foods that would be served.

The Sterling family stood in the middle of Tea Time Tea Shop, admiring Bailey's handiwork. "This is lovely, darling," said her mother, taking in the tables covered with lace tablecloths and topped with small vases filled with daisies and pink carnations.

A pink ceramic wall clock shaped like a teapot hung on one wall, and the anniversary clock her mother had gotten for her sat on top of the glass display case that housed a mouthwatering array of baked goodies and Sweet Dreams chocolates. In the shop section, all manner of teapots, tea accessories and fancy jams and teas were displayed on shelves and on little white tables decorated with vintage crocheted doilies.

At one point Bailey had talked with Cecily about selling some of her homemade lavender sachets. There were no sachets anywhere on the shelves. And there was no sign of Cecily.

"Cec said she was going to be here, right?" she asked Samantha for the tenth time.

Her sister frowned. "That's what she said."

A knock on the front door raised her hopes, until she opened it and found Kevin from Lupine Floral bearing a gigantic floral arrangement.

"A little something from Heinrich and me for your big day," he said as she let him in. "Oh, look at this," he gushed as he handed it over. "You are going to do such fabulous business!"

She thanked him and set the arrangement on the glass display case. "I hope you're going to stay for our party."

"Oh, darling, free food? Just try and keep me away. And I'm going to insist Heinrich tear himself away from his workroom and come see this. It's simply divine."

A fresh knock on the door shot her hopes up again.

It was Todd, and he, too, had flowers from Lupine Floral. "Long time no see," he joked with Kevin. Then he turned to Bailey. "You look great," he said, nodding at her simple green summer dress and vintage ruffled apron. "Fresh as a…"

"Daisy," she supplied. She felt more like a *wilted* daisy. She'd been working here since eight, getting everything ready, and had run back to Samantha's house only to freshen up and change. Normally, excitement would have carried her along, but her disappointment over not seeing Cecily had sapped her energy.

"I'm thinking more 'cream puff.' In fact, you look good enough to eat," he whispered and kissed her.

Her kiss must have been as wilted as she felt. Todd studied her. "What's wrong?"

"Nothing," she lied, trying to sound perky.

He glanced around, seeing Samantha and Muriel and Blake, all checking out the merchandise. "Where's Cec?" he asked, frowning.

Bailey's eyes filled with tears, and she shook her head.

His frown deepened, and his jaw tightened. "Well, never mind. This is going to be great." He set the flowers next to the arrangement from Lupine Floral and said hello to the rest of the family, then returned to her. "What do you want me to do?"

In light of all the cash he'd laid out and all the manual labor, she said, "Nothing. You can help me talk this place up."

"That won't be hard. I'd say it speaks for itself."

"I hope so." She really wanted her tea shop to succeed.

She also really wanted her sister here, but that was

out of her control. She slipped into the kitchen to see how Amber and Ginny were doing as they finished prepping the serving trays.

They, too, were wearing vintage aprons. Ginny smiled at Bailey as she entered the kitchen. "Don't worry," she said. "We're just about done."

A mix of vintage china and silver serving platters covered every inch of counter space, all loaded with scones and cookies and tea sandwiches. And Bailey had more in containers in the cooler to replenish the supply. Two large drink dispensers filled with lemonade and lavender iced tea stood ready to quench visitors' thirsts.

"We can handle this," Ginny said, giving her a little push back into the main room. "Get out there and open the door."

It was time. Bailey's palms suddenly felt damp. She wiped them on her apron and went to let people in.

Olivia Wallace was the first to show up. She came bearing a card and the Bless This Kitchen sign that had hung in her kitchen at the Icicle Creek Lodge. "My kitchen has been blessed," she said, kissing Bailey's cheek. "Now it's time to pass the blessing on."

Bailey hugged her. "Thank you, Olivia," she whispered. "For everything."

"You're going to do really well. I just know it," Olivia said, patting her cheek.

Right behind her came Dot Morrison. "Hey, kiddo, it's gorgeous in here," she said and handed Bailey a card. She lowered her voice. "There's a little something in there for unexpected business expenses."

Knowing Dot, that "little something" would be a

big something. Bailey hugged her, too. "Dot, you're the best."

"You got that right," Dot cracked and went to join Olivia and Muriel.

Ginny and Amber put out the goodies as more people flooded in. Her mother's admirer, Arnie Amundsen, brought flowers. So did Todd's brother, Devon.

"Whoever painted your outside trim sure did a good job," he said with a wink.

"You were a big help," she told him, "especially with hanging the lace curtains."

"Don't say that too loud," he said, pretending to recoil in horror.

She kissed him on the cheek.

At that moment Todd arrived at her side, and Devon held up both hands. "I wasn't hitting on your girl. I promise."

Tina Swift came next, bringing some lace doilies. "I thought you could use these on your tables." She looked around, studying everything. "It's so pretty in here. You're going to be turning people away."

"Thanks," Bailey said, as she thought, *Thank you for firing me.* Now, instead of working in someone else's shop, she had her own business.

Ed York and Pat Wilder came bearing more flowers, and Stacy Morris, who had recently opened Timeless Treasures Gifts and Antiques, brought Bailey a chintz teapot. The gifts and guests kept arriving—Cass Wilkes, Charley and Dan Masters, Chita and Ken Wolfe, Elena from the Sweet Dreams office, Gerhardt Geissel from Gerhardt's Gasthaus. In fact, everyone from the chamber of commerce was on hand to help celebrate. The place was getting packed. But where was Cecily?

Bailey hugged and shook hands with well-wishers and smiled, all the while watching the door for her sister. She wasn't going to come, and as time passed it became increasingly difficult to keep that smile in place. This day should have tasted so sweet, but her sister's boycott made it sour as lemons.

"Please, call her," Bailey begged Samantha.

"I have. She's not answering her cell." Samantha looked both sad and angry. "There's nothing we can do right now. Don't let this spoil your day."

Too late. It already had.

Cecily found her car at the Sea-Tac airport parking lot and put her suitcase in the car trunk, then fell behind the wheel. She'd gotten a flight out, but it had been cursed. The kid sitting next to her hadn't gotten to his air-sickness bag in time and had used Cecily's lap instead. She'd cleaned off as best she could but still smelled faintly like barf. She'd have to change when she got home. What was the traffic like? She'd check Google Maps on her phone and see.

Her phone! Where was her phone?

Bailey's mouth ached from smiling, but not as badly as her heart ached. All the compliments and good wishes in the world couldn't make up for the fact that she'd lost her sister. She went into the kitchen to get another serving tray of cookies and discovered Todd on his cell.

"I don't care how pissed you are at me. Get your butt over here."

She came up and laid a hand on his arm, making him jump and his face turn red. "Oh. Hi. I had to make a call."

"I heard. It's really sweet of you, but it won't work. She's not coming."

"She's a bitch."

"No, she's not. She's never been like this."

"Well, the new her is no improvement," Todd said furiously. "She's ruining this day for you."

Ruining someone's day was probably nothing compared to ruining someone's life—and that was what she'd done to her sister.

The crowd ebbed and flowed. Luke Goodman arrived with his mother and little girl. She heard him asking Samantha, "Where's Cec? I thought she was coming back for this?"

"She was supposed to," Samantha said, her voice peppered with irritation.

She wasn't coming. Bailey got the message loud and clear. *I'm through with you.*

They couldn't go on like this. A sister wasn't just a sister. She was also a best friend, someone you stayed connected with all your life. Bailey couldn't allow that connection to be broken permanently. And there was only one way to fix it.

She sneaked out onto the back porch with her cell. Of course, she got voice mail. Her eyes stung with tears as she spoke. "Cec, I'm sorry. Please, forgive me. I'll do anything to make things right. I…I love Todd, but I can't be with him like this, not with us never speaking. I'll do anything you ask. I'll leave town. I'll—"

"No, you won't," said an angry voice behind her.

Todd snatched the phone out of her hand and ended the call. "Damn it all, Bailey, did you mean that or didn't you? Do you love me?"

Tears were pouring down her face now. "Yes," she cried. "I do. But…"

"No buts. Do you think you can just shut this off like a faucet, that if you leave I won't follow you? I'm not some—" he threw his hands up in the air "—pair of shoes you borrowed and didn't give back. You can't hand me off."

"I don't know what to do," Bailey wailed. "She's my *sister*."

"Then she'd better start acting like one," he growled. Bailey was sobbing in earnest now, and he took her in his arms and softened his voice. "Come on, now. Don't cry. You don't want to ruin your big day worrying about something that's going to work out."

"It's too late. It's already ruined," she said.

"Only if you let it."

She looked up at him. He'd been a great partner and had turned into a great friend and lover. But he wasn't a sister. "I don't know how to explain," she began.

"You don't have to. I get it. Well, as much as a man can get women," he added. "But we've still got twenty minutes left. Anything could have happened. Her flight could have been delayed. She could have hit traffic."

"On a Saturday? And why didn't she call?"

He shook his head. "I don't know, but don't write her off yet. If you guys are as close as you claim to be, she'll come through."

Which was why he'd been calling her earlier? "You don't really believe that, do you?" Bailey said in a small voice.

"I want to. I hope she doesn't let us down. Now, we need to get out there and get back to businss."

She nodded, took the tissue he gave her and blew her nose. Twenty more minutes.

Back in the shop, she discovered that one final late-afternoon wave of people had rushed in. But her sister wasn't one of them. She rang up a jar of black cherry preserves for Hildy Johnson, greeted Mayor Stone and scanned the crowd. Now not only her sister was missing but Todd, as well.

Her mother was next to buy something, insisting on paying for a box of chocolate mint tea. "I think your business is going to be a success, darling," she said.

Bailey nodded and tried to smile. What good was business success if you failed with your family?

Cecily had gone home to clean up, throw on jeans and a ruffled top and was on her way to the door when someone banged on it. She opened it to find Luke Goodman standing there. "Oh, hi," she said. "I was just leaving."

"For your sister's grand opening," he supplied. "Everyone's been wondering where you were."

Cecily ducked her head, embarrassed to look him in the eye. "I had some trouble getting here." *I had some trouble getting to the point where I wanted to be here.*

"Well, the party's still going on," he said, but instead of ushering her out the door, he closed it behind him. "First, we have some business to settle." Then, before she could say anything, he pulled her against him and kissed her. It wasn't a polite kiss or even a romantic kiss. It was a force of nature, impossible to resist. And he didn't stop there; he backed her up against the wall and put his tongue to good use. She felt one of his big hands slide up her midriff, setting off her zing-o-meter. Good Lord, what was going on here? Something was catching fire, and she suspected it might be her panties.

"I don't care what you think about Todd Black and you," he said, his mouth against her cheek. "You're wrong. He's not the man for you, and, deep down, you know it. We're done playing games." He kissed her again, and then his lips began to blaze a trail down her neck while his hands went…other places. "Are we still just friends?"

Why had she thought they didn't have any chemistry together? What was wrong with her? Oh, yeah, that half-a-brain thing. "Maybe I was wrong," she said faintly.

"No 'maybe' about it."

Now there was a fresh banging at the front door. Luke swore and yanked it open.

There stood Todd. His irritated expression turned mocking, and he gave her a cynical smile. "I don't suppose you could tear yourself away from what you're doing to come to your sister's grand opening."

"We were just on our way," Cecily said with as much dignity as she could muster.

"Nice of you to let someone know," Todd snapped. "Do you have any idea how many people have left messages on your cell?"

"I lost it on the plane," she said as they started for the stairs to the parking lot.

Todd shook his head and shot down the stairs ahead of them. "Yeah, and the dog ate my homework."

"It's true!" Cecily insisted.

"Whatever," he said.

"Remind me what I ever saw in you," she muttered to his back.

"My charm," he growled.

"Come on," Luke said. "I'll drive you over." Once they were in his hybrid, he echoed, "I don't know what you saw in that guy."

Blind. She'd been blind.

"You and I—we're not done," he added.

"That's fine with me."

The angry caveman expression had vanished, and now he was the honest, kind family man she'd known for years, smiling tenderly at her. "You remember I had a crush on you in high school?" he murmured.

"Why didn't you do something about it back then?"

"I could never quite get up the nerve. Anyway, you always had a boyfriend." He shrugged. "Then you moved away, and I moved on. And I was happy. I had a great marriage. But once I lost her—" He stopped for a moment, getting control of himself. "It's been hard. and when you came back to town, I thought, *Here's my chance*. I decided to try again." He gnawed his lip for a minute. "I'm not a mover and shaker like Blake. I'm not the best-looking guy in town."

"Way to sell yourself," she teased.

They were on Lavender Lane now. He parked his car and turned to face her. "I'm a regular guy—that's all. But there's nothing I won't do to make you happy. We could be good together, and after we're done with this party I'm going to show you just *how* good."

That sent a tingle shooting up her spine. Her mother had been right. Cecily had found someone who was perfect for her, and he'd been there under her nose all along.

Bailey must have seen her coming because Cecily had barely started up the front walk when her sister hurtled down it toward her. She picked up her pace, and they ran into each other's arms, both crying and saying, "I'm sorry."

"I thought I'd lost you as my sister," Bailey said around her sobs. "I'm sorry."

"Me, too. I was being insecure. And you know what? I knew you two were a match, but I didn't want to admit it. Please, forgive me."

"Thank God," said Todd, who'd been directly behind them. "Maybe we can get on with the grand opening now."

Cecily and Bailey smiled at each other and, arm in arm, went back up the walk, the two men falling in behind them. "I should have figured out my own love life a lot sooner," Cecily said as they climbed the steps to the front porch, "especially when Todd talked about you being his best friend." She glanced over her shoulder and smiled at Luke.

"I'm smart that way," Todd joked, and Cecily stuck out her tongue at him.

"Really. What *did* I see in you?"

"Nothing you won't get more of with me," Luke said, opening the door for her and giving her a look that sent her zing-o-meter into orbit.

Samantha was out on the front porch now, waiting for them. "About time you got here," she said to Cecily.

"I had a problem with my flight." Actually, she'd had a whole bunch of problems, but they were fixed now.

After the last guest had left, and everything had been cleaned up, the Sterling sisters, their men and their mother all pulled extra chairs around a table by the window and sat down to talk.

"This place is going to do okay," Blake predicted. "Of course, I knew that right off when I saw your business plan," he told Todd.

"Olivia, Dot and Pat and I are going to be among your first customers," Mom said. She smiled at all three of her daughters. "I'm so proud of my girls."

Cecily realized she hadn't given her mother much to be proud of lately, and she felt the hot flush of shame on her cheeks. "Some of us don't always deserve it."

"None of us are perfect," Mom said gently.

"Wait a minute," Todd joked. "I thought this was a perfect family."

"Not hardly," Samantha said. "But we love each other anyway."

Cecily reached over and took her little sister's hand. "Yes, we do."

Loving Happily Ever After

Spring had returned to Icicle Falls, and May was in full bloom when family, friends and neighbors packed the Icicle Falls Community Church to witness the union of Cecily Sterling and Luke Goodman. The mothers of the bride and groom sat teary-eyed as little Serena Goodman walked down the aisle, scattering silk rose petals, while on Muriel's lap baby Rose Preston looked on in wide-eyed wonder. After her came Bailey Sterling, carrying a small bouquet of spring flowers and wearing a pale green sheath that showed off her auburn hair. She was wearing an engagement ring on her left hand. Next, Ella O'Brien, Cecily's friend, who'd flown in for the wedding along with her husband, Jake, walked up the aisle. Following her was Samantha, the matron of honor, dressed in chocolate-brown. Her husband, Blake, one of the groomsmen, smiled proudly. Next to him stood Todd, the future brother-in-law, also smiling.

And then came the bride in an off-the-shoulder wedding gown, her face radiant behind her veil. Everyone present later agreed that although all brides were beautiful, this one truly was the most beautiful they'd ever seen.

Jake O'Brien sang a wedding song he'd written as the couple lit a unity candle. Vows were exchanged, and finally Luke was allowed to kiss his bride. The kiss he gave her was enough to wilt every flower in the sanctuary and was rewarded with hoots and clapping.

The reception, held in the dining room at the Icicle Creek Lodge, was catered by Bailey, with the help of Olivia Wallace and her staff. Even though all the partitions had been folded back and the tables packed in, there was barely enough room to hold everyone.

Samantha gave a speech, talking about how well suited Luke and Cecily were. "Of course, with my sister's gift for matching people up, we knew she'd figure it out eventually," she added, making Cecily blush and the wedding guests chuckle.

Her speech was followed by the best man's. Luke's longtime friend Joe Coyote looked handsome in his black tux. His toast was short but to the point. "When it comes to women, some of us guys have a hard time getting it right but not Luke. You got it right again, buddy, and I know you two are gonna be happy."

Luke squeezed Cecily's hand, and her heart fluttered. Looking back, she could only shake her head at how long it had taken her to realize how special he was and how perfect for her.

Now the speeches were at an end, but there was one more that needed to be given. Cecily stood and asked for the microphone, and the surprised best man handed it over.

"I know brides don't usually give speeches at their weddings," she said, "but I want to say how thankful I am that you're all here to help us celebrate. True love

is a gift, and it's best enjoyed with friends and family."
She smiled down at Bailey. "And especially sisters."

Because in all of life's ups and downs, no matter
who loved you or who broke your heart, no matter
what you did, no matter how foolish you were, there
was one thing you could count on—you always had
your sister.

* * * * *

A Little About Tea

Hi, everyone! I'm really enjoying my tea shop. Everyone in Icicle Falls has been so supportive! Especially Cecily, who comes in and lends a hand serving when I'm short-staffed. I'm selling her lavender sachets now. We package them in vintage teacups and they're really popular. In fact, she's having a hard time keeping up with demand. I've learned a lot about tea, too. Here are a few facts you might enjoy. In England high tea is actually dinner and tends to be on the heavier side. Afternoon tea, however, is something much more fun and girlie. Afternoon teas come in three different varieties:

Cream tea, which offers tea, scones, jam and cream;
Light tea, which gives you tea, scones and sweets; and
Full tea, with tea, savories, sweets and dessert—yum!

To steep a perfect cup of tea…

Use boiling water for black, dark oolong and herbal teas. This will break down the leaf and release the flavor and antioxidants. Steep for three to five minutes. This is why, when you're using a teapot, you should have a tea cozy over it to keep everything nice and hot. Don't steep any longer than that or your tea will become too astringent. If you're making a more delicate tea such as green, green oolong or white tea, use slightly cooler water.

Serve tea…

With milk, not cream—better for the hips! Cream is too heavy and can mask the taste of the tea.

When serving lemon with tea, lemon slices are preferable to wedges—much daintier! Don't forget to provide a small fork, or lemon fork, for your guests. And never add lemon with milk since the lemon's citric acid will cause the milk to curdle.

Drink it up…

With your pinkie out. What's that about? I guess originally all porcelain teacups were made in China. They were small and had no handles. So to keep from spilling on themselves, tea drinkers had to hold the cup with the thumb at six o'clock and the index and middle fingers at twelve o'clock. Then they'd raise the pinkie for balance. Well, we're still using the pinkie for balance. Holding your pinkie finger out a little helps avoid spills.

Make time for tea because it's good for you! Tea contains polyphenols, antioxidants that repair cells and may help our bodies fight off sickness. And it's not just green tea that's good for you. Black, white and red tea also have flavonoids and polyphenols. One of my personal faves is Rooibos. So, go ahead—enjoy that cup of tea!

And here are some of my favorite recipes from Tea Time. I hope you like them.

Bailey

Lavender Honey
(Courtesy of Elizabeth Schultz)

Ingredients:
1 cup honey
1 tsp. lavender buds

Directions:
In a small pan bring the honey and lavender buds to a boil. Remove from heat and cool to room temp. Then let it rest covered for a day for the flavors to meld. Strain out the buds and store covered in a dark place.

Lavender–White Chocolate Scones

Ingredients:
2 cups flour
1 tbsp. baking powder
¼ tsp. baking soda
¼ tsp. salt
2 tsp. crushed lavender buds
⅓ cup sugar
½ cup white chocolate chips
1 stick (½ cup) butter (cold)
⅔ cup milk
lavender sugar (available in most kitchen specialty stores)

Directions:
Sift flour, baking powder, soda and salt into a large mixing bowl. Add sugar, lavender and white chocolate chips and mix. Cut in stick of butter as for piecrust, then add milk and stir with a fork until mixture becomes dough. Divide dough into two balls, then turn out onto a floured

surface, knead lightly and form into mounded rounds. Cut each round into quarters then place on an ungreased baking sheet. Sprinkle with lavender sugar and bake for 12–15 minutes at 425. Cool on wire rack. Makes 8–12, depending on the size of your scones.

Chocolate Cookies

Ingredients:
1 cup butter
½ cup granulated sugar
¼ cup cocoa
2 cups flour
½ cup mini chocolate chips
½ cup chopped nuts
1 tsp. vanilla
powdered sugar for coating

Directions:
Cream butter, sugar and vanilla. Add flour, chopped nuts and mini chocolate chips and mix well. Form into 1-inch balls and bake on ungreased cookie sheet at 350 for 10–12 minutes. Makes approximately 2 dozen.

Lavender Cake

Ingredients:
2 ¼ cups cake flour
2 ½ tsp. baking powder
1 tsp. salt
1 ½ cup sugar
1 cup milk
1 tsp. vanilla

1–1 ½ tsp. lavender buds, crushed
½ cup butter, room temperature
2 eggs
1 tbsp. oil (for added moistness)

Directions:
Sift dry ingredients into a large mixing bowl. Add sugar, butter and two-thirds of the milk and beat at medium speed for two minutes. Add remaining milk, eggs and oil and beat until blended. Pour into cake pans and bake at 350 for 25 minutes. Remove from oven when cake springs back when touched or when a toothpick inserted comes out clean.

Lavender Cake Frosting

Ingredients:
1 stick butter
1 cup granulated pure cane sugar
8 tbsp. shortening
3 tbsp. flour
⅔ cup milk at room temp
1 tsp. vanilla

Directions:
Combine, one at a time, the butter, shortening, sugar and flour, mixing well after each addition. Add milk and vanilla and beat well. Frost cake and sprinkle with lavender sugar. (Which you can purchase at most kitchen shops or lavender specialty stores.)

Acknowledgments

I enjoyed my return to Icicle Falls, and much of that is due to the people who've been with me on the journey. I want to thank Cindy Hassinger, owner of the Alpen Rose in Leavenworth, WA, for giving me insight into the business of running a place like Olivia's Icicle Creek Lodge. Cindy and her crew make it look easy! As always, I'm indebted to my wonderful editor, Paula Eykelhof, and the rest of the Harlequin team for their expertise and support and to my agent, Paige Wheeler, to whom I probably owe chocolate for life. Thanks also to the brain trust, my good pals in literary adventure: Susan Wiggs, Lois Dyer, Kate Breslin, Elsa Watson and Anjali Banerjee. Getting to work with all of you is a large part of what makes writing so fun!

Love and scandal are the best sweeteners of tea.
—Henry James

*Turn the page for an excerpt
from Sheila's upcoming book,
THE LODGE ON HOLLY ROAD.*

*Coming from Harlequin MIRA
in November 2014!*

Jolly Old Saint Nicholas

The toddler wasn't simply crying. Oh, no. These were the kind of earsplitting screams that would make the strongest department-store Santa want to run for his sleigh. Her face was a perfect match for James Claussen's red Santa suit, and both her eyes and her nose had the spigot turned on full blast.

What was he doing here sitting on this uncomfortable throne, ruling over a kingdom of fake snow, candy canes and mechanical reindeer? What had possessed him to agree to come back to work? He didn't want to be jolly, not even imitation jolly.

"Come on, Joy," coaxed the little girl's mother from her spot on the sidelines of Santa Land. "Smile for Mommy."

"Waaah," Joy responded.

I understand how you feel, James thought. "Joy—that's a pretty name for a pretty little girl. Can you give your mommy a big smile?"

"Waaah," Joy shrieked and began kicking her feet. The black patent leather shoes turned those little feet into lethal weapons. Come tomorrow, he'd have a bruise on the inside of his left thigh.

"Ho, ho, ho," James tried and the shrieks got louder.

Okay, this was as good as the picture with Santa was going to get. He stood and handed off the child, who was still kicking and crying, barely dodging an assault to the family jewels in the process. The jewels weren't so perfect now that he was sixty-six, but they were still valuable to him and he wanted to keep them.

Shauna Sullivan, his loyal elf, sent him a sympathetic look and brought over the next child, a baby girl carried by her mother. Rosy-cheeked and alert, probably just up from a nap, the baby was all dolled up in a red velvet dress with white bootees on her feet and a headband decorated with a red flower. She was old enough to smile and coo, but not quite old enough to walk or, thank God, kick Santa where it would hurt.

This baby girl reminded him of his daughter, Brooke, when she was a baby, all smiles and dimples. Big brown eyes that gazed at him in delighted wonder. Oh, those were the days, when his kids were small and Faith was still...

Don't go there.

"And what would this little dumpling like for Christmas?" he asked, settling the baby on his lap.

For a moment it looked as if she was actually concentrating on an answer. But then a sound anyone who'd had children could easily recognize, followed by a foul odor, told him she'd been concentrating on something else. Oh, man.

"Smile, Santa," Krystal the photographer teased, and the smelly baby on his lap gurgled happily.

James had never been good with poopy diapers,

but he gave it his best effort and hoped he looked like a proper Santa.

Finally, they were down to the last kid in line. Thank God. After this, Santa was going home to enjoy a cold beer.

That was about the only thing he'd enjoy. Oh, he'd turn on the TV to some cop show, but he wouldn't really watch it. Then he'd go to bed and wish the days wouldn't keep coming, forcing him to move on.

He especially wasn't looking forward to the next day, December 24. How he wished he could skip right to New Year's Day. Or better yet, go backward to New Year's Day two years ago, when he and Faith were planning their European cruise.

Stay in the moment, he told himself. *Stay in character.* He put on his jolliest Santa face and held out a welcoming arm to the next child.

This one was going to be a terror; he could tell by the scowl on the kid's freckled face as he approached. He was a big, hefty burger of a boy, wearing jeans and an oversize T-shirt, and could have been anywhere between the ages of ten and thirteen. Logic ruled out the older end of the spectrum. Usually by about eight or nine, kids stopped believing.

"And who have we got here?" James asked in his jolly *I love kids* voice.

Normally he did love kids and he loved playing Santa, had been doing it since his children were small. He'd always had the husky build for it, although when he was younger Faith had padded him out with a pillow. No pillow necessary now. And no need for a fake beard, either. Mother Nature had turned his beard white over the past few years.

These days he wasn't into the role, wasn't into Christmas, period. Santa had lost his holiday spirit and he was starting to lose his patience, too. Very unSanta-like. He should never have agreed to fill in today, should have told Holiday Memories to find another Santa.

His new customer didn't answer him.

"What's your name, son?" he asked, trying again.

"Richie," said the boy and landed on James's leg like a ton of coal.

"And how old are you, Richie?"

"Too old for this. This is stupid." The kid crossed his arms and glared at his mother.

"So you're twelve?" James guessed.

"I'm ten and I know there's no such thing as Santa. You're a big fake."

Boy, he had that right.

"And that's fake, too," Richie added.

James was usually prepared for rotten-kid beard assaults, but this year his game was off and Richie got a handful of beard before James could stop him and yanked, hard enough to nearly separate James's jawbone from the rest of his skull. For a moment there he saw stars and two Richies. As if one wasn't bad enough.

"Whoa, there, son, that's real," James said, rubbing his chin, his eyes watering. "Let's take it easy on old Santa."

Now Richie's mother was glaring, too—as though it were James's fault she'd spawned a monster.

"Look, Richie," he said, lowering his voice, "we're both men here. We know this is all pretend."

And Christmas is a crock and life sucks. So deal with it, you little fart.

James reeled in his bad Santa before he could do any damage. Good Santa continued, "But your mom wants this picture. One last picture she can send to your relatives and brag about what a great kid you are." *Not.* "Can you man up and pose so she can have a nice picture of you for Christmas?"

Richie frowned at him suspiciously, and James sweetened the holiday pot. "I bet if you do, you'll get what you want for Christmas." Now the kid seemed less adversarial. James pressed his advantage. "Come on, kid. One smile and we can both get out of here. Whaddya say?"

Richie grunted and managed half a smile and Krystal captured it. "But you're still a fake," Richie said.

And you're still a little fart. "Ho, ho, ho," James boomed and rocketed the boy off his leg, sending him flying.

"Hey, he shoved me," Richie said to his mother. He pointed an accusing finger at James.

"Trick leg," James said apologetically. "Old war injury. Merry Christmas," he called and, with a wave, abdicated his holiday throne.

"Okay," he said to Shauna, "I'm out of here." Thank God this day was over. He was never doing this again. He didn't care if every Santa on the planet was home with the flu.

"You can't go yet," she protested and began looking desperately around the mall.

After a ten-hour day? Oh, yeah, he could. "No kids, and it's ten minutes till the end of our shift. We'll be okay. Right, Krystal?"

Krystal shrugged uncertainly. "Well..."

It was nearly five o'clock. All the moms and kiddies were on their way home to make dinner. The next Santa crew would arrive soon to deal with the evening crowd. All they had to do was put up the Santa Will Be Back sign. What was the problem? Maybe the girls felt guilty stealing a couple of extra minutes from work.

Not James. He'd worked hard all his life and he had no qualms about stealing a few minutes for himself now. For forty years he'd been a welder for Boeing. Then he'd come home and worked some more, putting that addition on the house, mowing the lawn, cleaning the garage, repairing broken faucets.

Of course, he'd also realized the importance of playing—backyard baseball with the kids, Frisbee at the park, The Game of Life on a rainy Sunday afternoon. And real life had taught him that you should take advantage of everything good, even little things like getting off ten minutes early. Because you never knew what cosmic pie in the face was waiting for you around the corner.

"Come on, ladies," he said, putting an arm around each of them and trying to move them in the direction of the Starbucks. "The eggnog lattes are on me." They still balked. He'd never known the girls to turn down a latte. He glanced from one to the other. "Okay, what's going on?"

"It's a surprise," said Shauna.

James frowned. He hated surprises, had hated them ever since Faith got sick.

"It's a good one," Krystal added.

And then he saw his daughter hurrying down the mall toward him and the heaviness that was trying to settle over him was blown away. There she came, his brown-eyed girl, all bundled up in boots and black leggings and a winter coat, her hair falling to her shoulders in a stylish light brown sheet. Once upon a time it had been curly and so cute. Then suddenly she'd decided she needed to straighten her hair. He never could understand why the curls had to go. But then, he'd never understood women's fashion.

He also never understood why she thought her face was too round or why she thought she was fat. Her face was sweet. And she was just curvy. As far as he was concerned, she was the prettiest young woman in Seattle. That wasn't fatherly prejudice. It was fact, plain and simple.

"Daddy," she called and waved and began to run toward him.

Krystal had been right. This *was* a good surprise.

"Hello there, angel," he greeted her and gave her a big hug. "Did you come to let your old man take you out to dinner?"

"I came to take my old man somewhere special for Christmas," she said. "Thanks for not letting him get away," she told his holiday helpers.

"No problem," said Shauna. "Have a great time."

"For Christmas?" James repeated as Brooke linked her arm through his and started them walking toward the shopping mall's main entrance.

They were going somewhere for Christmas on the twenty-third? Did that mean she wasn't going to spend Christmas with him and Dylan? It was their first Christmas without Faith (well, technically their second since she'd died on December 24 the year before). He'd assumed he and his son and daughter would all be together to help each other through the holidays.

But she was an adult. She could do what she wanted. Maybe she'd made plans with friends. If she had, he couldn't blame her for wanting to run away from unpleasant memories. Maybe she'd found someone in the past couple of weeks and wanted to be with him. She shouldn't have to babysit her dad.

"Don't worry, Daddy," she said. "I've got it all under control."

He didn't doubt that. Like her mother, Brooke was a planner and an organizer. She'd organized their Thanksgiving dinner, gathering his sister and his cousin and her husband, assigning everyone dishes to bring.

But what was she talking about? "Got what under control?"

"You'll see," she said with a Santa-like twinkle in her eyes.

Oh, boy, another surprise. "What are you up to, angel?"

"I'm not telling, but trust me, you'll like it."

He doubted he'd like anything this season, but he decided to play along. "Okay, lead on."

He hoped she hadn't spent too much money. Kindergarten teachers didn't make a lot and he hated to think of her spending a fortune on some fancy meal. He'd be happy enough with a hamburger. Anyway, he'd rather eat in the car than go into a restaurant dressed like he was.

They were out of the mall now and at her trusty SUV. She complained about her gas mileage, but he was secretly glad she had it. The thing had all-wheel drive and handled well in the snow, which meant he didn't have to worry about her when she was driving in bad weather. Seattle rarely got much of the white stuff, but they'd had a couple of inches earlier in the month and the weatherman was predicting more by New Year's.

James had always loved it when they had a white Christmas. He remembered snowball fights with the kids and hot chocolate afterward. Faith used to lace his and hers with peppermint schnapps.

"No frowning allowed," Brooke said as they got in.

"Who's frowning? Santa doesn't frown."

"He never used to," Brooke said softly.

"Well, Santa's getting too grumpy for this job. I think it's about time for the old boy to pack it in."

His daughter shot a startled look in his direction. "Daddy, are you crazy?"

"No, I'm just..." *Sick of this "ho, ho, ho" crap.* It would never do to say such a cynical thing to his daughter. "Ready for a break," he improvised.

"You can't take a break," she protested as she drove out of the parking lot. "You're Santa."

James looked at the crowd of cars rushing around them, people busy running errands, going places, preparing for holiday gatherings with loved ones. Most of the men in Seattle would be out the following day, frantically finding something for their wives or girlfriends. He wished he was going to be one of them.

He reminded himself that he still had his kids. He had a lot to be thankful for, and if Brooke had other plans for Christmas, well, he and Dylan could make turkey TV dinners and eat the last of the cookies she'd baked for them, then watch a movie like *Bad Santa*. Heh, heh, heh.

Now they were on the southbound freeway. Where were they going? Knowing his daughter, it would be someplace special.

He couldn't help smiling as he thought about the contrast between her and his son. Dylan would come up with something at the last minute, most likely a six-pack of beer and a bag of nachos, their favorite football food. Naturally, Dylan would help him consume it all.

James was just wondering which downtown Seattle spot his daughter had picked for dinner and was hoping it was in the Pike Place Market when they exited off I-5 onto I-90, heading east out of Seattle. "Dinner in Bellevue?"

"Maybe," she said, obviously determined to be mysterious.

They passed Bellevue. And then Issaquah, getting increasingly farther from the city. Where the heck was she taking him?

When they reached North Bend at the foot of the Cascades, he said, "So, we're eating here?"

"Actually, dinner is in the backseat," she said, nodding over her shoulder at a little red cooler. "I've got roast beef sandwiches and apples and a beer for you if you want it."

If they weren't going out to dinner, then where were they going? Now he began to feel uneasy. How long was he going to be stuck in this suit? "Okay," he said, making his tone of voice serious so she'd know he was done fooling around. "What's going on?"

"We're going to Icicle Falls," she said brightly.

"What?"

"This is a kidnapping."

That was not funny. "Brooke," he said sternly. "I'm not going to Icicle Falls."

"Daddy," she said just as sternly. "We're all going to Icicle Falls. For Christmas. I booked us rooms at the Icicle Creek Lodge."

"You can't just spring this on me, baby girl," he said. "I don't even have a change of clothes."

"Not to worry. Dylan's bringing clothes when he comes up later."

He should have known she'd thought of that. She'd probably given her younger brother a detailed list. He tried another argument. "I can't leave my car at the mall."

"Dylan's picking it up after work and driving it up. See? Everything's under control."

No, it wasn't. It wasn't even remotely under control. James was getting hauled off to some stupid Bavarian village that would be chock-full of Christmas lights and happy tourists when all he'd wanted was to spend Christmas at home with his kids. Being depressed because his wife wasn't there with them. And making the kids feel bad. Ho, ho, ho.

"We thought we should do something different this year," Brooke added gently.

Maybe she was right. They could have tried to celebrate the way they'd always done with a big dinner on Christmas Eve followed by a candlelight service at church and then pancakes and presents in the morning and friends over in the afternoon to sing Christmas carols and eat cookies, but it would have all been hollow and empty.

Still, he'd planned on trying. He'd bought a bunch of Christmas movies for them to watch and stocked up on cocoa, had put up the tree and stuck their gift cards in among the branches. "I just thought we'd have Christmas at home," he said. Now he sounded like an ingrate and he didn't want to do that. Anyway, it was too late now. They were halfway to Icicle Falls. The Polar Express had left the station.

"I think this will be good," Brooke said. "It's our gift to you."

"Your gift?" Staying in some lodge would be expensive. "Oh, no. I'll take care of it."

"Daddy," she said firmly. "You've always taken care of us. And you've always been Santa," she added, smiling at him. "Now it's our turn to play Santa. So don't ruin the game."

He sighed and looked out the window at the stands of evergreens they were rushing past. He guessed he could play along.

As long as nobody asked him to be Santa this year. Because Santa had lost his Christmas spirit and he didn't care if he ever found it again.

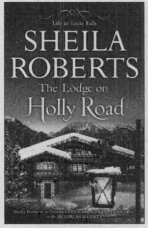

Life in Icicle Falls

SHEILA ROBERTS

The Lodge on Holly Road

Sheila Roberts is Phenomenal for her stocking-stuffer tale!
— *PUBLISHERS WEEKLY*

$7.99 U.S./$8.99 CAN.

Limited time offer!

$1.00 OFF

The Lodge on Holly Road
by

SHEILA ROBERTS

Sometimes the best gifts are the
ones you don't expect...

*Available October 28, 2014,
wherever books are sold!*

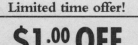

HARLEQUIN® MIRA®
www.Harlequin.com

$1.00 OFF

**the purchase price of
THE LODGE ON HOLLY ROAD by Sheila Roberts**

Offer valid from October 28, 2014, to November 25, 2014. Redeemable
at participating retail outlets. Limit one coupon per purchase.
Valid in the U.S.A. and Canada only.

52611621

5 65373 00076 2 (8100)0 11939

MSR1661CPN

Life In Icicle Falls

SHEILA ROBERTS

Can a book change your life?

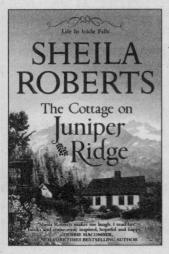

Yes! When it's *Simplicity,* a guide to plain living. In fact, it inspires Jen Heath to leave her stressful life in Seattle and move to Icicle Falls, where she rents a lovely little cottage on Juniper Ridge. There, Jen enjoys simple pleasures—like joining the local book club—and *complicated* ones, like falling in love with her sexy landlord….

Her sister Toni is ready for a change, too. She has a teenage daughter who's constantly texting, a husband who's more involved with his computer than he is with her, and a son who's consumed by video games. Toni wants her family to grow closer—to return to a simpler way of life.

But sometimes life simply happens. It doesn't always happen simply!

Available now, wherever books are sold!

REQUEST YOUR FREE BOOKS!

2 FREE NOVELS
FROM THE ROMANCE COLLECTION
PLUS 2 FREE GIFTS!

YES! Please send me 2 FREE novels from the Romance Collection and my 2 FREE gifts (gifts are worth about $10). After receiving them, if I don't wish to receive any more books, I can return the shipping statement marked "cancel." If I don't cancel, I will receive 4 brand-new novels every month and be billed just $6.24 per book in the U.S. or $6.74 per book in Canada. That's a savings of at least 22% off the cover price. It's quite a bargain! Shipping and handling is just 50¢ per book in the U.S. and 75¢ per book in Canada.* I understand that accepting the 2 free books and gifts places me under no obligation to buy anything. I can always return a shipment and cancel at any time. Even if I never buy another book, the two free books and gifts are mine to keep forever.

194/394 MDN F4XY

Name _____ (PLEASE PRINT) _____

Address _____ Apt. # _____

City _____ State/Prov. _____ Zip/Postal Code _____

Signature (if under 18, a parent or guardian must sign)

Mail to the Harlequin® Reader Service:
IN U.S.A.: P.O. Box 1867, Buffalo, NY 14240-1867
IN CANADA: P.O. Box 609, Fort Erie, Ontario L2A 5X3

Want to try two free books from another line?
Call 1-800-873-8635 or visit www.ReaderService.com.

* Terms and prices subject to change without notice. Prices do not include applicable taxes. Sales tax applicable in N.Y. Canadian residents will be charged applicable taxes. Offer not valid in Quebec. This offer is limited to one order per household. Not valid for current subscribers to the Romance Collection or the Romance/Suspense Collection. All orders subject to credit approval. Credit or debit balances in a customer's account(s) may be offset by any other outstanding balance owed by or to the customer. Please allow 4 to 6 weeks for delivery. Offer available while quantities last.

Your Privacy—The Harlequin® Reader Service is committed to protecting your privacy. Our Privacy Policy is available online at www.ReaderService.com or upon request from the Harlequin Reader Service.

We make a portion of our mailing list available to reputable third parties that offer products we believe may interest you. If you prefer that we not exchange your name with third parties, or if you wish to clarify or modify your communication preferences, please visit us at www.ReaderService.com/consumerschoice or write to us at Harlequin Reader Service Preference Service, P.O. Box 9062, Buffalo, NY 14269. Include your complete name and address.

ROM13R

SHEILA ROBERTS

31470	MERRY EX-MAS	___ $7.99 U.S.	___ $8.99 CAN.
31454	THE COTTAGE ON	___ $7.99 U.S.	___ $8.99 CAN.
	JUNIPER RIDGE		
31432	WHAT SHE WANTS	___ $7.99 U.S.	___ $9.99 CAN.

(limited quantities available)

TOTAL AMOUNT	$ _____
POSTAGE & HANDLING	$ _____
($1.00 for 1 book, 50¢ for each additional)	
APPLICABLE TAXES*	$ _____
TOTAL PAYABLE	$ _____

(check or money order—please do not send cash)

To order, complete this form and send it, along with a check or money order for the total amount, payable to Harlequin MIRA, to: **In the U.S.:** 3010 Walden Avenue, P.O. Box 9077, Buffalo, NY 14269-9077; **In Canada:** P.O. Box 636, Fort Erie, Ontario, L2A 5X3.

Name: _____
Address: _____ City: _____
State/Prov.: _____ Zip/Postal Code: _____
Account Number (if applicable): _____

075 CSAS

*New York residents remit applicable sales taxes.
*Canadian residents remit applicable GST and provincial taxes.

HARLEQUIN® MIRA®
www.Harlequin.com

MSR0714BL